MW01127922

UNDER MY HEEL

The Kurtherian Gambit 06

MICHAEL ANDERLE

COPYRIGHT

Under My Heel (this book) is a work of fiction.

All of the characters, organizations, and events portrayed in this novel are either products of the author's imagination or are used fictitiously. Sometimes both.

Copyright © 2016 Michael T. Anderle
Cover art by Andrew Dobell - Creative Edge Studios -
http://creativeedgestudios.co.uk
Cover copyright © LMBPN Publishing

LMBPN Publishing supports the right to free expression and the value of copyright. The purpose of copyright is to encourage writers and artists to produce the creative works that enrich our culture.

The distribution of this book without permission is a theft of the author's intellectual property. If you would like permission to use material from the book (other than for review purposes), please contact info@kurtherianbooks.com. Thank you for your support of the author's rights.

LMBPN Publishing
PMB 196, 2540 South Maryland Pkwy
Las Vegas, NV 89109

First US edition, 2016
Version 2.00 Edition (Edited by Ellen Campbell) February 2017
Version 2.04 June 2017

The Kurtherian Gambit (and what happens within/characters/situations/worlds) are copyright © 2017 by Michael T. Anderle.

DEDICATION

To Family, Friends and
Those Who Love
To Read.
May We All Enjoy Grace
To Live The Life We Are
Called.

**Under My Heel - The Kurtherian Gambit 06
Street Team**

Arthur DeForest
Dorene Johnson
Mike Lucas
Scott Paul
Diane Velasquez

Editors

Stephen Russell version 1.02
Ellen Campbell version 2.0

CHAPTER ONE

Washington, D.C. USA

Mary Brennan was silently suffering. Her husband, Martin, had been killed some months before in the basement parking garage of his office building.

It had been a gruesome and painful death. Oh, Brandin, Martin's second in command had tried to hide the truth from her in the beginning, to save her pain she was sure. But you don't stay the spouse of a government intelligence group member without learning a few tricks of your own. She had the autopsy report, she knew her husband had died in pain. More pain than she would allow herself to consider.

Martin had been her rock. The man she was going to live the rest of her life with. They had plans to retire to a beach or at least to someplace warm. She loved the Atlantic City coast, but it was still too cold and miserable too much of the year for her. Martin had promised her... he had promised her. Now, he was dead and she had no way to track down who had killed him or why.

She finished putting on her makeup. Every Sunday, Tuesday and Friday she would get ready to visit Martin. She would take the single rose she had picked out the night before from the corner market and get into her eight-year-old Mercedes Benz.

She wiped a tear from her eye as she picked up the rose and left for her drive to the cemetery.

It took her twenty-two minutes exactly. She had timed every trip. She left at 8:15 AM every time and arrived at 8:37 AM. Occasionally she would be a couple of minutes late, if she got behind someone slow. But you could usually set your clock by her.

She parked in the same spot for every visit. If it had snowed, the helpful caretakers would have cleared the parking spot. Those same caretakers had noticed her arrival every week, month after month.

Reaching over to the passenger's seat, she picked up this morning's rose.

The morning was crisp and cool, all of the sounds muted on this side of the cemetery. She rarely met anyone as she walked along the path.

She came around the final turn, looked up the lonely little hill towards Martin's gravestone, and stopped in her tracks. Martin wasn't alone. There were a couple of men standing about fifty yards away. They were big guys, they looked professional, and they seemed to be watching over a woman.

Her eyes were drawn to the woman standing with her back to Mary. The lady was dressed in slacks, and a full-length black winter coat came down to her knees. She seemed to be wiping tears away from her face, her shoulders hitched a little. The lady was crying. If Mary was any judge, she had been crying for a while.

Mary started walking, a little faster this time. Who was this woman and why was she crying at Martin's grave? She approached her, slowing down, coughing a little so as to not surprise her.

Mary watched as the woman put a tissue to her eye one more time and turned to face her. Mary's eyes widened in shock.

A dead woman was crying for her husband.

Mary fainted. Bethany Anne deftly caught her, and the rose that had fallen from her hand, before either hit the ground.

Somewhere in France

David picked up the throw away phone. Until he knew where Michael was, he was going to be just as anal about security as Anton had been.

Not that it had helped him in the end. Perhaps, David thought, Anton shouldn't have hosted lavish parties that put a big target on his back. For such a devious ass, Anton was blind at times to his own inadequacies. Anton frequently harassed him about his castle, only to die himself in one of his own homes.

David hadn't gotten the full story, but he had been made aware that Anton was very, very dead.

Apparently this little female of Michael's was still being a resolute pain in the ass.

David called one of his contacts in America. The voice on the other end of the line was abrupt, pushy. "Hello? Who is this?"

"It is David."

The voice on the other end became less abrupt. "Oh, good to hear from you. I take it you know about Anton?"

"Yes. That is the reason for my call. We need to up the pressure on this annoying brat Bethany Anne. I want you to move forward with the plans to push for a no-support vote against Gerry. Can you swing that?"

"Possibly. He's made it harder since the test with the troublemakers has been successful so far. I'll start planting rumors. We should be able to at least cause the council to deadlock. Once we're deadlocked, Gerry's powers are minimized and I can move forward to get him tossed out. I'll have a figurehead take control. No reason for my head to go on the chopping block if Michael comes back around."

"If Michael comes back around, I imagine the safest place will be anywhere he is not. Don't forget Valentine's Day."

"I won't forget, that's the reason I agreed to work with you in the first place. Don't forget you needed me to take care of this for you, when it all finally works out."

"Of course not, I remember my friends."

"Good." They said their good-byes.

David looked down at the pieces of the phone he had just crushed in his hand. "Of course, I would have to count you as a friend, first."

He dropped the crushed remains into the trash basket next to his chair and wiped his hands together to get the dust off.

He picked up the next phone and looked up the number he needed.

———

Mary woke up slowly, cradled in a woman's arms. Her memory a little foggy, she opened her eyes to look up… into the face of an angel, someone who shouldn't be holding her right now. Who shouldn't be here, period.

"Bethany Anne?" Mary reached up to touch Bethany Anne's face, lit with a compassionate smile. Even with tear streaks running down her face, she still looked beautiful.

"Yes, it's me. I've come to pay Martin the respect he was due. I didn't want to speak to him until I had taken care of those responsible for his death."

Mary looked around her; there were four new people on the other side of the grave. Two more men accompanied by two women. The two men that she had seen before were still scanning the area, definitely protection. The other men and the two women were looking at her.

"Can you stand?" Bethany Anne asked her.

She nodded. She felt a little woozy, but with Bethany Anne's help she got her feet back under her again. Bethany Anne kept an arm around her shoulders.

Mary's mind caught up to what Bethany Anne had said. "You took care of who? Who was responsible for Martin's death?"

Bethany Anne's smile turned sad. "It was a group that was looking for me. I had helped another government agency in the Everglades. The operation went bad, but I was able to help and turn things around. That led to another operation in Miami and that caused the other group to start investigating me. They tracked me to Martin and he was killed as a result."

"I, I thought you were dead? I know Martin said that you were alive, that no one else would have sent him that shoe. But the doctors gave you no chance, and you've been gone… well, almost a year?"

"Pretty much. I was moved into a clandestine… group. This group had the medical capability, in Europe, to heal me. But it changed me." Bethany Anne let go of Mary, watching her in case she needed support again. She started pacing in front of the gravesite. "It took six months to make me better. Since then, I've been involved in different things. My main goal for the last six months has been tracking down Martin's killers, and their boss, and so on up the chain." She stopped to look Mary in the eyes. "Mary, my team and I have killed every person related, or even tangentially connected, to what happened to Martin. We have hunted down and killed the person who killed Martin here in D.C.. We tracked his boss in Costa Rica and then her boss in Argentina. I'm tracking another person over in Europe and I know who's going to take care of him, too. Me and my team will not stop until every person in that group is under my heel, ground into the dust of the earth and washed into the oceans, never to be heard from again. That's my promise."

Mary heard the biggest guy there murmur, "Ad Aeternitatem."

Bethany Anne looked over the grave at the man and nodded her head once, sharply.

Bethany Anne looked back at her. "I'm sorry Martin got entangled in this mess. I had no idea anyone was going to track me back to my old life."

Mary looked down at her feet. "So, Martin was killed in the line of duty, then?" A tear had just started to form in Mary's right eye.

"Yes. He was killed because I was involved in operations sanctioned by the U.S. Government."

Mary continued to weep softly. "Why didn't the government admit it? They claimed it was a random act."

Bethany Anne held out a fresh tissue.

"You know that Martin's group was almost black, right?" Mary nodded. "Well, next is black and then beyond black is the group I'm in now." Bethany Anne stepped over to Mary and used a finger to gently tilt her head up, to look her in the eyes. "Mary, Martin might not have died if he had given the killer information about me. He died to protect me. He was so sure I was alive that he gave his life to protect me without any evidence but a shoe."

Mary used the tissue to wipe her eyes. That was her husband. That was the man she loved and that was the man he was when he died. He was a protector. He protected those he loved even when she had thought he was grasping at ghosts.

The ghost, it seemed, was real. She smiled at Bethany Anne. "Then he didn't die in vain, did he?"

"Boss?"

Mary watched Bethany Anne turn to the large man again and raise an eyebrow.

"I'd like to speak if I could?"

Bethany Anne stepped beside Mary, nodded, and wrapped an arm around her waist. The huge man came around and stood in front of Mary. "Ma'am. My name is John Grimes. I would have died in that Everglades operation if Bethany Anne hadn't come onto the scene. In fact," he turned around a little and waved at the people on the other side of the grave, "every man here would have died on that operation." He turned back and faced Mary. "I owe my life, my future and my hope to Bethany Anne. By extension, I owe my life, my future and my hope to one of the men that made Bethany Anne the person she is today and that is your husband. So, from the bottom of my heart, thank you for his devotion to duty, devotion to life and devotion to those he loved. I am honored to say that I was there helping take down the killer. On behalf of me and my men, we will finish the job. Every person who belongs to this group of slime will be ground into dust."

As John was finishing his statement, Ecaterina stepped up behind him. John shook Mary's hand and Ecaterina then took his place.

"This woman," she nodded at Bethany Anne, "Is responsible for too much good in my life for me to share right now. I was there when Martin's killer was taken down. I am also one of the two who pulled the trigger to execute his ultimate leader. This is the least I can offer in appreciation for all your husband did to make her the woman she is today. Ad Aeternitatem."

By now, Mary was openly weeping, tears that she couldn't shed while she tried to understand Martin's murder, finally fell. Martin's life had not been useless. Rather, he had invested a part of his life in the woman standing with her, holding her, right now.

Next came Darryl, Scott and Eric. Finally, the woman named Gabrielle came and spoke with her.

Every person there was teary as Gabrielle finished her story. Mary hugged Gabrielle, then Ecaterina, Scott, Darryl, Eric and John. Finally, she turned to Bethany Anne. Pointing between herself and Bethany Anne she said, "I know we haven't spoken much. But as often as Martin spoke of you, I feel like you are a lost daughter. One that has come home and given me help to understand why, and the gift of knowing that his murderers have gotten justice." She moved over and hugged the younger, taller, woman. "I would wish I could see you more often, just to chat." She pulled back and looked up at Bethany Anne who was trying to smile through her tears.

"You come visit me any time. I might not be close to where you live, but you are always welcome in my home, do you understand?"

Bethany Anne hugged her back. "We might be closer than you think. Ok?"

Mary mumbled agreement, not really sure what she meant. Bethany Anne handed her the rose that she'd brought to the gravesite. She and Bethany Anne each laid a rose down. Then, to her surprise, each of the team members followed suit. That day, Martin's grave had eight roses on it.

When Mary walked back to her car, the weight of the emotions lifted off of her shoulders for the first time since Martin had been killed. She pulled off her coat and opened her door. She noticed a legal sized envelope addressed to her in the driver's seat. She grabbed the envelope, tossed in her coat and got in. She started the car and turned the heat on.

It took her a few minutes to figure out the contents.

She had been deeded a house in Key Biscayne, Florida.

A personal note inside said: Please accept this gift, it is the least I can do. Trust that I want you to know that Martin's promises, the dreams he shared with me, that you and your husband spoke about were never in vain. This home is paid for, furnished, and all the taxes and fees paid for until you die or sell the house. I would be honored if you accept this and come live near me. All my love, Bethany Anne.

Tears fell one more time from Mary Brennan's face, the ink on the personal note smearing just a little.

———

Key Biscayne, FL USA

Scott was walking along the edge of the water, thinking about the trip to Martin's gravesite. He had been involved with the takedown of Adrian, the vampire responsible for killing Martin. He'd also been involved, at least in the action plan, with the effort to get Clarita. He would have been involved with the fight for the Polarus, but Jean Dukes and her team had made very short work of the boat attacking them that night.

He was standing, looking at the evening sunset over the water when Darryl caught up to him. Scott had heard him and waited until his partner stood beside him, sharing the view. He spoke, "Beautiful, isn't it."

Darryl nodded, it wasn't so much a question between the two men who had fought together, bled together and made it out the other side together, as it was a simple 'hello.'

They stood in companionable silence for a couple of minutes, Darryl letting his partner take his time.

Scott finally broke the silence. "Are we going to be enough, Darryl?"

"Enough for what?"

"Enough to see her to the other side of all this?" Scott threw his hand out to the horizon. "Enough to protect her from what's coming?"

Darryl considered his response. Scott was the odd guy out in the Queen's Guard. He came to them from the NYPD. He wasn't ex-military like most of the others. Scott had been involved in a bad outcome with a Nosferatu in an apartment building and Dan had somehow pulled strings to let the man join their team. He had been a solid part of the four for a while now.

"Brother, what do you think is coming up?" To Darryl,

every one of his team was his brother. Three guys, now four if you counted Gabrielle, who he knew would never leave him behind even if the brass had other ideas. Hell, his brass was Bethany Anne. That lady would risk dying in a foreign dimension to try to save one of her own.

"You know the score. We have to get this Forsaken bullshit behind us. Team BMW is going to get those rockets working. I don't think it will take much time before they're working in atmosphere and then working out of atmosphere. After that it won't be too much longer before we really will be able to move into low earth orbit. That's going to piss off some really powerful people."

Darryl nodded his agreement. "Scott, we're going to have to be enough. She's a tough woman, don't get me wrong, but she can't be looking everywhere at the same time."

Scott snorted. "Remember San Jose?"

Darryl grinned, remembering the fight in the park. "We got her through that."

Scott turned his head to look up at his partner. "Who was trying to get whom through that? We were a unit. The absolute best I've ever been a part of and she left us in her dust. We have to up our game or we're going to be holding her back."

It was Darryl's turn to be quiet and think about what Scott had just said. The guys had heard about the fight on the Ad Aeternitatem. Pete's team paired with Todd's Marines had a short and bloody fight of their own. But the big news was Pete himself turning into the first standing werewolf in centuries as he and his team had fought for Bethany Anne. Perhaps John could take Pete in a fight, but John had been maxed out by... "You want to go John's route, don't you?"

Like before, while phrased as a question, it was a statement from one person who knew the other all too well.

Scott nodded. "I've thought about it a lot since we helped the reporter in San Jose." Scott scanned the horizon. "When those douchebags shot at us and Gabrielle, I stopped thinking in terms of us, them, nations whatever. It became my team, my team members, my mission. We have one goal. We have to save the world." Scott looked back over at Darryl. "If I need to take a bullet to make sure Bethany Anne crosses the finish line? I won't hesitate. But, if I could shrug it back off so I'm not out of the game? Well, bring it on motherfuckers, bring it on." Scott turned back to viewing the horizon.

"That was a little plebian." Darryl smirked.

Scott smiled at that. "Yeah, let's just hope she isn't listening or I'll have to drop and give her fifty. Wait!" Scott turned back to Darryl, "No one has used just 'motherfucker' that I can remember in months. That should check out ok, I'm thinking."

Darryl shook his head. "You want to try that on her?"

"Fuck no."

"What do you think is our next step?"

"Eric, then John and then Gabrielle."

Scott hadn't really asked Darryl if he wanted to go this route. These guys had been human the whole time. John wasn't, not really. No one was exactly sure what he was, but if he was still human he had to be damn near a perfect specimen.

But they had all been saved in one way or another by Bethany Anne. Now, Scott wanted to make sure he had the ability to truly be the asset she needed when the chips were down.

His brother from another mother didn't need to voice his agreement. He already had.

It was time the Queen's Guards upped their game.

CHAPTER TWO

The Queen Bitch's Ship Ad Aeternitatem
En Route to the Mediterranean

Three men were sitting at a table in the compartment the boat's crew was kind enough to call "Team BMW's Garage." Until the team was able to produce a working craft, they were going to suffer from the kidding. Bobcat took it in stride and Marcus was bemused by the whole experience. While Marcus was familiar with getting the short stick from other scientists, he considered the fun loving antics just that, fun loving.

William didn't have the same opinion. Perhaps due to the gravestone he had been presented with. The crew had created it after their initial effort plummeted through the first barge. The rocket sank so fast into the depths of the ocean that it took the bubbles at least half a minute to make it to the surface. Or maybe it was because he had been accustomed to being the 'supreme mechanic' no matter what the military had him work on.

UNDER MY HEEL

Bethany Anne threw a damn spaceship at William, and then told his boss and a rocket scientist to make her a personal attack craft.

So he would. First, he would do it because winning the battle with machines is what he did. The second reason was because he wanted to know he had been a part of the team that built the first ship out of alien technology.

The third, and perhaps *the* most important reason, was that he wouldn't let Bethany Anne down again. He had screwed up back in Miami and he would do whatever it took to make sure he didn't let her down again.

Including not drinking alcohol until they were successful.

That prohibition wasn't something his boss and his teammate ascribed to. There was a bucket of mental lubrication medicine between them. Bobcat and Marcus had just popped the tops off of their second longnecks, when the world's deadliest woman sauntered in with her big as hell white German Shepherd. Gabrielle followed Bethany Anne into the room. She wore tactical clothing and made it look like she was walking on a fashion runway.

Damn vampires could make anything look sexy. William lifted his Coke in their direction, he could drink to that.

So he did.

"William! How is my favorite mechanic this evening?" Bethany Anne pulled a chair out and turned it around, straddling it and looking at them. Gabrielle took up a position a few feet behind her and Ashur laid down right behind Bethany Anne's chair.

William noticed that both Bobcat and Marcus had lowered their bottles, neither one knowing why their boss had arrived unannounced. He smiled. "Doing fine, thank you very much. We are unsuccessfully trying to figure out how to handle a couple of these problems with the new engine." He scratched at his chin; he had a little stubble going again. "The…" He stopped when she put up her hand.

"You are about to start speaking the language of numbers, forces, metals or stresses. None of which I speak."

I DO

No shit, Sherlock. That's why we're here.

Oh? Do tell.

Well then listen the fuck in, why don't you? Stop interrupting and we can all learn at the same time.

Bully for you.

I swear to God, if the kitchen team is listening to something you're picking up, I will make them swim behind the Polarus for a few miles while I chum the water.

Tom was silent. That pretty much sealed the guilty verdict right there. She continued her conversation with the guys.

"I know someone who DOES speak those things and has a clue…" Marcus interrupted her.

"You're going to let us talk with Thales aren't you!"

Bethany Anne stared at the man until he corrected himself. "Fine, TOM it is. I still don't understand why you have this thing with calling him by his full name."

She could imagine Marcus kicking an imaginary rock as he said this.

"Consider it my prerogative to keep his name short. I refuse to walk around calling him 'Thales of Miletus' or even 'Thales.' TOM he started and TOM he will be."

She leaned over to the bucket and grabbed a beer. Bobcat reached into his pocket to pull out his knife so she could use the bottle top tool. As he reached, she put her thumb under the top, flicked it off and took a swig. Bobcat put the knife back in his pocket. He considered her ability to just pop a bottle top off like that had to be useful as hell.

She made a face and put the bottle back on the table. "Oh hell, that is horrible!" She turned the bottle around and looked over at Bobcat. "Believe it or not, I think vampire taste buds don't like this."

Bobcat shook his head. "Sorry, then count me out if it ever comes time to offer me a chance at changing. If I can't enjoy nature's brew, life just isn't worth living." He punctuated that comment by draining his beer.

She shoved the bottle away. "Marcus, you asked a few weeks ago to talk with TOM. I've been trying to figure out a way to accomplish that and we might have a solution." Marcus had moved his bottle aside and picked up his pen and paper. "You know how this stuff," she waved around the room at the engines and different pieces of technology they had strewn about, "works through the Etheric dimension?" He nodded his agreement. "Well, we should be able to move communications through the Etheric to a computer that's secure. When I see your questions, I'll be able to type the responses."

"So, kind of like a chat channel?"

"Yes. You'll have to wait for responses depending on how busy I am, but it will be better than waiting until I get a chance to drop by here."

Why don't we just connect the computer I have right here through the Etheric directly to a laptop like we did for Frank?

Because the last time we talked about that, you said it would require another trip to the pod-doc.

Well, yes. But it would be a very small surgery to facilitate your ability to connect.

I'm not plugging a wire into my head.

It won't be a wire. It will be a micro... really, really micro... analog and digital transceiver.

So, I can be fried or hacked by an external group? No thanks.

Please, like there would be any ability to hack an alien computer system. This isn't Hollywood, you know.

Bethany Anne had watched Independence Day with TOM. She had to stop the movie when the two heroes plugged their computer straight into the spaceship's computer system and sent a worm into the alien's computer. TOM wouldn't shut the hell up explaining all the myriad different reasons why that wouldn't work.

Marcus sat back in his chair, obviously less enthused over the solution than he might have been. Of course, Marcus wanted to speak directly to TOM if he could but Bethany Anne wasn't willing to open that can of worms.

They got busy figuring out how to set up two laptops to work through the Etheric. With TOM's help, they had it covered in fifteen minutes.

Bethany Anne stood up and turned the chair back around. "Get with either Ecaterina or Patricia to order the laptops. Have them delivered to the Florida house and I'll bring them with me next time."

They said their goodbyes and stepped back out of the room, closing the door behind them.

William spoke to no one in particular. "Don't say anything. You've had a little beer and they can still hear you. We know they are attractive and God forbid you say something you will regret in the morning."

Bobcat just tipped his bottle in appreciation. He knew the warning wasn't for him. It was Marcus that couldn't hold his booze for shit.

Marcus just closed his mouth, not so far gone he couldn't recognize sage advice.

———

Ad Aeternitatem

Todd Jenkins was having trouble controlling his anger. The three Marines sitting with him at the table were having the same problem.

Todd, Chet Nichols, Kevin Russel and Paul Stephens were watching the aftermath of a terrorist attack in France.

It was pissing them off.

When you're in the military, you have to follow the commands of those above you. They follow the commands of those above them until, eventually, you end up at the top person who is usually an elected commander in chief. Sometimes the person holding the position is respected, sometimes they are not. Hopefully, the position is respected or you end up with societies that can change at the whim of those who have the most charisma and the biggest guns.

That doesn't mean that the people in the trenches and those who support them don't wish they could be released to cause mayhem and screw the 'political realities.'

The four Marines were barely restraining their anger as they watched the videos of the massacres that were running on the newscast again.

The news had made it around the Ad Aeternitatem pretty quickly. A few of the Marines had casually commented that 'France is on the way to the Mediterranean, right?' Wishful thinking, they knew. They had their task and it was to get

Stephen, the new owner of the two ships, back near his country so that they could continue their efforts to take care of the Forsaken and prepare to move to low earth orbit.

Pete and the Guardians walked into the mess, coming off of one of their training sessions. Every Were could easily smell the pheromones rife around the ship. Pete broke off from his team to go to Todd's table. They would be working out with Todd's team in a couple of hours. Since the boarding action a few weeks back, Todd and Pete had become close friends and both teams worked and trained hard together.

The Marines leaned towards using their guns and the Guardians leaned towards fast and ferocious close quarters killing.

Together, the two teams were taking their skills up another notch or five.

Todd turned his head, acknowledging Pete.

Pete asked, "What's going on? The whole ship smells angry, but it's really thick in here with you guys."

Chet answered the question without taking his eyes off of the T.V. on the wall. "Fucking terrorists went walking around the city, killing indiscriminately. One group went into a packed concert and started blasting away before they had a police standoff and two of them detonated suicide vests. Probably over a hundred killed and many hundreds wounded. Cocksucking pricks won't stand up and fight like fucking men, they have to send kids to go kill themselves. Mind-fuckers just twist the words of their religion to get the young to do what they want."

Pete raised an eyebrow at Todd, who shrugged. Pete looked over at Chet. "Damn Chet, why don't you tell me what you really think?"

Todd jumped in. "Nothing that any of the rest of us aren't

thinking, we want a chance at these assholes so bad we can taste it."

Pete shrugged. "So? Why don't we ask if it can be done?"

A voice asked from right beside Pete, "If what can be done?"

Pete, who had supernatural hearing, damn near jumped out of his skin. Stephen had come up beside him and spoken close enough that Pete could feel his breath in the air. He twisted around looking at the older, much older, vampire. "Dammit, Stephen! God, you're going to give me a fucking heart attack!"

Stephen smiled at the young Were. "Pete, there isn't a chance I could scare you so badly that you couldn't regenerate the damage. I'm just using you for practice."

Todd was happy those two were talking for a minute. It gave him a moment to get his own heart under control. Todd had Pete in his vision, so he knew for a fact that Stephen had just appeared out of nothing or as close to it that he couldn't tell the difference. Chet and Kevin hadn't even flinched. He wasn't sure if they were even aware of the conversation going on around them. Paul was trying to pretend he hadn't just jumped a foot out of his own chair.

Pete grumped back, "Can't you choose someone like Gabrielle or Bethany Anne for that?"

Stephen waved away his question. "Bethany Anne always knows where I am and Gabrielle learned my tricks a couple of centuries ago."

Sensing a chance to earn some money, Pete asked Stephen, "Really? How many centuries ago?" There was a very hush-hush bounty on Gabrielle's age. Rumor had it that the amount was now ten grand and a few people were whispering that it was Bethany Anne herself who was willing to pay the bounty. No questions asked.

Stephen turned to look at Pete's guileless face, a perfect mask of innocence. "Peter, you will have to do much, much better than that to find out Gabrielle's age." Stephen detected just the barest flinch in Pete's eyes.

Pete said, "No, just curious how long it took her to learn your tricks."

Stephen turned to look at the table, everyone sitting there was now riveted on his conversation with Pete. "So, what is it that you wish to know could be done?"

Pete threw answering over to Todd. The two of them were getting good enough that they didn't need to talk, just that telepathic abilities friends acquired whenever they were around each other long enough.

Todd mentally answered a '*you dick*' at Pete, who smiled his acknowledgment of the barb.

Todd pointed his thumb back over his shoulder at the T.V. on the wall. "These cocksuckers… Er, sorry." Unlike Bethany Anne, Stephen wasn't so loose with the cursing when he spoke. "The terrorists over in France. We were wishing that we could get a chance to pin their asses to the wall. Any chance your contacts could dig up an M249 for us?"

"Oooh oooh, How about a jeep with a Gau-17/A?" Kevin asked with his hand up, bouncing in his seat.

Chet bopped him on the head. "You ass."

Stephen looked up at the television and watched it for a few seconds. In his centuries of living, he had witnessed atrocities that made this seem minor by comparison. Then again, all that evil needed to prosper was for good men and women to do nothing. Or, he considered, not be allowed to do something. His face turned thoughtful and Todd risked a glance over at Pete who shrugged.

Now, all of Pete's team had joined Todd's group. Stephen looked around and noticed he had some of the ship's crew watching him as well. He measured the emotions on all of their faces.

"I take it, this," he waved his hand at the television, "is something that angers you, turns your sense of justice into a desire for revenge?"

Todd answered, "Not revenge, retribution."

Stephen turned back to look down at his Marine lead. "They have been judged as deserving of punishment for their actions and you would like to know if that is something that is within our operational parameters?"

Todd wasn't sure how to answer that. He knew Stephen would never go against Bethany Anne's wishes. No hope but to admit what he wanted and see how the dice rolled. "Pretty much, yeah."

There were grunts of agreement from around Stephen. Oh yes, these people were angry at the atrocities they watched unfold on the television.

Stephen looked back at the T.V. while everyone in the dining room looked at him. He smiled, a malicious smile, causing a few to want to take a step back. Most had thought Stephen a fun-loving vampire who rarely raised his voice.

The face of the vampire in front of them right then would have caused nightmares for most, had they been younger. "My Queen has appointed, to me, the responsibility of cleaning up Europe. I believe her intent is to make Europe a safe haven in anticipation of the upheaval that will happen when we move to our next stage. I believe that ridding Europe of this pestilence would be within my understanding of her instructions."

He looked at the two commanders. "Let's call a meeting

with Dan and the captains of the ships. If it is agreed that an operation is practical and it is something we want a chance at…" Stephen pointed to the T.V., "Then these… cocksuckers?" Stephen raised an eyebrow at Todd who nodded. "Then these cocksuckers will learn what it means to find themselves as the focus of the Queen Bitch's Navy."

Stephen walked out of the dining room to the cheering of a group of men and women who saw a chance for retribution come within their reach.

———

Somewhere in Germany

It took David three days to locate the appropriate available contact in the U.S. military. Those damn Americans could be an ethical pain-in-the-ass. Finally, one of his contacts in the German military was able to provide a contact that was at least malleable in their efforts to protect the U.S.. Further, they were high enough up to be able to execute the orders he wanted given.

Then it was only five minutes to assure the contact that a problem in Syria was going to occur, and that he would be provided an outside force to deal with it. He just needed to make sure that the outside force wasn't given air support after they arrived.

The two agreed on a price and hung up.

David smiled. Too bad the outside force wouldn't be called until AFTER the contact sacrificed a few of his own men first.

David crushed the phone over the trashcan, and wiped his hands together to get rid of the small pieces. Now, if this

Bethany Anne worked like Michael, they would come to the rescue if a large Nosferatu outbreak happened.

David stood up and grabbed his coat; it was time he took a trip to Syria. It had been a while since he had drunk enough blood to turn young again. That was one benefit of creating a large Nosferatu group, you had a lot of blood to drink in the process and one always looked really good after the effort.

CHAPTER THREE

The Queen Bitch's Ship Ad Aeternitatem

Marcus was looking down at his scratch pad and up at the drawings they had taped to the whiteboard on the wall.

Bobcat and William were in a heated discussion over something to do with fins. Something wasn't right and Marcus couldn't grasp it, yet.

"Gentleman." He spoke a little louder, "Gentleman!" Bobcat and William turned to face him. Marcus pointed to the sketches. "Why are we using three as the assumed number of people on the rocket?"

Bobcat answered, "That's how many Bethany Anne asked for, two and a pilot."

Marcus walked up to the whiteboard and looked through the sketches. They all looked like some variation of the old V-2 rockets from World War II. "Who would we need to ask if that's the right decision?"

Bobcat's eyes stopped tracking Marcus and looked over their designs. "Probably Dan at first, but also Todd and Pete."

Marcus looked over his shoulder at Bobcat. "Not Bethany Anne's group?"

William snorted. "Why would she take something slow like this?"

Marcus's mouth dropped open. "Slow? Do you realize just how fast this can actually go? We are talking up to Mach 42 and that's just in the atmosphere." There was a new hypersonic private jet concept out of Bombardier that was possibly going to do Mach 24, so humans were going to catch up with this craft eventually, but it wouldn't be as agile or safe as theirs.

William shrugged. "Yeah? But if you can step 7,000 miles in a second even Mach 42 might be a tad on the slow side."

Marcus's face scrunched up. He had tried to ask her about her Etheric walking, but she politely pointed him back to this task and told him, "One Nobel prize winning project at a time, Marcus." Before he wiped the shit-eating grin off of his face, she was out of the room.

Marcus shrugged, nothing he could do about *that* curiosity at the moment.

Bobcat started his question by drawing out his first word, "Soooooooo…. You're wanting to figure out if Bethany Anne has made the right decision on how many people should be in the craft?" It was Bobcat's turn to think about the question. "Fuck if I know. Let's ask Dan and the guys what they want. We had better get this done pronto, though."

———

Marcus, Bobcat and William were walking down the hallway when they caught sight of Tim Kinley, from the Guardians. He was the easiest one for Bobcat to remember, as he was the tallest of the group.

"Tim!" Bobcat called out.

Tim turned his head as he continued down the hallway. "Yeah?"

"Have you seen Pete or Todd?"

He pointed the direction he was walking. "This way. They're with Dan, Stephen and the captains in the meeting room."

"Meeting room?" Marcus asked, looking between his teammates.

"BT FOOM," said William, shrugging.

Marcus's face was comical as he tried to parse the letters. Bobcat took pity on the scientist. "Beats-the-fuck-out-of-me."

"Ah." Marcus figured it would take him another lifetime to learn all of the acronyms his new military friends used.

They got to the meeting room and were surprised to see a group of eleven crew standing around the door talking to each other.

As they walked up, the door opened and Dan stuck his head out. "Can someone go get—" He spotted Bobcat walking up. "Just the man I wanted, can you three join us, please?"

He left the door open and they followed Dan into the room.

It was a pretty large room. It hadn't started as a conference room, but rather a medium sized holding area for some expensive toy or another. The team had dropped in a couple of tables and twenty chairs. Typically, they would have held the meeting in the nicer rooms on the Polarus, but most of the people were here on the Ad Aeternitatem, so Dan, Captain Thomas and Jean Dukes had joined Captain Wagner, Todd, Pete and Stephen, who was sitting at the head of the table.

The three men sat down, clueless as to what was happening.

———

Buenos Aires, Argentina

Michael was working through the papers in Anton's main house. He was disgusted by what he had found over the last few weeks.

Moreover, he was ashamed that he had allowed it to go on as long as he had.

His first efforts had been to find, and get rid of, the research apparatus and people that Anton had built over the decades since he had run from Germany. Michael had been ruthless when he learned some of the scientists had been old Nazis that Anton had helped keep alive far longer than their normal lifespan.

He had even taken a couple of days to track down one who had heard of the 'change in management' and fled to Chile. When Michael had someone executed on his orders, he required the head to be brought back to him as proof. He wasn't going to take any chances.

He wasn't as trusting as he might have been before his altercation with David. His hubris had certainly caught up with him and he now trusted only a few.

Three of Anton's main people had to be eliminated. They had tried to talk the talk without taking a step in the right direction. Unfortunately for them, Michael could hear their thoughts on the matter. Most of the time he would allow them to make a mistake, not just judge them on their inner musings. It helped others to believe he was being fair.

Of course, a few wondered how Michael always seemed to be around when the offenders were breaking his rules.

He was going through each of the files in Anton's desk. He had come across some notes related to his contacts in South America and set them aside for later review. He had created another pile for Anton's banking information.

Anton had little notes all over the place. Often, they would only have a few words on them scrawled in a scratchy way Michael found difficult to decipher. Anton's handwriting had always been horrible and becoming a vampire, Michael admitted, did nothing to help.

He had found a U.S. folder and was able to decipher a few short notes on a plan related to banking in Miami. He thought this must be the effort Bethany Anne had interrupted. He called Bethany Anne's phone and was surprised when Ecaterina answered for her. It seemed Bethany Anne had left her phone in her room when she stepped over to the ship from Miami, with Gabrielle. Michael decided he didn't need Bethany Anne specifically to answer his question when Ecaterina told him that John Grimes was in the house.

Pity that.

John was able to confirm the information and Michael hung up.

Michael had almost ignored some writing in the corner of a worksheet as useless until he caught 'Were contact.'

Michael turned the paper sideways to try and browbeat the lines into a semblance of understanding.

That effort was useless.

He went searching and found a few more cryptic notes. He wasn't able to glean a name, but he was able to learn one bit of information.

The American Pack Council had a Forsaken mole in their midst.

CHAPTER FOUR

Key Biscayne, FL USA

Lance was relaxing on the patio outside Bethany Anne's main house in Key Biscayne. He was sipping on a beer when the patio door opened and Patricia stepped out with a white wine in her hand.

Lance smiled at the woman, she had been everything he had needed and more. He pushed out the chair next to him in invitation and she smiled in response and sat down, setting her wine on the table.

"Penny for your thoughts?" she asked.

"I can't believe it's done." The sun was going down and it would get unseasonably cold this evening. For both Patricia and Lance, it wasn't uncomfortable at all. They had spent most of their lives in Colorado and were well acquainted with cold weather. Miami didn't have anything close to cold in its temperature range.

She took a sip from her wine, a nice Riesling. When she

went back in, she would see if the fridge had a cheese that would go with it. "The base?" She often knew exactly what Lance was thinking after so many years working together.

"Yes." He said no more.

"What's bothering you?"

He looked over at the woman beside him and sighed. "There isn't any hiding stuff from you, is there?"

She communed with her wine for a second. "Of course you can. I didn't realize the owner of this beautiful house, the CEO of the corporation was your own daughter." The sunset light was playing in her wine, mesmerizing colors swirling around.

Lance smiled. "Ha! That's probably the only thing I was able to hide from you and thank God it was only for a day. It helped that you thought she was." Lance turned back to look out over the water.

Patricia looked up. "You're probably right. I'm being too hard on myself. My lack of perfection was starting to grate on my nerves for a minute. I appreciate you reminding me that you only succeeded because you were working for the undead." Patricia took a deep breath; sometimes she forgot to close her damn mouth around this man.

Fortunately, Lance took it as the joke she intended. "That's right! I guess you could say that I've worked for the undead in both versions of the meaning." Lance rubbed his hands together. "I can't wait to spring that on old futz and guts."

Patricia's face was elegantly confused. "Who?" Before Lance could respond, she made her best guess, "Frank?"

Lance continued looking out over the water, but waved his hand in her direction. "That's why I needed you so much. I don't have to explain the little things."

She resolved to circle back around to Frank later. "Why

are you surprised we got the base back and what has you so melancholy over it?"

"Surprised because I thought it would be another couple of years, melancholic because I'm the asshole corporate raider that helped close it down. I would never, in my life, have thought that I would be the cause of good men and women in the service needing to move from that location."

Patricia understood what was causing Lance's unease. He blamed himself for the base closing the military operation and going private. "We have open calls for those who want to leave the Army and help with the new base, changes, and security, to stay in the area. It looks like we're going to be re-sourced pretty well. Both on security and on the engineering side."

Lance looked over at Patricia and raised an eyebrow.

"Probably a hundred percent of our short term needs and seventy percent of our long term needs for security are going to be staying with us."

Hot damn, Lance thought, the eyebrow worked!

He asked, "How did you get that many to make the change?"

"There was a rumor going around about the new corporation. Apparently they're moving their corporate headquarters, and highly valuable research and development. It appears that they have a 'military history.'"

"You didn't!"

Patricia looked at her fingernails, admiring the manicure she had done just this morning. She let Lance sit for another few seconds before answering, "You're right, I didn't."

Lance grunted and turned back towards the view.

"Kevin did."

Lance swung his head back towards her, shock on his

face. "Kevin knows? You told Kevin?"

Patricia looked dead into Lance's eyes. Sometimes she wished she could use a bat, this man was that blind to the obvious. "No. I didn't tell Kevin. Kevin is a little quicker on the uptake than you. He knows I wouldn't quit my job and move to Florida for just anyone, so I assume he is making a very educated guess."

Lance was working on her statement. He knew there were two discussions going on, but he couldn't connect the first because the comment about Kevin held his attention. Well, hell, he would come back to it.

He turned back again. Maybe taking over his old base wouldn't be such a bad thing.

_____

Key Biscayne, FL USA

Bethany Anne, Gabrielle and Ashur arrived back in her suite. This time, Ashur ignored her shoes and walked to the door. Gabrielle did the honors and Ashur took off ahead of them, down the stairs.

Gabrielle waved over her shoulder as she walked ahead of Bethany Anne. "I'm heading next door. I'll send John and Eric over." Gabrielle was out the front door before Bethany Anne had made it down the steps. She could hear her dad and Patricia in the back. It sounded like they were possibly having a personal moment, so she turned around and headed back upstairs. No need to spray any gasoline on that little fire right now. Bethany Anne hadn't decided whether she was going to get personally involved in that relationship or not.

Ecaterina and Nathan's dance had been fun to watch, and even more fun to poke and prod at every once in a while. Bethany Anne wasn't sure whether to have fun at her father's expense, always tempting, or find a moment to slap her father upside his overly thick, caveman skull. Unfortunately, she shouldn't tell him that Patricia wouldn't wait forever because to date, she already had.

As she went back into her room she heard her phone go off. She walked over to her nightstand to pick it up. Ecaterina would kill her if she realized that she had left it behind.

When she answered, she could smell that Ecaterina had already picked up her phone. Looks like she was in for a lecture in Ecaterina's Romanian accent. Bethany Anne had a hard time feeling 'talked at' when the person talking to you sounded sexy as shit.

"Hey Michael." Bethany Anne sat on her bed. The back patio was not an option. She didn't want to intrude on what might become a personal moment. She considered her other options for a place to hold this conversation. She stood back up to get a jacket and go out. Damn shame Shelly wasn't around.

"Hello Bethany Anne, how are you?" Michael was like that. He was ever the polite person with her, no matter how much she tried to poke the bear, his aloofness making it hard to settle into any sort of relationship. She was no longer the woman who needed his help. With TOM's information, she often understood more about what was going on with their abilities than Michael did.

She considered how she could poke the man one more time, and keep poking him to see what would get a reaction out of him.

"I'm not late, that's how I am." There, take that. Next time you come rushing to rescue the damsel who-wasn't-in-distress be on *time*.

"That's nice. I didn't realize that still occurred since your change."

Gott Verdammt. That *motherfucker* just dinged her and got a point in. Fucking prick!

Shit, she had no retort for that statement. He was getting better, time to up her game. Can't have a thousand-year-old walking aristocrat thinking he's got game.

Then again, she had seen him without a shirt, so he had at least *some* game. Not that she would ever admit that to Michael, his overgrown ego would explode.

"Lots of things you don't know about me since my change. Come to think about it, you didn't know me well before my change either. But, enough about my mysteriousness. Whatcha' got?"

Damn, Michael thought, he was sure he was going to get under her skin with that comment. Time to figure out how to up his game, as Stephen would say. "I've been going through Anton's records and I found some notes that suggest he has a contact on the American Pack Council."

Bethany Anne's face clouded up. "Seriously?"

"Yes."

Bethany Anne grabbed her purse and headed out the door of her suite. She heard the front door open, so her shadows had arrived. She boosted her speed to meet John as he entered the house. She quickly slid between John and the half-open door, his face moving from startled to resigned as his boss left him behind.

He closed the door behind her.

Bethany Anne walked over to one of the SUVs and jumped in the back.

John called out, "Where are we going?"

Bethany Anne answered Michael. "I wish that asshole was still alive so I could kick his nuts hard enough he would suffocate."

Eric looked over at John and mouthed, "Anton?" John shrugged and nodded that was his guess as well.

Bethany Anne answered John's question, "Take me to someplace that sells Bugattis. I feel a need for speed."

Eric took out his phone. "Hot damn, car shopping!"

John wasn't too happy. "Those cars have four seats, right?"

Eric shrugged, "Beats the fuck out of me, if they have two seats then Miss Moneybags… Oww!" Eric spun around in his seat after his ear blazed with a sharp, intense pain. Bethany Anne was sitting in the back seat, looking out her window ignoring the byplay of her guards up front. Eric turned back around while rubbing his sore earlobe. "Then our beloved leader, Bethany Anne, will need to purchase two so her ever-dependable and long-suffering…" Eric slammed his hand back over his ear, but nothing happened. "Guards will be able to keep up."

John smiled, he decided he could support that argument. "Then hurry up with the directions, we are wasting valuable daylight, my good man."

Michael continued the conversation from his side. He had heard everything including the infinitesimal sound when Bethany Anne flicked her guard's ear. He was trying to understand why she allowed what seemed like disrespect from her guards. He couldn't, however, deny that all of them would put their own life on the line to save hers. Maybe he had a few things to learn, yet. "Yes, well Ecaterina and Killian made short work of him. His death was too quick. He deserved far worse."

"I thought you were ambivalent about Anton? I know you have a hard-on for David…"

"I do NOT have a 'hard-on' for David."

Bethany Anne snickered, point for her.

"Sorry." No she wasn't. "Turn of phrase. I mean I know you want David's death to be significant, but I thought you didn't care about Anton's as much."

Dammit, that was a point, he was sure she got a point in there. She often got him by using vernacular he wasn't used to hearing. When he pulled out a phrase from the 1980s it took her three minutes to stop laughing. He had almost hung up except that would have given her extra bonus something or other. "I've been having to deal with, and clean up, Anton's mess for the last few weeks. I have a fresh appreciation for his evil."

Bethany Anne grew somber. "Thank you, Michael. I do appreciate you taking this on." Michael felt her sincerity thousands of miles away as if he was there in the car with her.

Just like that, Michael's irritation at Bethany Anne evaporated. "It is mine to clean up. I still owe you, for you having to deal with everything while I was… indisposed."

Bethany Anne was aware Michael had a problem with admitting how weak he had been while in David's captivity. He still didn't like it when he had to refer to his time in the vessel. He never would tell Bethany Anne how he had been trapped. When she cornered Stephen, he hadn't known either.

"The past is just the past, Michael. What do you think we need to do about the American Pack Council?"

"Kill them all?"

Gott Verdammt! Bethany Anne was ready to give Michael both barrels about how killing everyone wasn't the only option, when she heard the silent chuckle escape his lips.

She bit back her first words and instead said, "You ass-riding scrotum king!" This time, Michael didn't try to hold back his laughter. Nor the laughter when she kept calling him names. "You flipping slut-sucking experimental nipple dictator!" She stopped calling him names when she realized he had put his hand over the phone and was howling with glee.

Eric was busy, typing furiously on his phone. John looked over at him. "Duplicate?" Eric pressed the return key, "Hell no, how the... uh, stuff does she come up with so many?"

She waited, and waited, and fucking waited. Mind you, what seemed like forever was probably only fifteen seconds. Michael wasn't usually comfortable letting loose very much. She could almost imagine him daintily wiping a tear away from his eye.

When he returned to the phone call, he was as much the ever reserved ass-munch he had been when she first met him. "So, if that isn't an option, what would you suggest?"

She was tempted to tell him 'kill them all' as a joke, but he might take that as permission. "Call Gerry and set up a meeting for the council, leave the reason for the meeting vague and show up to find out who the guilty party is. Then keep the punishment to a minimum. I'm not really fond of using death as the only punishment for all crimes. Kind of sucks when minor littering is death, jaywalking is death, running a yellow light is death..."

Michael sniffed. "Perhaps, but it makes the punishment phase very easy."

"A little lazy, but I understand." Bethany Anne noticed they were on the South Dixie Highway and she was hungry. She leaned forward and covered the phone, more for appearances than keeping the vampire on the line from hearing anything. "Hey, pause the Bugatti run. I *needs* me some Joe's dogs."

John smiled. Bethany Anne had been buying Joe's ever since they first met her and she had convinced the proprietor to swing by and feed Dan's group. If by convince you meant dropping twenty-five large ones on him. His place was on the main road into Miami proper from her house and damn near every time she went near the place she would have them swing through.

Eric knew that once they finished stuffing their faces, Bethany Anne would probably be over the 'need for speed' feeling. "So close." He muttered under his breath.

Michael considered her response. "Ok. Do you want me to come up there for this?"

Bethany Anne returned to her conversation with Michael. "Not sure, I'll talk with Gerry and Nathan and see what we need to do. If you show up, we're liable to have people jumping out of the windows." Michael kept quiet, she could be right.

They said their good-byes as John pulled up. The red food trailer didn't presently have anyone in line. Before he could come to a complete stop, Bethany Anne was out of the SUV and heading to the window.

Eric looked over at John. "Can't we get her back on track? Do you know how much a Bugatti costs? We would have made Guard's Hall of Fame for the sickest ride ever. Those things are a cool million for used." Eric looked back at his boss who was talking with the guy in the trailer. "Damn. So close." Eric and John got out of the SUV and walked over to say hi to their friend.

———

The Queen Bitch's Ship Ad Aeternitatem

Stephen allowed everyone to chat for a minute. It wasn't a secret why they were meeting—well, except to Bobcat's team. They had been sequestered and didn't have any external T.V. connection. But now, Todd and Pete had brought all three of them up to date.

"It has been said…" Stephen, like most vampires, could layer emotions into the air with his vocal cords. He understood it to be a method of affecting humans, and used it now while he talked. He didn't employ it often, but he had been affected himself by Michael's use of it back in Argentina and now considered it a very useful tool. Here he was layering enough 'danger' into his voice that everyone immediately stopped talking and quickly tried to find the source.

He quit doing it and repeated himself into the now silent room. "It has been said that for evil to prosper, all it takes is for good men and women to do nothing. I would modify that to say all it takes is for good men and women to not be permitted to do something."

He had everyone's attention. He looked over the team that Bethany Anne had entrusted him with. It had been many, many decades since he had more than himself to be concerned with. Even in World War II he had been an independent. Fortunately, the skill of leading people, however many centuries ago it might have been when you first learned it, didn't just evaporate. "I interrupted two of us discussing the actions of the terrorists in France. One was wishing to have the opportunity to 'do something' while the other, perhaps in ignorance, simply asked 'why can't we?'

"I asked all of you to come to this meeting to ask if you believe that our mission would be served if we 'do something.'

Is it worth the risks, the potential loss of lives, your lives, to get involved?"

Captain Thomas spoke up, "Do you believe it's something that Bethany Anne would want us to get involved in?"

Stephen smiled. "Do you mean, would Bethany Anne see all of the innocents killed, maimed and injured and feel a righteous anger and a desire to right the wrongs done against them?"

Captain Thomas shook his head quickly. No one believed Bethany Anne wouldn't have a burning desire to help those who suffered, and put paid to those responsible for the heinous acts. "No, we all know that answer. I'm asking would Bethany Anne consider the effort to get involved worth the risk. Both to the people and to the Ad Aeternitatem?"

Stephen pursed his lips. "When I first met Bethany Anne, she changed my future. She asked me, after I drank from her, to be her eyes and ears in Europe. I took responsibility for the UnknownWorld in Europe. Now, Europe is my protectorate. You are charged with helping me. Our mission, in the end, is to save the Earth. We are going to cause many changes in the near future. If, through the changes we bring about, we create more fear these… people… will use it and we will have hurt those we are trying to help. I have seen atrocities that make what has happened in France seem like a family squabble. I am not the right person to judge if what has happened warrants our involvement."

He looked around at all of those in the room with him. He could hear the breathing of the many crew standing outside the door. "Our Queen was willing to gamble the fate of the world's future on her ability to come and rescue one person… me." He stopped looking at people and remembered how he had lain on the floor, pain racking his body, as Reginald stood over him. He could see her as she exited his hallway, two pistols in her hands and mouthing the words that sealed the doom of both Terence and Reginald.

Stephen stood up. "But, if you ask me, I'll tell you that I believe those cock-tip sucking, fudge-loving, fucking retarded clusterfuck, shit-faced ass jackers need to be sent to whatever heaven they believe in, sooner, rather than later. They don't represent their faith, they represent hate and hate will kill the world just as quickly as any aliens might."

Shouts of agreement reverberated throughout the ships. It seemed Captain Thomas had left his communications gear that kept him in contact with the Polarus on and sending.

The details needed to be ironed out, but the Queen Bitch's Navy would be going to war.

CHAPTER FIVE

Las Vegas, NV USA

Tom and Jeffrey were finished with the data upload that ADAM had requested. They had shot the forty-three requests over to Nathan and Bethany Anne. She only asked to leave off anything with recent history and they got busy pulling the rest of the data. Unfortunately, it meant a lot of data cleaning to keep the information as close to the requested subjects as possible.

They failed on one of the books and ADAM was quick to ask for more about, of all things possible, Bugs Bunny cartoons. One of the books had used Bugs Bunny cartoons as examples to discuss different physics problems.

After some back and forth, it was decided to ignore that request. They could imagine Bugs Bunny progressing to Wile E. Coyote and the Road Runner, Marvin the Martian and many other characters, which would open up the requests to too many variables.

They had no idea that their decision to leave out uploading those cartoons would play a role in ADAM's future.

ADAM's communication skills were getting better although it still required a fair amount of typing on Tom's part. Jeffrey was a poor typist and Tom had hundreds of thousands of lines of code under his belt. His typing speed was pretty high.

After some conversation, they decided that they would stick with typed commands instead of trying to interface voice communications. The main concern was mistranslation issues from the humans back into the computer for ADAM. The secondary concern was if something happened to be said while the system was on, but the communication hadn't been meant for ADAM. Jeffrey figured that the last problem he wanted to deal with was ADAM wanting to know what 'go fuck yourself' meant should Tom mouth off to him.

Just a few miles away, inside the grounds of Nellis Air Force Base there was a party given to the outgoing cyber-security and intelligence officer. Their new officer had arrived that afternoon from Hurlburt Field, Florida.

As Captain Benjamin G. Stockton got settled into his new post, he overheard two of the enlisted personnel discuss the massive amount of downloads happening at the bunkers outside the fence.

Data Bunkers? That sounded ominous. He wrote down a note to follow up on that comment later in the week.

Turkey

David was in the back seat of the Mercedes-Benz SUV. All of the back windows had been blacked out, in case his driver could not locate an appropriate stopping point before sunrise. They had landed in Istanbul, and had driven from there. They should hit Konya before morning.

David was looking for just the right location. A town with enough people that he had a chance to procure enough fresh blood without causing too much confusion right away. Yet it had to be small enough and far enough from supporting towns that a trap could be set.

Preferably it would be in a location that his contacts in the PKK would be able to get approval for a focused attack, to help their own effort against the Turkish government.

For his plan to have the best chance of success, he wanted one near the Syrian border. That would cause the U.S. forces in the region to jump at the chance, if a neutral military partner was selected as the group to liberate the small town.

Small town, small force. They would be weakened by his Nosferatu and then finished by the PKK.

———

Key Biscayne, FL USA

Bethany Anne was resting on the bed in her suite. She wasn't tired, thanks to the large consumption of Coke an hour ago.

She was feeling anxious. Something was bothering her and she couldn't tell what it was. Something subconscious…

Tom?

Yes.

Are you doing anything that would cause me to feel anxious?

No, I'm not doing anything that should affect your emotions. I am working with the computer, but that

hasn't caused you any problems recently. Not that I am aware of.

No, me neither. Bethany Anne stared at her ceiling. *What are you running?*

I'm trying to determine how to best communicate with Marcus without you getting involved. It does get a bit lonely in here from time to time and I will admit that I am looking forward to working on the math involved with the engineering for the ships.

Bethany Anne considered that for a minute. Tom had never admitted to being lonely, at least not that she could remember. Now, he was getting involved in helping design the ships with Team BMW, and she was the limiting factor.

All because she had a fear of getting into the pod-doc again. She studied that feeling and tried to figure out why she felt that way.

No control, plain and simple.

Bethany Anne was a control freak about her body now. She had a large amount to be thankful for from the changes that TOM, and by extension the Kurtherians, had made. But she didn't like that she didn't know exactly what was going to happen. The first time she woke up, she had an alien tag-along.

TOM, what is the absolute best way to make this communication with Marcus happen as seamlessly as possible?

With or without going into the pod-doc?

The absolute best way.

There is a way to add a micro-miniature communication device that can operate through the Etheric, using very little energy, and communicate with anything here on your world. Most of the time, we would use a repeater that has a connection to your Internet.

How do we make sure nothing can attack the computer in my head?

Seriously? Didn't I make this argument when we watched Independence Day?

Humor me, it isn't like you have anywhere to go. Bethany Anne sighed. *I'm sorry, TOM. That was uncalled for.*

What are you talking about? I can't go anywhere because I chose to 'hitch a ride,' as you call it, without permission. I've at least got to accept that responsibility.

Bethany Anne sat up in bed and used her palms to rub her eyes. *It's not that, TOM.* She looked around her suite, everything in place and yet still cold. She thought back to her earlier plan of buying a Bugatti and racing around Miami.

She was running. Running from the responsibility of moving forward with the connectivity. It was the best solution to get the little ships going quickly and she was being a big fat…

I'm scared, TOM.

Of?

Losing control. Not knowing and approving everything that goes on when I go in the pod-doc.

Bethany Anne, I'm sorry for failing to get your permission to…

Stop, just stop. This isn't about that. At least, not anymore. I understand why you did what you did. I've got to own up that I've been treating you as a second class citizen. I've been using 'you hitching a ride' as a bludgeon to beat you back into a safe box. No more, it ends right now. We are either partners who will make it to the end together or we fail together. I refuse to treat you as any less than my closest friend. That's figurative, you're already my closest friend literally.

She smiled at that thought. Not even a lover could be any closer than TOM.

She sat up, and Ashur's big head poked itself above the end of her bed, watching her. She smiled at the dog, and whispered, "We're going to sneak out, make sure no one is in the hall."

Ashur turned around and went over to the suite door and stuck a nose to the floorboard, and then cocked his head to get an ear by it. When Ashur looked back at her he gave her a soft 'woof.'

She pointed to the closet and Ashur padded silently over to the room and went in.

She followed and closed the door gently behind her and locked it.

Bethany Anne? What are you doing?

We. What are we doing.

TOM was silent for a moment. He knew something momentous had just occurred, but he wasn't sure what it meant for his future.

Ok, what are *we* doing?

We're sneaking over to the Ad Aeternitatem and jumping in the pod-doc before anyone knows we're gone and then sneaking back. This won't take long, right?

No, probably a couple of hours.

Bethany Anne thought about that. She should be good for three, maybe four, hours before anyone had a reason to bother her.

What about taking the phone?

Fuck me. Yeah, if anyone calls and it just rings someone will eventually come looking. She gently opened the door and went over to her nightstand and picked up her phone. She didn't bother putting any clothes on as she would just be taking them off in the ship.

Besides, no one was supposed to see her.

She closed the door again and locked it. Reaching over she snagged Ashur by his neck and they disappeared.

———

Anton's former residence
Buenos Aires Argentina

Michael was tapping his chin as he studied the banking information he had set aside earlier. Anton had been into a lot of businesses. He actually had quite a stake in a lot of Michael's own companies.

If he read Anton's notes correctly, he had made a killing in local oil companies over the decades and had stolen a large percentage of a country's GDP.

Michael was trying to figure out how to get a significant portion of the money back to the people to whom it truly belonged.

In years past, he would have added it to his own holdings and figured that being under his management was better than what had happened previously.

But that wasn't Bethany Anne's way of doing things and annoyingly enough, it mattered to Michael what she might think. So he considered how to mitigate Anton's dealings here in South America. The latest Argentinian government had dropped capital controls. Now a bunch of people were selling the peso and purchasing dollars. This action was causing the devaluation of the peso at an alarming rate.

Maybe it was time he used the massive amount of funds from Anton's reserves to see if he could first help support Argentina and, from a good base here, the rest of South America.

Michael smiled. It wasn't going to be easy, but he had the beginnings of a plan and damned if he didn't feel good about doing it as well.

Not a chance he would mention *that* fact to Bethany Anne should it ever come up.

Now, he had to figure out who the movers and shakers in the financial industry were and start the long process of finding people who could be trusted.

Michael made a disgusted face and tossed his pencil on the desk. He needed help. He had learned what David had done to Carl. David had delighted, in fact, in telling Michael multiple times how he had tortured Carl for information. Now, how was he going to find another Carl quickly enough?

He reached for his phone, to call Bethany Anne.

CHAPTER SIX

Nellis AFB, Las Vegas NV USA

Captain Benjamin G. Stockton had taken a couple of days to get acquainted with his people and basically get caught up on what was happening on and around the base.

Now, it was time to follow up on what he had found out about Patriarch Research. He grabbed his notes and the folder that had been dropped on his desk and started reading through the highlights.

It didn't look like a big deal at first glance. Captain Billings had gone outside the gate and had dropped by unannounced. He had met the two principals while they were in the middle of setting up some equipment, and their story had checked out when followed up.

But, when the phrase 'data bunker' had been spoken about their location, it set off an alarm for some reason. Might be something, might be nothing, but he would figure out why it bugged him.

Key Biscayne, FL USA

Bethany Anne and Ashur appeared back in the closet. She listened for a moment and confirmed no one was in her room.

She had played hooky and gotten away with it.

Her phone buzzed and she just about jumped through the ceiling. She had been so worked up sneaking out and back that she was on edge. She laughed off the adrenaline rush and looked down to see who the caller was.

Michael was asking for a video call. She looked down at her chest and considered what he would say, but decided not to chance it right then. She hit the voice only button. "Hello Michael, what's up?"

"Not me." Bethany Anne's mouth dropped open in shock, the man was using a double entendre. "I'm sitting behind Anton's desk." Her mouth closed again, that old man knew enough to be oh-so-right while sounding oh-so-wrong.

Ass.

She unlocked the closet door and walked into her bedroom and got back into bed. "Ok, other than you sitting at a desk and taking comments way too literally. Here's a thought, act a few centuries younger. It might do you some good."

Score! She knew that would annoy him.

She heard a grunt from her phone. "Yes, well when you have as much wisdom as I do, you find that leaving a few centuries behind might make you as brash as a baby sometimes. Prone to running off at the mouth and getting into situations a calmer mind might have seen a way clear of. Perhaps without destroying an 1836 piano."

"Are you seriously blaming me for breaking that piano at

Anton's party? I might remind you, I was thrown over that balcony. It wasn't like you were at the bottom to catch my ass."

She could have sworn that she had heard an 'if only.' Had she? No, he didn't talk like that. Possibly wishful thinking on her part? Dammit, she had to get old fussbudgets out of her mind. Why she was even thinking about him as anything but a tactical partner was beyond her.

She had gone out with Ben the previous week. It had been a nice little dinner, but you could see that it was a 'bucket list' check for him. He had gotten back on the horse and ridden it. He'd voiced his appreciation for her help getting him and Tabitha out of the Miami operation. He had been pretty sure that they would have been killed, had her team not busted the operation.

At the end of the dinner it was time to take him to Nathan on the Polarus. They drugged him as they approached their private plane. It took about ten minutes for the drugs to take effect and then Bethany Anne, John and Eric translocated with Ben through the Etheric to the Polarus. They took the snoozing guy to Nathan who left him in his stateroom and promised to make up an appropriate story of how he got on the ship so quickly.

It wouldn't matter; if Nathan trusted Ben enough to work with him it wouldn't be too long before Ben knew many secrets. At that point he would be able to guess how they had transported him to the middle of the ocean so quickly.

Michael brought her wandering thoughts back on track. "No, but you couldn't dodge just a little? That piano was worth a small fortune."

"I'll try to find something a little less expensive to break my fall the next time, you ass. Now, did you call to complain about the piano or do you have a legitimate reason to interrupt my sleep?"

"Please, you were not sleeping. I heard you unlock a door and walk to your bed. In fact, I would hazard a guess that you went somewhere without your team." Michael didn't personally care if she had or hadn't gone somewhere with her team, but she wouldn't want her team to know she had snuck out. That was what made him smile on his side of the phone.

Damn the man and his vampire hearing. "Whatever. My point is, you called me. For what?" If at first you don't succeed, blow off his logic.

"I'm going to need to work with a lot of people and agencies down here that I am completely unfamiliar with. I'm going to need to fill Carl's position. Do you have any suggestions on who I should talk with to accomplish this? Normally, I would call Frank and I suppose that is a choice. Nathan might be another good choice. Just seeking some advice, that's all."

She narrowed her eyes, it was never 'that's all' with Michael. The man could have plans within plans within... Oh, hell. He could be a conniving bastard if he chose to be. A small grin started to form on her face. "You know what Michael? I do happen to have a good suggestion. But let me talk with Nathan before we reach out to them. I'm not sure what this person's status is right now, but they are already familiar with the UnknownWorld so that isn't an issue. I'll probably rope Frank into the conversation, to vet this person as well, before they are chosen. If they work out, I'll have them on a plane and down to you within forty-eight hours."

"On a plane? You aren't willing to bring him to me?"

"What do you think I am, your taxi?" The two of them had tried to teach each other their Etheric tricks. But Bethany

Anne couldn't get the hang of turning to myst and Michael wasn't able to Etherically walk. It bugged Bethany Anne that she couldn't turn to myst and spy on people. Well, yuck. Not like her dad or anything.

"No, I think of you as the leader of our team who would recognize the desperate need of one of her partners. A resource he needs, to be able to move forward and accomplish a goal that she had set out for him."

"Right, your taxi. Ok, I'll consider it. Until they get vetted it doesn't matter." He had made an excellent point, actually. He did need someone to replace Carl. "Oh, hell. Yes, yes. If they work out, I'll bring them down."

"Thank you."

"You're welcome. Is that all? Can I get my beauty sleep now?"

"Yes, do plan to get a full night's sleep to help, why don't you?" She wanted to reach through the phone and slap the shitty grin she heard through the phone right off his face. She should accidentally, on purpose, hit the video button. Show him a strategically placed breast, with just a touch of nipple, to make his eyes come out of his head. Then, she could take a screen-capture of his face before his old heart exploded on him.

She rolled her eyes, what the hell was wrong with her? Where were all of these thoughts coming from? She was becoming a phone slut? It had to be Gabrielle's fault. Probably giving her bad ideas with the stories about relationships across the centuries. Damn, damn, damn. Since she was the one who kept prying into Gabrielle's love life she only had herself to blame. She was going to have to go cold turkey and cold showers.

Wait a second…

TOM, can you shut off my emotions?

Not shut off completely. At least not most of the time. I can add to or subtract from your emotions, why do you ask?

Hold on, I've got to get back to Michael.

Something TOM had just said was trying to make itself known…

Gott Verdammt TOM, are you screwing with my emotions!

Aaaahhhh, what?

I said…

"Bethany Anne?"

I'll get back to you in a minute.

"Sorry Michael, your lame effort to annoy me has been duly noted and I will get back to you with an appropriate response in a reasonable time." There, suck on that persimmon for a minute you bag of bones. Chippendale quality bones but …

Dammit TOM, what the fuck are you playing with?

Huh? I'm not playing with… oh. Oh! Oh, my bad. I'm sorry Bethany Anne. Oh, holy crap. This is bad… this is bad. Wait, my bad… Sorry, this is my bad!

Well, whatever the fuck it is, stop doing it for one fucking minute so I can have a decent phone call without making a slutty fangirl of myself. You're making me think I want to join MAS for fuck's sake.

MAS?

Yeah, your Michael Adoration Society. You're the founding, and only, member right now.

She got silence from TOM. She must have hit some point of truth in that conversation.

"I'm sure I'll be sleepless tonight with anticipation. I

appreciate you taking the phone call, and I'll let you get back to your much needed rest. Have a good night, Bethany Anne."

"The same to you, Michael." They hung up.

Now, back to her little miscreant alien symbiont.

Her phone rang again and she was about to stab the button and yell at Michael when she realized it was Stephen calling her.

She put the phone to her ear. "Hello! How is my favorite vampire?"

Stephen's smile came through the phone, "I wonder what my daughter would say about that?"

"Nothing, I tell her all the time that you're my favorite."

"Is that because she won't tell you her secrets?"

"Of course! I'm trying hard to wear her down but her stamina is pretty substantial for being a cold-hearted blood sucking fiend."

"I did train her well."

"Wait! Can I get you to say that again? I didn't have the recorder on." Bethany Anne appreciated how easily Stephen could bring a smile to her face.

Stephen laughed "Maybe after our call."

"Deal. Ok, what do you have for me?"

"Have you been paying attention to the situation in France?"

"Huh? No. I've... not been around a T.V. for a while, what's going on?"

Stephen took Bethany Anne through the situation in France in the last few hours. By the time he finished, she was *livid*.

"Those senile goat-fucking cum-nut, jizz-swallowing, rectal bastards!" By the time she was at the end of her diatribe, she was practically spitting the words out. Bethany

Anne was thinking about what it must have been like to be sitting in a cafe when some twisted dick wanker came walking around spraying bullets, the fear they would have felt…

"Pretty much our feelings over here. I'm calling to get your okay to go and do something about it."

Bethany Anne brought her mind back on track. "Wait, what? You want to go after them?"

"Well, actually both ships' crews are spitting mad and they want to get a little of their own back."

Bethany Anne pursed her lips. She didn't have an issue with this. "Come clean with me, Stephen. What are your feelings on this situation?"

"My Queen, they did this in my land. I'm paraphrasing a little, but the best quote I've got is 'that evil will prosper if good men and women aren't permitted to do something.' What is the use of protecting the Earth from aliens if the terrorists have already destroyed the people here?"

There was a pause. Bethany Anne replied after a few seconds, "The priority is the safety of TOM's ship. So long as that is taken care of, then you have my full support and will have my team on call if you need us. Have Frank and Nathan find those fuckers for you. They think they know terror? They can't imagine real terror."

She thought more about all the senseless killing these assholes had done. The brothers, sisters, fathers and mothers that weren't coming home, ever again. Her voice turned dark, angry and violent. Her eyes turned blood red, her fangs started to grow.

"Stephen, tell those on your ships Bethany Anne unleashes the Dogs of War."

UNDER MY HEEL

The Queen Bitch's Ship Polarus

Frank was in his stateroom on the Polarus, working on his book about Bethany Anne in his off time. With Nathan working to get ungodly amounts of connectivity options on the ship, he was in the middle of the action and could easily keep his ear to the… well, ground wasn't the right word.

For the last few hours he had been reading the reports coming out of France. Most of them were diplomatic communications for the people back in D.C., but he would occasionally get a military update in the bunch.

He had requested two monitors and now he had the same setup that he'd enjoyed back in the subterranean office in D.C., without the cold.

He noticed his dashboard had a red file flagged. Interesting, he thought. He clicked on the file and started to read.

Turkey was having a problem in one of their small towns near their border with Syria and had sent in some men.

Those men had died. So Turkey had reached out to their partners in NATO for assistance. Most of Turkey's present resources were deployed to be the 'bully boys' for the other European countries. They were to interdict the flow of refugees coming into Europe proper. Because of these efforts, Turkey didn't have enough additional resources to send a military response into the town.

The U.S. had dropped a couple of fire teams to see what was going on. The teams reported a silent town and dead bodies everywhere. They found a lot of tracks going up into the mountains that surrounded the town and followed the tracks into a large cave.

Two fire teams, eight men, went into the cave. Two men staggered out and one of them died of his wounds in the small town below. The last man had found a working cell phone and had called in the report.

He claimed there were zombies in the caves. Dead townspeople who had come back to life.

Night had fallen shortly after the first report. They had not heard from the soldier since the first call.

This wasn't a zombie infestation, Frank knew. This was a Nosferatu attack. Frank and Dan had talked together a couple of times wondering what David would do. Well, now they had the answer.

David was creating Nosferatu in a remote location. Perhaps hoping the infestation would get large enough to be self-replicating.

Frank wasn't sure why David would do that. Without a true vampire, the Nosferatu were rarely able to create additional Nosferatu.

What was David's plan here?

There was a knock on his door. Frank called out, "Come in."

Nathan stuck his head in. "Hey. Stephen and Dan are requesting our services to locate these asshole terrorists. Got a minute?"

Frank started unplugging his external monitors. His mind was abuzz, his gut told him he was missing some pieces. But, until he got more information, he would just have to push his way through for the short term.

"Yes, I've got time. Hey, did you hear about the Nosferatu attack in Turkey?"

"What? Nosferatu in Turkey? Dammit, when it rains, it pours." Nathan pulled out of the doorway so Frank could exit his room.

Frank closed his door and they walked towards the

smaller meeting room. "Yes. I haven't received any official request for help yet, but I imagine I'll get a call sometime soon. The U.S. just lost eight soldiers on the Syrian border. I think it's probably David starting something. I just can't figure out what his strategy is yet. Maybe he thinks Michael will come take care of the problem? Try to keep Michael busy while he works somewhere else?"

Nathan shrugged. His life had been significantly less busy before he had met Bethany Anne. With his almost nine decades, he had learned how to handle bad news and not freak out. "I'm sure we'll find out. I'll get Ben to start tracking more information out of Turkey. I've got him backtracking the attacks, combing through all of the server logs. We're losing a lot of connections in or near Russia, they're just disappearing. Weird shit."

Frank asked, "How is Ben doing?"

The men made it to the meeting room, rapped on the door and stepped in. They were the first to arrive. They both took a seat. "Pretty well. It isn't like he didn't have a clue before. He had tried to track down more information so it was pretty fortuitous that he didn't find out too much before he came onboard."

Frank made himself comfortable and set up his laptop. "Huh, he must be pretty good because he didn't trigger any of my alarms."

"He *is* good. I'll give him credit. But he isn't that smart in the relationship area. He tried a date with Bethany Anne but he admitted that he could hardly keep up a conversation with her. When he saw her again something in his croc-brain went ape-shit, and it took all of his focus not to run, he said. I've talked to Bethany Anne and she said he just seemed zoned out."

"I'm surprised she didn't listen to his heart rate, that should have told her what was going on."

Nathan shrugged. "I talked with John. He thinks she was trying to have a 'normal' time that night. Leave all of the specialness behind and just be a woman for an hour or two."

"So, she tries to be a normal Nellie and she gets William the wax paper cut-out for a date? Figures."

Frank had everything back up on his laptop, so he started trying to find out more about the Turkish flare up. "You would think if she wanted a date, that Stephen or Michael would be good…"

"Watch your mouth!" Nathan exclaimed.

Frank looked up, astonished. "What? I know that Stephen is her vassal or something…" Nathan stuck a hand up.

"Not my worry there. I'm more concerned about something between Bethany Anne and Michael."

"Why?"

Nathan leaned towards Frank. "Because right now, the only person in the world who keeps Michael in check is Bethany Anne."

"Yeah, so? She would keep him in check regardless."

"Who keeps Bethany Anne in check?"

"Well, I suppose…" Frank got quiet. "None of us really keep her in check, do we? It isn't like she's done anything that we actively oppose."

Nathan shook his head. "Not really what I was trying to say. Maybe this is just my decades of experience freaking out, but having two of the strongest vampires in existence as a couple seems like a monumentally bad idea."

"I don't think you're giving either one enough credit."

Nathan put his hands to his face. "Yeah. That's the same thing that Ecaterina tells me. I do try and realize that the

Michael I met a few weeks ago isn't the same guy I had to work with P.B.A."

Frank searched his mental archives and drew a blank. "P.B.A.?"

"Pre-Bethany Anne. When I first met her, I thought she was either ignorant or psychotic when she would talk about slapping Michael's head off or any of the dozens of other things she was going to do when she finally saw him again. Now, I'm not sure that she isn't the more powerful of the two, and if she went bonkers... So, can you imagine if she's in a relationship with Michael and he pissed her off? Even the best of us can say something to upset our better half."

"Spoken like a man who has recently encountered this situation."

Nathan opened his mouth, then shut it without saying a word. He had to admit that he was starting to sound like an alarmist. Maybe Ecaterina was right and his vampire racism was rearing its ugly head.

Frank tried to see it from Nathan's point of view for a second. He tried to get Nathan to see it from another angle. "If not Michael or Stephen, then who? Are you saying that she's better off alone? Do you trust a human not on our team?"

"Hell no."

"How about a Were that isn't in our group?"

"Hell, I don't trust a Were that's IN our group. Maybe Pete, but I think that he's too young for her."

"Ok, out of the humans in our group, did you have one in mind? If she 'gets pissed off' at a human, are you ready for what would happen if she forgets, even for a micro-second, and hits them harder than she should?"

He shook his head.

"Not even John?"

Nathan shrugged. "Talked to him already. He said he would die for her, just didn't want to die in bed because of her."

"So, no humans, no Weres... that leaves vampires. Stephen is out because I know he doesn't think that he is the appropriate relationship for his Queen to be in." Frank let his words drift off.

Nathan sighed, "Are you being nice and pointing out that I'm being an ass?"

"Are you?"

Their conversation was interrupted when Dan knocked on the door and joined them at the table.

Frank typed a couple of quick sentences into a secured notebook he had open for instances just like this. Little reminders for scenes in his book.

Dan got the meeting started. "Gentleman, we have a new war footing designation, it seems. Bethany Anne has officially, created a 'unleash the dogs of war' designation. So, I'm asking you to find where the terrorists that we need to visit are." He looked up with a sardonic smile on his face. "I can't just release the dogs anywhere, can I?"

After their meeting, Nathan went to go talk with Ben while Frank told Dan about the unfolding situation in Turkey.

———

Key Biscayne, FL USA

TOM, we need to get you hooked up. We're going to need those new attack ships sooner, not later.

I've been testing the computer connectivity through

the Etheric to my ship. My ship easily has the capability to use the connections to the internet from the Ad Aeternitatem or the Polarus. It can even grab connections whenever there's a jet or cell phone tower within range. Not that there's a cell phone tower within range right now.

Yeah, I guess no one can call you in the middle of the Atlantic.

I think they're in the Mediterranean right now.

Wherever. Can you get on the internet?

Yes.

Wait, how is it that you can connect to our internet, but we aren't supposed to be able to connect to your computers?

Because I've been studying your communications for many decades and the ship's capabilities are significantly ahead of what this world has right now. It's pretty laughable.

Yeah, well just because it hasn't happened don't be stupid. Humans are known to be good at figuring shit out.

TOM considered how easily Bethany Anne had started working with the Etheric and took her advice to heart. I'll put in place some measures to… uh… defend against intruders.

I think Nathan calls them firewalls.

But fire doesn't exist in digital signals.

Tell that to a guy when his wife finds out he has a girlfriend.

TOM chalked this up to something he wasn't going to get across to Bethany Anne. He made a mental note to call his defensive efforts firewalls and dropped it.

CHAPTER SEVEN

The Queen Bitch's Ship Ad Aeternitatem, Mediterranean Sea

Bobcat stepped through the door into the 'garage' and saw Marcus unwrapping a box. "What'cha got?"

Marcus looked up as he tore off a flap. "Laptop that I can use to talk to TOM."

Bobcat stopped a few feet away from the table. The complete lack of care Marcus was displaying while he ripped open the box told Bobcat one thing. This laptop couldn't be returned. Hopefully it would work and they wouldn't be stuck with it. Fortunately, when Marcus got into the main part of the wrapping he slowed down and they didn't have to pick up foam pieces. Bobcat heard the door open behind him so he looked over his shoulder and nodded at William. He turned back around to see Marcus plugging the laptop into an outlet. "Do you have any idea how to reach out to him?"

Marcus looked confused for a second as he parsed Bobcat's question. "To TOM?"

William sidled up next to Bobcat. "What's going on?"

Bobcat nodded at Marcus. "Rocket scientist is about to wet his pants in anticipation of talking with Bethany Anne's alien friend. But he didn't think about getting a phone number."

"Reminds me of a girl one time…"

"Stop!" Bobcat looked up at his old friend. "This is a girl-friend-free discussion zone. Shelly took all of my cash before I met Bethany Anne and I've been going nonstop since then. Now I have the cash and not the time." He turned to face Marcus who was watching them talk. "Of course, if I had the time, considering where we are, it's not like there are a lot of bars or places to meet someone in the middle of the ocean."

Marcus got a glint in his eyes. "Men, these craft we are building will allow us to get to the nicest and hottest cities in the world in the amount of time it takes to drive from Miami to Orlando. You could meet girls in Rome on Friday night, Oslo on Saturday and Rio de Janeiro on Sunday. There won't be a beach you can't hit and still be back in time for the next shift. But first, I need to talk with an alien. Do you have any ideas?"

"Why the hell didn't you say that before?" Bobcat and William came up beside Marcus and started looking at the laptop to see if there were any clues to what needed to be done.

There was a knock on the door. Bobcat looked up from the laptop. "Who is it?"

"Nathan."

"Come on in." He returned to looking at the laptop screen. "What's going on?"

Bobcat almost jumped out of his pants. "Damn Nathan! Don't sneak up on a guy like that." He returned his focus to the laptop.

Nathan was confused. First, he hadn't snuck up on anyone. Second, all the guys were staring at a normal laptop screen. "What are you looking for?"

Marcus grumped, "How to talk with TOM."

Nathan considered letting them search around the vanilla Windows install for a while. He then considered what Bethany Anne might do, to him, if she needed them online sooner rather than later. "Guys, it isn't on the laptop yet. I've got the chat program with me."

Nathan took a step back when all three men turned as one and started eyeing him like he was the Thanksgiving turkey.

Marcus' voice was quiet, yet oozed impatience. "I need that program, young man." He was acting like a druggie.

Nathan reached into his pocket and pulled out a USB drive. "Got it right here. Give me some room…" All three men jumped back, Marcus holding the chair for him. Marcus was impatiently pointing from Nathan to the chair.

"Get with it, man! I'm not getting any younger."

Nathan noticed Bobcat, behind Marcus, mouthing 'aliens.'

Ok, Nathan could understand Marcus being impatient because he wanted to speak with TOM. What about these other two clowns? Nathan sat down and plugged the USB drive into the laptop. With a couple of simple commands, he started the installation process. He needed to load a set of usernames and passwords, all with the appropriate credentials. "So, what has you and William so anxious, Bobcat?"

William grunted, "Women."

"Bars," added Bobcat.

Nathan turned to look over his shoulder. "What? The chat program is locked into a unique communication protocol.

You aren't going to find women on this laptop."

Bobcat barked a laugh. "Although funny, what he meant is that, once we have these ships running, Marcus tells us we can hit any of the hottest beaches in the world for dates within three hours."

Nathan turned back around. "So, saving the world from alien invaders isn't enough? But, getting to a beach in Brazil to pick up a super-hottie in three hours is enough to get your drive up to… err … peak performance… No, that isn't right…"

"Hell-to-the-yes." That was William, ever to the point.

Marcus took up the conversation. "I wanted help. I figured that I needed to find a motivational force. Something that would provide an ever present, and useful, encouragement for younger men. Something that would bring about a renewed enthusiasm for completing the task more quickly."

Nathan pulled the USB drive out of the laptop. "Well, that's it for the laptop. Let's not let it outside of this room and for sure not off this boat. Not that it probably matters, it isn't like there's any proprietary data." He stood up. "Don't put any other programs on here. If something happens, just turn it off. If that happens, you will then need a new password that I will have to give you. So, if you disconnect it from the wall and it runs out of juice you'll need to find me, understood?"

The men all agreed they understood, so Nathan left them.

Before he met Ecaterina, Nathan had been chased by enough women that he considered dating a chore. Since he had met Ecaterina he had no desire to be chasing women. So, he logically understood Bobcat and William's interest, but that was all.

Speaking of Ecaterina, he had an hour to spare before his meeting with Ben. He headed off whistling, to hitch a ride back to the Polarus.

Back in the garage, Marcus was sitting in the chair in front of the laptop. He had the chat window open, staring at it.

Behind him, Bobcat looked over at William who shrugged his shoulders. Bobcat looked down at the scientist. "What's the problem, Doc?"

"What do I say?"

William said, "You're not dating him, say hello and let's get this rocket stuff moving."

Marcus typed into the laptop's chat window
>Hello?
The chat window was immediately filled with a response.
>>Hello, this is TOM. Who am I addressing?
>This is Dr. Marcus Cambridge.
>>Hello, Dr. Cambridge. Or would you prefer Marcus?
>Marcus is fine, thank you.
>>No need to be so polite, Marcus.
>I'm sorry, it has just been a passion of mine to meet an alien and now I'm actually communicating with one.

Marcus jerked around and looked up at both men. Both looked at him, confused. He said, "You guys aren't punking me, are you?"

"No. Although that would be funny as hell." Bobcat replied while William chuckled.

Mollified, Marcus turned back to the chat window where a response waited for him.

>>Marcus, not to put this too bluntly, but you're not my first. My first human contact was over a thousand years ago. So, I'm not a virgin.

Bobcat burst out laughing behind him.

Marcus smiled. He recognized an effort to put him at ease. Shrugging his shoulders, he wrapped his fingers together and cracked his knuckles. "Let's get to work, gentleman. We have some serious hot rods to build!"

The men spent the next three hours working with TOM on the ship's capabilities and drive specifications. TOM explained things and Marcus translated them into what would help define their ship's design parameters. At the end of the session, Marcus told TOM 'goodbye for now' and he sat back, amazed.

Marcus had his head tilted back, staring at the ceiling. "I'll be damned."

Bobcat put the bucket of beers on the table and reached in to get one. There was a Coke in the bucket for William. Marcus waved off Bobcat's offer. "Not yet."

Opening his bottle, Bobcat took a swig. "Why are you going to be damned?"

Marcus stood up and tried to pop his back. It felt stiff and sore from sitting so long. "It's an anti-gravity device. If Podkletnov could see even half of this information he would shit bricks, I'm sure." Marcus walked over to the whiteboard. The guys had written down some information for him while he was chatting with TOM. "Right here, this calculation that William wrote down almost verifies his and Modanese's calculations for anti-gravity pulses at sixty-four c."

Bobcat interrupted Marcus, "Doc, remember not all of us know your shorthand."

Marcus picked up the green dry-erase marker. "Speed of light. Sixty-four c is sixty-four times the speed of light." Marcus added a couple of mathematical notations. "The only thing is, TOM's people had the ability to make it quadruple in capacity. So they can go two hundred and fifty-six c for short bursts of time."

William opened his Coke carefully. Bobcat had 'accidentally' shaken one up on him more than once. William had to go and take a shower to get the sticky stuff off. "Wouldn't you die from the acceleration?"

"Good question, but no." Marcus grabbed the red marker. "Here are the notations on how to build a locally transitive gravity shield so that the effects warp around using a gravity sphere." The mathematical notations might as well have been Sanskrit to the other two.

William looked over at Bobcat. "Is he punking us?"

This time, it was Marcus that barked a laugh. "Gentleman, if we can fabricate the right shielding I could get you to Brazil in five minutes. Of course, you'd probably destroy anything within a quarter mile of your vehicle from the shock waves." He turned back to the whiteboard using the marker to scratch the back of his head. "Guess that means a limiter for atmospheric travel."

It was another hour before the doctor sat down and accepted his first beer of the night. He was officially the most knowledgeable scientist in the world related to anti-gravity and light-speed travel between the stars. And, it annoyed him that except for these two men and one alien, no one had a clue.

Well, they would soon enough.

———

Key Biscayne, FL USA

Bethany Anne had Nathan and Frank on a conference call.

"So that about sums it up. Both of you say that Tabitha

is solid and she's an almost terrifyingly good hacker. She passed your background check, Frank. And Nathan, you also have Ben's opinion to back up performance reviews from her bosses, right?"

Nathan said, "Yes. Although her bosses are just about as happy with you taking Tabitha as they were when I took Ben away from them."

Bethany Anne replied, "Can't be helped. I need someone really good that's already been exposed to the Unknown-World, and she fits the bill perfectly."

Nathan knew there was something else going on with this. He thought he could feel an undercurrent of mischie-vousness in Bethany Anne's voice. "Boss, anything else you need to know about Tabitha?"

"Yes. Is she snarky? Maybe a bit of a pain in the ass?"

Nathan looked over the table at Frank, who shrugged but answered as best he could. "The background check showed a few run-ins with the law before she was eighteen. She has a bit of a chip on her shoulder. Is that a problem?"

"Fuck no, not for me anyway. I think she's perfect!"

Nathan wanted to bounce his head against the table a couple of times. "Boss, who is going to be utilizing Tabitha's skills?" Frank's eyes started to open wide and his mouth made a little 'o.'

"Guys, I thought you knew? Michael has asked for some help to find someone who can replace Carl. He needs a per-son to fill the technical liaison role for him in South Ameri-ca." Her answer was so smooth Nathan was sure that she was doing her best to not laugh out loud.

Nathan agreed to get Tabitha and her traveling clothes ready. Paul would go and pick her up in Texas. Bethany Anne would take her down to Michael after she arrived in Florida.

They said their good-byes and hung up.

Nathan stared at Frank.

Tabitha and Michael together? Oh god in heaven, what was Bethany Anne up to?

———

Michael was standing in the house where Anton had held his last party. He was looking down off of the balcony to the floor where Bethany Anne had killed the two Nosferatu that Anton's scientists had created. It was the location that Bethany Anne could most easily remember. It would be her target when she translocated from Miami down to Argentina.

He was staring at the spot where he expected Bethany Anne, and the guy who would become his new technical support specialist, to appear.

His face was carefully controlled. He didn't want Bethany Anne to get any ideas from the fact that he had actually arrived five minutes early. He wanted time to make sure that he was in the perfect place to witness her arrival. When she arrived she wouldn't immediately be able to see his face, yet he would be able to see hers.

Which was a good thing, if not for the reason he had expected. As it happened, she didn't see his carefully schooled expression turn to one of shock. Three women and Ashur appeared, and Michael realized that his new technical liaison was a *she* not a *he*.

And she had a nose piercing and tattoos.

God in heaven, what had he done to this woman to make her hate him so?

CHAPTER EIGHT

Buenos Aries, Argentina

Bethany Anne listened to find Michael up on the balcony looking down. His face was so smooth she was sure he had locked every muscle. He didn't, however, manage to keep his eyes from widening a little in shock.

Got you! Bethany Anne smiled up at Michael. "Why are you up there? Come on down and meet the newest member of Team Michael."

Ashur left the group to make a quick run through the house. Gabrielle decided that Ashur had a good idea. She wasn't that comfortable around Michael and if the two of them couldn't handle an attack, Gabrielle's skills probably weren't going to be the deciding factor for the next few minutes.

But you can bet your ass she was going to be listening in on their conversation. Gabrielle smiled and waved to Michael who acknowledged the greeting with a raised hand. He watched as the woman walked out of the room, following the German Shepherd.

That left two.

The woman who remained beside Bethany Anne was lean and just slightly shorter. She had blond hair with… black ends? Michael looked a little closer as he got nearer. She must have naturally blond hair, but had dyed it black at one point. Wasn't blond considered the most attractive color for women? When had black become the preferred color?

With a nose ring. Michael had seen a lot of earrings and many of them were very pretty. It did tend to draw the eye to their neck, which, he considered, was a fine feature. But their nose? Let's not, he thought, get started with the tattoos on her chest and shoulders. None on the arms, though.

Michael finished coming down the stairs and smiled at the two women. Bethany Anne's smile was honest, warm and deceptively innocent. Michael replayed their conversation when he had asked for technical help. Not once had she mentioned the person who she had in mind was a male. It was always 'they' or 'them.'

He had been shown the price of his gender assumptions and she was standing next to Bethany Anne staring at him with calm, cool intelligence.

Like he was a bug that she was judging for her collection.

He turned his eyes to her face and allowed his skill at emotional influence into his voice, "Ladies…"

The new technician's eyes widened with fear. Then Michael's left arm stung like crazy and a crack resounded off of the walls. Bethany Anne took a step into his personal space while looking up into his eyes, getting his attention. "None. Of. That. Michael."

It took an effort not to reach over and rub his arm where

she slapped it. That woman had a mean slap.

Michael cut off the emotional overlay in his voice. "My apologies." He didn't step back. Bethany Anne had stepped into his space, she could damn well step back out, too.

She squinted up at him one more time before turning toward the new woman and taking a step back. "Tabitha, let me introduce you to Michael. No last name, but then in the UnknownWorld…"

Tabitha's eyes went from surprise and caution to happiness and amazement. "Michael? THE Michael? Oh. My. GOD!" She even squealed like a teenager as she grabbed Michael's hand and started pumping it like she was shaking a pom-pom. Michael looked over at Bethany Anne in bewilderment, hoping for an explanation, but Bethany Anne's face was… priceless!

Bethany Anne was staring at Tabitha like she had brought the *wrong* young lady to South America. Michael's face went from shock to satisfaction as he gently voiced, just loud enough for a vampire (or dog, had he thought about it). "You might want to close your mouth, Bethany Anne. You might catch a bug."

Bethany Anne's mouth snapped shut as her head turned sharply, daggers shooting from her eyes at Michael who turned to give Tabitha his undivided attention.

Michael returned Tabitha's question with a question, "I'm not sure if I am the right Michael, maybe you can provide me with a synopsis of the Michael you think I am?"

Tabitha dropped Michael's hand and swung the low-riding backpack off of her back and onto the floor. She bent down and unzipped it and then started to rummage through it. Michael snuck a quick peek at Bethany Anne who had a look of consternation on her face, watching the twenty-something.

"Got it!" Tabitha came back up with a small notebook that had a pen pushed into the rings. She opened it and flipped through a few pages. "Here, 'The Michael,'" the fingers of her free hand making air quotes, "that I'm talking about is the assumed head of all the vampires and was the one who turned Anton." With this, she looked up at Michael, "Douchebag move, if you did that." She went back to her notes. Michael snuck another quick look at Bethany Anne, whose look of incredulity was starting to smooth back a little, towards one of pleasure. Tabitha continued, "Also is the parent of a Steven, David and Howard…"

Michael said under his breath, "It's Hugo."

Tabitha looked up at Michael, a gleam in her eye. "Got ya!" She turned the notebook around and Michael felt Bethany Anne's shoulder touch his as she joined him in looking at Tabitha's notebook.

There was the list, Michael was first, then Steven, David, Hugo, Anton, Peter and Barnabas.

Bethany Anne pointed to the list, "It's actually 'Stephen,' not 'Steven.'" Bethany Anne's smile was back full force.

Tabitha turned the notebook back so she could read it. "Really?"

Both of the vampires nodded.

"Well, slap a bitch and make her howl." She pulled the pen off of the notebook and made the correction.

Michael could hear Bethany Anne's voice, ever so soft, "You're going to catch a bug like that, Michael." He closed his mouth. Bethany Anne whistled and Ashur came running back. Gabrielle followed a moment later, from the other direction.

Bethany Anne looked over at Gabrielle. "Sorry, I wasn't whistling for you, I forgot about your good hearing."

Gabrielle answered, "I bet." She reached down to pet Ashur for a second before hugging Tabitha good-bye.

Bethany Anne was next. "You take good care of old what's-his-face over here, ok?"

Tabitha smiled at them. "No worries, I've got his back, and Bethany Anne?"

Bethany Anne had just grabbed Ashur's neck. She turned to face Tabitha again, "Yes?"

"Thanks, for everything, especially for Miami, ok?" Tabitha's earlier protective walls were gone. In front of Bethany Anne was the young woman who had been rescued out of a dire situation in Miami and given a second chance. Her expression hinted at the powerfully adept support that she would provide the teams and especially Michael.

Bethany Anne dropped her hold of Ashur and took a step back to Tabitha and opened her arms. Tabitha stepped into Bethany Anne's embrace and listened while Bethany Anne spoke to her. "You have already paid me back for something that wasn't your fault. I'm glad that you were good in Texas and I appreciate you taking on this effort with Michael. It can be dangerous, so while he can be an egotistical wank-sack, he can and will protect you, ok?"

Michael retorted, "I am not now, nor have I ever been an 'egotistical wank-sack…'"

Michael was surprised by Gabrielle butting into the conversation. "No, no… I have to agree with Bethany Anne on this one…" Then, Gabrielle's eyes got big as she realized she *HAD* spoken that out loud.

The two hugging women laughed as they parted.

"Call me if you need anything. Or have Michael call me, understand?" Tabitha nodded.

Michael looked down at the backpack and single

overnight bag Tabitha had brought. "Not to interrupt, but no clothes?"

Tabitha answered, "Need to look local, so I don't stand out. There are just enough clothes and unmentionables in there for a couple of days. So, shopping?"

Bethany Anne winked at Michael as she grabbed Ashur and Gabrielle's arm and disappeared.

Damn that woman!

———

Key Biscayne, FL USA

Bethany Anne let go of Ashur as Gabrielle unlocked the door. Ashur bolted out of the room, heading downstairs.

Gabrielle turned to her boss. "You need to have a talk with your dad."

Bethany Anne stopped and gave consideration to what had happened recently. She drew a blank, there was nothing that came to mind that should require her to talk to him. "About what?"

Gabrielle put a hand on her hip. "Don't tell me you don't see how much Patricia likes the man."

"No, I know about that. Why? What is he… wait a sec. It isn't what he is doing, it's that he doesn't have a clue, isn't it?"

Gabrielle pursed her lips and nodded.

"How bad has it been?" Bethany Anne went around her bed to pick up her phone, she had forgotten it here again. There had to be a reason that she was doing it, she was never this forgetful in the past.

"He needs a 2x4 upside the head he's so blind. Really, he needs to be clued in so he can, what do they say around here… fish or cut bait?"

Bethany Anne rolled her head around, hearing the bones pop. Damn, that felt good. "Yeah. I was trying to not be cupid on this. He needs to get his head out of being the top in the chain of command."

"He needs to get his head out of his ass, you mean."

"Fuck. Really Gabrielle, don't sugar coat your opinion." Bethany Anne smiled at the older woman. "Yeah, you're right. He's probably aware, at least subconsciously. Maybe there's more than one person scared of the future."

"Why, who is the other one besides him and me?"

Bethany Anne looked over at Gabrielle, no smile on her face. "You're scared?"

Gabrielle walked over and sat on the couch. She hadn't meant to start this conversation. "Yes. Aren't you? I've lived for… Ok, lots of years."

Bethany Anne snapped her fingers, so close!

"It was a wild ride before I met you. But you take this, saving the world, seriously. You're trying to make it better for so many people at the same time. I'm scared of a lot of things, but you losing your mind is probably my chief concern."

Bethany Anne sat with Gabrielle, pulling one leg up underneath her and sitting on her foot. "Losing my mind? Have I been making bad decisions?"

Gabrielle shook her head. "No, and that's more troubling. We all make mistakes. But I worry that the longer you go without making a mistake, the bigger the mistake will be."

"Like some kind of Karma equation? Make lots of small mistakes or you save up the results for a big explosion?"

"Maybe? Maybe not. I'm not sure. Do you realize that we took out one of Michael's children? And as soon as we find that fucker David, his ass will be gone too. I've lived my... more than a hundred, less than a thousand, years with those two as pinnacles. You only got higher by going to Michael. And, I just got through watching him take on a female technician and *he didn't know what to do about it*. You have the Patriarch, the absolute top of vampires, who was never long-suffering to begin with, working with you as a partner. He even calls you for *advice*. Michael has never, before you, called anyone for *advice*."

"You did hear how that got him stuck in 'the container of death,' right? He had a long time to think about it, it seems to have changed him."

"Change. Maybe that's my problem?" Gabrielle sat back against the couch, arms crossed over her eyes. "When you are as... traditional... as I am."

"You mean old-as-fuck, right?" Bethany Anne let the smile creep into her voice.

Gabrielle lifted her right arm to peek out and stab Bethany Anne with a look that would wither a lesser woman. "That right there is what appeals to me, and scares me. You are so young to have so much on your shoulders, what if those shoulders break?"

There it was. That was what was bothering Bethany Anne. That was what she hadn't been able to put her finger on. What if her shoulders broke?

They are as strong as titanium, Bethany Anne. Well, not entirely, but it made for a good metaphor TOM thought.

What?

Remember? We adjusted your bone structure. Let the enemy come at us, we won't bend, we won't break, we will stand resolute and then, kick their ass.

Bethany Anne whispered, "And let God sort them out, TOM?"

And let your deity of choice sort them out.

Gabrielle understood that Bethany Anne was having an internal discussion with TOM. But it was an existential moment as she watched the woman in front of her go from Bethany Anne the friend, to Bethany Anne, leader. This was the woman who had first attracted her.

Bethany Anne's eyes flashed fire and her smile returned. "I've been so informed that it's damn near impossible for my Kurtherian enhanced shoulders to break. And we will take each challenge head on and steamroll the fuckers if they can't get with the program. If they will talk, we will talk. If they want to yell, well then, we'll slap the shit out of them until they want to talk or their jaws are wired shut. If they want to fight? Fuck 'em. We have shit to do and no time to do it."

Gabrielle stared at her boss for a minute and then could feel the confidence seeping back in her bones. "You've been worried, haven't you?"

Bethany Anne nodded. "You know? I think I have. I've made some poor decisions lately, I might need to go to a confessional. But thanks to you and the rest of my team, I'll never bow, I'll never break. I will stand and let the fuckers come…"

Gabrielle finished for her, "And then kill them all and let God sort them out?"

"If they won't talk? Yup."

Gabrielle stood up and offered her hand down to Bethany Anne. "Come on, boss. Let's go find someone who needs to be fucked up." Bethany Anne smiled at Gabrielle who raised both hands in the air and turned around to walk out of the room. "Oh, for fuck's sake! I can't believe you turned that into a slut statement!"

Bethany Anne hopped up and raced to catch her Guards'

leader, slapping Gabrielle on her ass as she ran by. "Three is the magic number!"

Gabrielle stopped in the hallway, looking at the stairs where Bethany Anne had just disappeared.

A smile curled her lips a tiny, so very tiny whisper breathing through her lips. "It was four. A girl has to have at least one secret." She started walking again. "Well, at least one *more* secret." But, she had been very drunk, which had taken quite a lot of effort. So maybe it was two and she thought it was just two sets of twins? Crap, for all she could remember, it was possibly just a dream too.

––––––––

Bethany Anne didn't find her dad, but she did see Ashur lying out on the grass, enjoying the sun. She translocated over to her house next door. Unlocking the transfer closet, she poked her head out and said in a loud voice, "Hello the house?"

"I'm in the kitchen," her father replied. She could hear AC/DC blasting from the weight room in the converted garage, so that was probably where the rest of the team was.

Bethany Anne walked into the kitchen. "What are you doing?"

Her father closed the fridge door. He had bread on the counter and cold cuts in his hands. "Lunch," he said.

"Where's Patricia?"

"She had an 11:30 appointment at what she called the 'magical, magical' place. When I asked for clarification, I was informed my security clearance wasn't high enough. Imagine that, a general without a high enough security clearance."

Bethany Anne put out a hand, "Stop what you're doing.

We need to catch up and I don't want," she waved at his sandwich materials, "this. How about Joe's?"

Her dad smiled. "Damn, what a negotiator. Fine, fine, twist my arm and demand the concessions … I'll do it." Her dad finished putting away the bread and reached for the keys on the counter. "Which pair is going to shadow us?"

She shrugged. "Don't know, but we need to talk without extra ears, so they can take a second car."

"What are we going to talk about that those guys can't hear?"

"Father-daughter stuff."

Lance looked back at the kitchen, already wishing he hadn't been so quick to throw away his safety line.

As they came up to the front door Gabrielle walked in.

"Going to Joe's. Tell whoever to grab the next SUV. We'll drive the speed limit, so catch up."

Gabrielle saw the forlorn look on Lance's face, so she could guess he had an idea this wasn't normal business. "We'll be a couple of minutes behind you."

Lance was surprised when Bethany Anne jumped into the driver's seat. She so often had her security driving, he had rather forgotten that she could drive just fine. Sliding into the passenger seat, he watched as she started the SUV and hit the button to open their gate. She was a better driver than he remembered.

No time like the present to get the hard stuff out of the way. "What's going on, baby?"

"You, Dad."

"Me?"

"Yes, my loving father who is occasionally as dense as a howitzer barrel."

Lance considered what she had just said. Nothing he

should have figured out came to mind. "Did I forget a birthday? Do Nacht even have birthdays?"

"Dad! Women after a certain age don't have birthdays. They remind us that we're aging. Well, I guess I don't want to know how old I am. Wait, how did we make this about me? That's a woman's trick."

"Also a general's. Works to keep the younger officers on their toes."

"Good trick. Now, let's talk about you."

"That's what I'm avoiding."

"I can tell."

"So, let me know who I offended and I'll try to make it up to them."

"Who you offended?"

"Yeah, I can't think of anyone I've pissed off. That's something I probably would remember. So, I figure that I've been my usual tactless self and offended someone. But, I've got to tell you I wouldn't have believed I could offend any of your team, and I've tried."

"Patricia."

Lance was caught unprepared. He was expecting to have to play twenty questions. He never would have thought Patricia was the one person he would offend. He never would have wanted to do that. "How? When?"

"For the last umpteen years."

"Then why did she come work for me?" Lance was puzzled, he thought Patricia was happy. At least, she always seemed happy.

"Dad." Bethany Anne made sure she had his attention. "She loves you. You treat her like a secretary in the Army, friendly but untouchable."

Lance was shocked. His world just got twisted on its ear.

UNDER MY HEEL

Bethany Anne reached over and snapped her fingers to get him to focus. "Stay with me, Dad. You aren't in the Army anymore, you're private. You can have a relationship or not have a relationship. But what you can't do is not let Patricia know if you're available for a relationship. You can't continue to ignore the love she has for you."

Patricia was available? Patricia loved him?

Bethany Anne looked over again and noticed he wasn't tracking. She smiled and let him think about it for a couple of minutes.

"You said she loves me?"

The gruff Army general wasn't in the vehicle at the moment. Her *dad* was, and Bethany Anne couldn't be happier. "Yes, she certainly believes she does. But unless you're willing to return her affections and see if the relationship can go anywhere, she is going to love this ideal of you until the day she dies."

"Dies? Bethany Anne, can't you help like you did for Frank and me?"

"Certainly, but will she want that? Not everyone wants to take the oath to do whatever it takes to save the world. The benefits are great but the price is steep, Dad."

He nodded. He had a lot to think about. This wasn't the lunch conversation he had expected to have today. Or, frankly, ever.

The Queen Bitch's Ship Ad Aeternitatem

William got up early. He figured that the other two, after their quiet deliberation and a couple of beers last night, would follow him later.

He was surprised to find Marcus already in the garage, typing on the new laptop, communicating with TOM.

"What're you talking with TOM about, Doc?"

Marcus looked up and smiled. "Life the Universe and Everything." When he got no response from William, he continued, "Not a Douglas Adams fan?"

"Who? Is he another rocket scientist? Because I have to admit that you're my first, Doc. I've popped my cherry on you, my friend."

A laugh erupted from Marcus. "I'm your first rocket scientist, William? You guys have some of the most puerile humor. I love it." He looked back at the laptop.

"Puerile, Doc? Don't make me beat you senseless to find out it was something nice."

Marcus answered without looking up. "It means immature. I find the effort you and Bobcat make to keep your teenage humor alive enjoyable. As a scientist, too many of us spend our early years trying to be taken seriously. By the time we're old enough to wear serious correctly, we've lost the ability to enjoy the youth we left behind."

"That fucking sucks, Doc."

"That it does, William. That it does." Marcus was typing furiously.

William looked over the whiteboard. There wasn't anything new on it. He got out a fresh pad and pen, pulled a chair out across from the doc and started doodling.

William was perplexed. They had an original design for three people and after the big meeting with Stephen and the captains, the team had talked with Pete and Todd. They had decided that their fire teams were going to be limited to three, and a shitload of equipment.

That meant four per ship when you included the pilot.

"Damned shame that we have to put a pilot in these things."

"Hmmm?"

William hadn't been talking to Marcus, as Marcus was so absorbed in his communication with TOM. "I said, it's a bit of a shame that we have to have four people on the ships. When you include the three from the fire team, plus a pilot and all of the gear we might as well design an SUV for these guys."

Marcus looked up from his typing, his eyes losing the glazed over look of someone who is just now starting to pay attention to you. "SUV? What is that, a Support Utility Vehicle?"

Smiling, William replied, "No, Sport Utility Vehicle, like a truck?"

Marcus grimaced. "I'm sorry, William. My head was nodding but no one was listening. What were you asking?"

"I said, it's a shame that we have to have four people plus all of their gear. Shoving all of these requirements into a rocket design is limiting. What happens when they land? If we assume they're all standing up when the fins touch the ground, then they step off. If we try to land sideways, then that's all good, but taking off…"

William realized that their whole discussion from the previous evening had made their first designs a moot point.

"Doc, can you ask TOM what he would design for four people and a crap-ton of equipment as the most logical design for flight and for manufacturing?"

"Certainly." Marcus got to typing.

The door opened and Bobcat called out a good morning. William raised a hand. Bobcat wouldn't have a hangover. The man was too professional for that. But he'd be a little easier to talk with after a cup of the brown nectar.

Bobcat came over to the table and pulled out a chair next to William, setting his coffee down. "What's Doc up to?"

"Talking with TOM, asking him what the best design for four people and gear would be."

"Good idea, you come up with that?"

William grunted.

"Seriously?"

William grunted again.

"No way."

"Way."

Bobcat took another careful sip of his coffee, that shit was hot. "Good fucking idea. Five bucks says he comes back with a circle or sphere."

William looked over at the project lead. "Why?"

Bobcat shrugged. "It's in all of our stories, so there must be something to it. Best use of space for traveling through outer space? Couldn't tell you."

William was in. "I'll see your five and raise you five."

"Ok, deal. But why?"

"His design isn't a standard round orb. I think those are made when you don't have a clue what you need to fly through. Since he knows our atmosphere, he'll adapt."

"Ok, that works."

The two friends sat in silence while Marcus typed furiously.

Finally, Marcus sat back. "I'll be fucked."

Bobcat took a sip. "Why? Is it round?"

"Nope."

William smiled. "That's ten for me."

Bobcat reached for his wallet to pay up. "What design did the little alien genius come up with?"

Marcus scratched the back of his head, "You might not believe this, but he said 'buy something.'"

Bobcat said, "What?" William snatched the ten before Bobcat could recant the bet. Bobcat never noticed the ten leaving his fingers.

Marcus explained, "Yes. He said there are multiple problems with manufacturing something specific for this design in the time frame that Bethany Anne wants. If we want our first version flying soon, then we can buy an airplane or a helicopter and update the engines. That way, unless we foul up too badly it won't look like anything out of the ordinary."

"Genius." Bobcat smiled. "I want one for Shelly!"

William jumped up, his chair sliding backwards. "Hell yeah! That bird will be the baddest ass of badass helicopters in the world!" He started to do a dance to music only he could hear.

Bobcat's smile turned to a frown. "Wait, how is that going to work at speed? Shelly isn't aerodynamic for shit."

Marcus shrugged. "The aerodynamics help, but you can tune the engine to facilitate creating a shield that pushes the air out of the way, for the most part. We can't hit the highest speeds, but if the shield sphere is large enough, it would allow us to get somewhere quickly and then switch to regular mode to land."

William stopped his dancing. "So, we could build a huge metal box and that would fly?"

Marcus started typing. "Yes, it would in a pinch but no one would believe a flying box, you know?"

William started looking around the room, "Yeah, but think about all of the space here on the Ad Aeternitatem. How many boxes or... well, coffins do you think we could manufacture and fit on here?"

Bobcat looked around. "You're thinking single person craft?"

William nodded. "Yup."

"What about pilots?"

"We make sure everyone knows how to pilot?"

Marcus was busy typing. "TOM says that we can have AI controlled craft."

Bobcat asked. "AI? Like the stuff that Bethany Anne is working with?"

Marcus was reading, his eyes scanning text as it scrolled across his screen. "No, more like KI controlled."

"K?" William looked over at Bobcat who shrugged his response.

"Kurtherian. He says he can run all operations through his ship and a powerful computer that he has access to. It wouldn't take too much direction directly through the Etheric. Impossible to block and instantaneous."

Marcus looked up at them. "Would the men be ok with that? An alien driving?"

Bobcat answered, "You mean piloting? Shit, they're trusting his engines to work. It should only be a short step sideways for them to believe that the alien is the best pilot. Unless, we have a pilot, in which case all pilots have an itchy problem with others piloting." He paused, thinking. "But I still want to put one in Shelly."

William grabbed his pen and started drawing. "What about something where they're sitting down? I can't believe that anyone wants to fly on their back, or their stomach. We can build the front to open…"

"You mean like Urkel's car?"

"Yeah! The BMW Isetta."

Bobcat smiled. The Isetta. "Guys, new project name, the IZTA."

Marcus looked up from his typing. "What does that stand for?"

Bobcat shrugged. "Beats the fuck out of me, but give me time and I'll think of something."

William was busy pulling up old pictures of the Isetta to see if he could grab any of their engineering ideas for his own craft.

They had a plan.

CHAPTER NINE

Buenos Aries, Argentina

It had taken two days for Michael to outfit Tabitha. In those two days, he had gotten to know this young human female better than he had known any human in the last two centuries.

Tabitha had shared how Anton's people had found her on the dark web. How they learned enough about her to threaten those she loved. She had been so afraid of anyone finding out that she was alive, she hadn't even tried to reach out to her family.

Bethany Anne and Gabrielle had shared with her the destruction of Anton's group. And that Tabitha could reach out to her family again.

Tabitha had considered reaching out. But after a couple of hours back in Miami, she had decided not to do it. Her parents were divorced, she had lived with her mother and had been in and out of the home for most of her teenage life. Right now, she was ok. Her mother might have worried about her. Having been gone longer this time without coming back. But letting her know that she was alive wasn't going to provide her any comfort.

When Bethany Anne had asked Tabitha about what she knew of the UnknownWorld, she had held most of her cards close to her chest. She had acted the tough girl. One with a chip on her shoulder and a smartass attitude. It was her protection. Protection from guys who wanted more than she was willing to even think about giving. From adults who had wanted to 'protect' her when she was younger. She survived by learning and planning.

When she was in Anton's group, she had learned enough to start searching for the truth about vampires. And with what she had found she also learned that there were Weres. Not just stories, but in reality.

She had done it by hacking banks and financial institutions. From there, she tracked names and aliases through various companies. She knew she would need a place to start. She decided that there was one item she might be able to track... *age*. The people had to be old enough, she thought, to leave a trail and then she figured that they would be rich, rich, rich.

She had kept her notes on paper. She wasn't going to have her own files hacked as she had done to others. She wrapped her notes up in little hearts and fake stories. Her list of Michael and his children were under the heading, 'boyfriend name ideas.'

She had written scripts that would search the databases. Then they would leave the data, at drop points, in encrypted files on the dark web. She was careful when she picked up her data, always running through multiple cutouts to keep her tracks out of any server logs.

It had almost worked. When Michael was right in front of her, the proof of all of her hard work was staring at her. She had shrieked like a fangirl meeting her boy band idol. And she threw her information right out in front of Bethany Anne and Michael. It wasn't until after Bethany Anne left that Tabitha realized she could have been in deep trouble. What if they had been worried about her hacking and data gathering?

"Michael?"

"Hmm?" He was reading through notes he had pulled from Anton's files. He seemed constantly focused and working to understand the notes.

"Why didn't you or Bethany Anne get upset when I showed you my notes on your children?"

Michael looked up from his folder. Tabitha hadn't been bad so far, but he did find that she tried his patience from time to time. He thought about her question. "I didn't bother because you are with me. You are about to learn more about my life than you ever could have by hacking into databases across the world. I imagine that Bethany Anne didn't bother because it would be the same as punishing a bear for eating a deer."

Tabitha thought about that. "So, she didn't concern herself with a hacker, hacking?"

"It is what you are, Tabitha. You are inquisitive by nature and you have found it a security blanket, to try and control the world around you. Did you have any plans for what you would do with the information that you had acquired?"

"No. I just knew that if Anton were to come after me or my family I needed to have more information about him. Once I knew about vampires I got curious, and wanted to know the bigger picture. Bethany Anne scared the crap out of me in Miami. She came into the helicopter after they took us from the bank job and I would swear she had red eyes and fangs but maybe my memory was hazy. Then Nathan got us new names and jobs with his company…"

She trailed off as she realized the import of his question. "If I had talked, someone would have found me and killed me, right?"

"That was the rule, yes." He continued to regard her.

She made a face. "Kind of a douchebag rule if you ask me. Who wrote it, you?" The smile dropped off of Tabitha's face as she realized that Michael wasn't smiling along with her. How was she always sticking her foot in her mouth?

She gave him a small smile. "Um, sorry?"

Michael returned the barest hint of a smile. "No apologies necessary, this time. I've had a while to think about some of my rules in the last year. Don't pass this on to Bethany Anne, but it was a rather douchebag rule."

"Yeah! What is it with her? I mean, don't get me wrong but she doesn't act all that bloodthirsty and evil dead for being a wicked vampire." She pursed her lips, "Well, except that first time meeting her."

Michael closed his folder, keeping his finger between the papers he was reading. "Believe it or not, we aren't 'wicked vampires.' Anton and his brother David notwithstanding."

"I don't know, rules to kill humans if they know too much seems kinda wicked to me."

"Really? Pray tell what would you do if four billion humans went on a monster hunt looking to kill all of your kind if they learned the truth? Go on Oprah to talk about it?"

"So, you think the death of the one is worth it to protect the many?"

"Let's take you as an example. What if you should hack into a system? An act which by definition is illegal, and by-passes security measures that are meant to keep you out, and then you learn something that is life threatening to those who are trying to keep to themselves. Have you not argued for your own punishment?"

Tabitha kept her mouth shut for a minute. She wanted to argue, but she did understand. "You're saying I walked across the line that said, 'No trespassing, death to all who enter?' And now I don't want to accept my own responsibility?"

"More like culpability, but yes you have the salient points." Michael thought about it a few seconds. "Tabitha, you're playing for keeps here. Carl wasn't the first technician that has been killed because he worked for me. That being said, it's been a long time between the last person to lose their life and him being murdered. Carl is a reminder that your position is dangerous."

"What happens if I want to quit?"

"Do you want my answer, or Bethany Anne's?"

"What is the difference?"

"Probably not a lot in the end. My method, you would probably die without knowing why. With Bethany Anne's, you would at least know why and maybe make a couple of decisions to hide better."

"I don't understand."

"I would take your memories of us, away. Then I would set you up with enough money for you to live your life de-cently, so long as you don't gamble it all away. Bethany Anne would let you keep your memory, knowing that you would be hunted. There are a lot of other groups who are always on the lookout for people who are outside of our protection. It won't matter to them if you know anything or not. They will grab you once they find you. Then they will do anything it takes to pull anything you know out of you."

"So, I'm in a virtual prison of my own making?"

Michael considered that. "Perhaps you might consider it that way. Eventually, you would have been caught in your hacking. You would have been 'found and dealt with,' whatever that means. The Strictures, the rules that the Unknown-World have lived by for centuries, are in flux and we are rewriting them."

"What caused them to change?"

"You have met her already."

"Bethany Anne?"

"Yes."

"How come I never found anything on her? How old is she that she already has so much power, when I could only find you at the top?"

"That, my very young and nosy technician, is a story for another time."

Tabitha felt like her grandfather had just told her to go to bed. Her young and very scrumptious looking grandfather. "Hey, are you dating her?"

"No."

"Have you dated her? I mean, you two act like you've... uh..." Michael's penetrating eyes reminded her that sometimes, her mouth got ahead of her. "Never mind."

Michael opened his folder back up, and continued where he had left off.

Tabitha pulled her laptop over and sat it on her lap. Her latest scripts had been running. She had learned of the Queen Bitch's Guards and the operations in South America. Her first data dives had found all of the San Jose newspaper articles.

Now, her next level of scripts had found three files. They

were on a cloud service that provided secure personal cloud storage. Secure my ass, she thought.

This was interesting; it was assigned to the San Jose reporter. She opened the files and started reading.

"Michael?"

"Hmmm." He didn't look up from his reading.

"I found some information from a Giannini in San Jose. She has notes on Bethany Anne's team, including notes where she is trying to learn more about Gabrielle."

Michael looked up again. "I'm sorry, say that again? I wasn't in South America for these operations."

Tabitha read Michael most of the notes Giannini had in her folder.

Michael said, "She seems to know a lot about Bethany Anne and her team. I wonder why she's pulling this together?"

Tabitha looked through the notes again. "Don't know, but she has more information than I had about Bethany Anne... Bitch."

Michael's lips had the faintest of curves. That sounded like a professional annoyance. If he could nurture Tabitha in the right direction, she was going to turn into a fantastic intelligence agent. "I wonder how we can find out?"

"Why not just go visit her?"

Michael smiled, sometimes out of the mouth of babes. "What, you don't want to try and hack your way into all of her secrets?"

Tabitha was busy typing on her laptop. "Oh, her secrets will by my secrets by morning, trust me on that. What we need to do is ask her the reason she has the info. I haven't found where she has written any posts, so she hasn't gone public, yet."

UNDER MY HEEL

Michael stood up and stretched. "No time like the present. Order us a plane for Costa Rica." Michael started walking towards his room to get a suitcase packed.

Tabitha stared at Michael's back, and then down at her computer and then back at Michael. She raised her voice to the retreating man. "Uh, how?"

Michael stopped, counted to three and then turned around with a smile as he came back over. "Tabitha, what has been the largest amount of money you have ever been involved with?"

"Legal, or illegally?"

Michael raised an eyebrow. "Let's say legally, for now, but I'll want to know about Kensington later."

How the hell did he know about Kensington?

"A little over eight thousand after my first job with Anton's group."

"Ok, I'm going to give you access to an account that has a little over a million dollars. Please don't steal the money, embezzlement is a crime punishable by death."

The color drained from Tabitha's face. The casual way Michael said that spoke to his indifference to the sanctity of life. She needed to remember that under his hot body was a very dangerous man.

Michael provided the instructions and walked out of the room.

One, she realized, that could read her mind.

She put her head into her hands, how many times had she undressed him in her mind in the last two days? Oh my God, the tongue fantasy! She wasn't going to be able to stop blushing for a week now.

Then again, she could always create visuals to see if he would react. That might be fun! She sat back up. She considered how to test when he was or wasn't eavesdropping. There is one thing that is very similar between male and female hackers.

Both groups have very, very creative imaginations.

———

The Queen Bitch's Ship Polarus

Frank had requested that just about every one of the higher-ups help with the situation occurring in Turkey.

Around the table sat Stephen, Dan as head of Bethany Anne's military, Pete and Todd from the Ad Aeternitatem and both captains, along with Bobcat and Jean Dukes as the leads for air support and ship support, respectively.

Bethany Anne, Lance, Gabrielle and two of her team would be arriving shortly.

Frank was getting his maps ready to be displayed on the main screen. It was during this time that Bethany Anne, Gabrielle, Lance, John and Scott arrived. Scott took one look around the room and then stepped out to stand outside of the door.

Lance said hello to those already present and sat next to Dan. Gabrielle and John took positions in opposite corners of the room. John near the back, Gabrielle near the front.

Bethany Anne took the open chair to Frank's left.

Frank started, "Thank you everyone for coming. Before Bethany Anne was changed, Dan and I were part of a team that worked with each other to take care of Forsaken problems in the U.S.. And, occasionally I would have to deal with issues overseas. That was rare because David and Anton had South America and Africa sewed up pretty tightly. We had thought that Hugo was in control in Africa, but that wasn't the case. David has been ruthless about keeping his subordinates in check, while Anton was a little messier. Occasionally, Michael's group would have to go into Central and South America to deal with the odd flare up."

Frank flipped to the next slide, a map of Syria and Turkey with a red dot near the border. "Near the town of Yuceli, which is in a valley, is an even smaller outpost that's as old as anything in the Bible. The dot on the map represents a tribal area of maybe a few hundred people. Certainly less than a thousand. Many of whom are probably either dead or have been turned to Nosferatu. The town isn't on any major roads, but it sits in an area that contains a large number of caves."

John spoke up from the back, "A lot of areas to stay out of the sun, then."

Frank continued, "Yes. The Turkish military was called in and their people disappeared. They reached out to their NATO allies and the U.S. responded with a couple of fire teams. All of them, except for one person, were killed. We have lost contact with that last member, now assumed K.I.A."

Frank put up a satellite map with heat imaging. "We have one such cave that has activity around it during the day, and seems to be boarded up tightly at night."

Bethany Anne interrupted, "Why is David starting this now, if he hasn't done something like this before?"

Frank replied, "Oh, it's a trap, I'm sure. But is it for you, or for Michael?"

"Why me?"

"Because before, Michael always had a Bill to handle things like this for him. Also, this is a major outbreak. So, it's probably meant to draw at least one of our key players."

Stephen spoke up, "Maybe he's hoping to get both of them in there?"

Dan asked, "But why? They wouldn't be a challenge for Michael, much less the both of them.

Nathan was studying the map. "Michael's in South America cleaning that mess up. Could David want him out of the country for something?"

Frank nodded. "That could be. Same thing for Bethany Anne."

Lance spoke up, "If you keep your two biggest heavy hitters out of the mix, you're going to have higher casualties."

Todd spoke, "Can't be helped. With the new Guardians now active, we're a pretty formidable group."

"I'll be going to represent the Queen. This can't be permitted and David has attacked me as well." Stephen said.

"Something still stinks." Everyone turned to look at Nathan. "That's what, ten?"

Dan answered, "Yes. Nine with Pete and Todd's team, plus Stephen and transportation."

Bobcat said, "I've got transportation."

Bethany Anne cut him off. "Not this time, Bobcat." He jerked his head around in surprise. "You're too important to the ships project to go into action right now. You're going to have to pass the keys over to Chris."

Bobcat's face wasn't the only one showing surprise. Bethany Anne shrugged. "Sorry, can't be helped. This operation is pointing out how desperately we need to have those craft online."

Bobcat wasn't happy, but he nodded his understanding.

Dan took up the conversation. "Bobcat, is Chris an acceptable replacement?"

Bobcat thought about that. He had spent a lot of time with Chris in the last couple of months on Shelly. He had to admit the man was ready, but that didn't stop him from wishing that he could be in the hot seat. "Yes, he's ready."

Bethany Anne sat back, she was walking all over Dan's feet. She would have to apologize after the meeting.

Dan continued, "That gives us ten active plus one support."

Nathan spoke up again. "Actually, twelve. Ecaterina and I will be joining this party."

Bethany Anne was surprised to hear this, but then again that was the point of all of Ecaterina's workouts with the Guardians. Bethany Anne realized she would need to spend some time with Nathan before she left.

Dan nodded. "Ok, that leaves us protecting the ships. I'm comfortable with the Polarus covering us, but what about boarding actions?"

Gabrielle spoke up, "I can stay on the Ad Aeternitatem with Darryl and Scott as my backup. That leaves John and Eric covering Bethany Anne."

Dan looked over at Bethany Anne. "Where will you be?"

"My presence has been requested in Las Vegas. I'll take the Gulfstream there ASAP, but I'll be available if you need me. I'll have the guys and Ashur with me."

"Michael?"

Bethany Anne shrugged. "He'll be in South America as far as I know. I don't know what David is up to, or if David or one of his flunkies is the instigator of this. Just make sure there are enough medical supplies for everyone and a way back out."

Frank took that as his cue to continue. He flipped to the next slide, which drew everyone's attention back to the screen. "That gives us our force and a force-multiplier. We have the transportation so let's discuss the forward base. The U.S. group is about ten miles outside of the hills, or about fifteen miles from the hot spot. They have a couple of heavy artillery pieces, but Turkey isn't going to be giving any permission to use them on their soil."

Dan asked, "Then why do they have them?"

"They're close enough to the Syrian border that it makes the officer in charge there happy to have them." Frank went to the next slide. "They have a squad on the ground with a Sergeant McNichols in command."

Stephen asked the next question. "Aren't they going to question why a non-aligned military group is going in?"

Frank answered, "Good question. Normally they might, but they've lost eight men already. They know what is going on isn't normal. Enough of the men have seen unexplainable stuff in this area of the world in the last ten years. If someone higher up says 'hold for the exterminators,' then by god they will let someone else get their hand cut off. No one is itching to be sent home horizontally. The glory seekers have already been sent home and these guys have gotten their reward for keeping their heads down. They've stayed alive. They might be curious, but our team was asked for."

Dan followed up. "Asked for?"

Frank grimaced. "Poor choice of words. The brass knows that there's a black team for any of this unexplained stuff. It gets around. They just didn't realize that we haven't had to operate over in this part of the world."

The meeting went on for another thirty minutes before Dan felt he had a handle on the details. He asked Lance to stick around for a while so he could pick his brain. Lance did explain that his field experience was a couple of decades out of date, but he would answer Dan's questions as best he could.

Bethany Anne cornered Bobcat out in the hall.

"Bobcat, come with me for a second." She led him to an empty compartment and walked in. He followed. "Can you give me any idea where you guys are?"

"We have the engines in final design stages. Believe it or not, the manufacturing isn't the hard part, it will be the loading of the energy to get the engines primed the first time."

"What does TOM say?"

Why don't you ask TOM, he's right here.

Hush, I want to understand how well you guys are communicating.

Bobcat answered her. "He says that once we have the engines set up on the Ad Aeternitatem that, with your help, he'll be able to get them primed using his ship."

Bethany Anne considered that. "I wonder what the hell he's expecting me to do?"

"He hasn't told you?"

No he hasn't.

You didn't ask.

"No, I'm sure he didn't think it was important enough to inform me this early in the planning. I'll be sure to follow up with him, though. What are the parameters on the ship's construction? I understand that we can use off the shelf components?"

"Not exactly. What TOM suggested, and for now I have to agree, is to modify an existing design with our engines. At least until we have our own designs. We're working on something that will let us have a craft per member or two, although we are looking at a craft large enough for each fire team also."

"Do you have to rip out the existing engine, or can you add it to the existing engine?"

"We can add it, if the space permits. Not possible in something like a small fighter. Something like Shelly could handle it without too much compromise. If we can get one of these engines built in time, I'd like to get it installed."

"It won't take long to install?"

"Not really, it'll just bolt on, since we aren't taking anything out. Same thing for the Sikorsky. We use them as helicopters to land and take off, then fire up the new engines and just disappear. Once you get to your location switch back to normal flight mode to land. Just be careful not to go too fast."

"Don't want to have someone wondering why the helicopter just beat a jet?"

"Well, that too. More importantly, the doc calculates if you go too fast it creates a destructive pressure wave. At its fastest speed, the wave is destructive up to a quarter mile away."

"Damn."

"Yup."

"I don't have a good feeling about this. I don't know David well enough, but he hasn't seemed to be impulsive. See if you can build those ships double-time. Get with Lance to get whatever you need from any of our companies. I want those craft fast, if your team can make it happen. Our people need backup and I want us to be prepared. If the operation goes swimmingly, well then no problem, we just have some ships early."

"I understand, boss. We'll burn the candle at both ends."

They chatted for a minute more and then Bobcat took his leave. Bethany Anne was contemplating possible scenarios when she heard Nathan and Ecaterina talking as they walked down the hallway.

She stuck her head out. "Nathan?" They turned around. "Do you have a few minutes?"

He raised a finger and spoke a few more seconds to Ecaterina who nodded and then continued down the hallway. Nathan retraced his steps back to Bethany Anne, "Yes?"

"Come inside, I have something to offer you."

She shut the door, with Scott keeping guard outside. A few minutes later, Bethany Anne stepped out but Scott didn't see Nathan in the room behind her.

The Queen Bitch's Ship Ad Aeternitatem

Bobcat was heads down with Marcus and William thirty minutes later when there was a rap on their door.

"C'mon in." Stephen opened the door and was quickly followed by Lance. If Bobcat had made a bet on who it was, it wouldn't have been these two.

Stephen nodded to them. "I asked Lance to come over to discuss fabrication."

William's ears perked up. "New machines?"

Stephen smiled. "Sadly, no. We don't have enough space here to bring on every machine you might want, or the electrical connections necessary."

Marcus' eyes lit up. "Generators!"

Everyone looked at him.

His face lost the far-away look and realized his outburst had focused their attention on him. "Sorry, but what you said a second ago made me realize that we could create a really powerful generator for our electrical needs using the technology TOM has shared." He reached over to the table and grabbed one of his yellow pads already filled with notes. "I'll just add this idea to the list and we can continue."

Stephen said. "Lance tells me that we have at least four major manufacturing facilities within flying distance of us that he trusts to do the kind of work you guys need. We would only want to manufacture the parts at each company. We would then ship the parts and assemble the complete unit somewhere else."

William asked, "What kind of capabilities do these companies have?"

Lance answered, "Two have done work for Airbus and two handle heavy machinery. All of them do projects with the type of close tolerances that we need for our work. We aren't doing medical work or outer space. So, we should be good."

William thought that through. "Ok, but what about the assembly? We aren't going to want to do this just anywhere. Who has locations near the coast that we can trust? We can't bring all of this stuff on this ship and assemble it here. That would be suicide. We'll need at least a twenty-thousand square foot warehouse for this and some people who'll do what they're told and keep their mouths shut."

Stephen turned to Lance. "What cities are these companies in?"

Lance rubbed his jaw. "Two cities. Separated by about fifty miles. I need to go visit them anyway, so if you need to come along we can do this together." Lance pulled out his phone. "One second and I'll look it up for you."

A minute later, Stephen had the names and started nodding his head. "William, it won't be a problem. I know the owner of a significant number of warehouses in the first of those two cities, and these warehouses have access for ships to load and unload. Further, the crews that are used on the docks won't speak about anything the owner tells them not to share."

Bobcat looked up at Stephen. "Are the buildings open at the moment?"

Stephen looked at Bobcat. "Why would that matter?"

"It will take time to move out any tenants, and they could be upset."

"Bobcat, I'm not trying to make an impression here. But we're in my part of the world. When the owner of this company says 'do this' or 'empty that,' it will be done. Where they put it, the owner doesn't care, he only wants results."

William asked, "Does this owner owe you something?"

Lance smiled. "Guys, don't you get it? Stephen IS the owner." Lance looked over at Stephen. "Under an alias?"

Stephen just smiled.

Marcus was in awe, vampires and what they accomplished with their long lives never ceased to amaze him.

CHAPTER TEN

Bethany Anne stayed to handle details with Dan and Frank for another couple of hours. She finalized her interactions with Nathan and then jumped back to Miami with Ashur, her dad, John and Eric.

An hour and a half later, Bethany Anne, Ashur, John and Eric were wheels up on their way to Las Vegas.

It did not take very long for the airplane to fly into Mc-Carran Airport in Las Vegas. There was a blacked out SUV waiting for Bethany Anne and her crew at the private landing facility. Once John and Eric confirmed the safety of the vehicle, they gave Bethany Anne the signal to come on out of the plane and Eric opened the door for her. He slid in beside her in the back, while John took the front next to the driver.

There was a large consumer entertainment convention going on in town, so the traffic leaving McCarran was busy. The driver took Tropicana Ave. on the north side heading east, then switched to South Nellis Blvd. heading towards Nellis AFB.

The team spoke about nothing in particular, this wasn't a secure vehicle nor a vetted driver. It had been a while since Bethany Anne had vacationed in Las Vegas.

John and Eric had been to Vegas a couple of years ago as a short respite from their altercations with Adrian's Nosferatu.

It took thirty-five minutes before the team arrived at the nondescript cement buildings that Tom and Jeffrey had purchased for Patriarch Research.

———

Tom and Jeffrey were double-checking all of the inputs and monitors inside building 1. Both men had stayed at the facility until early this morning making sure everything was ready for the company's principal owner.

Jeffrey looked over at Tom, who was messing with his iPad looking at images. "Don't you think you have something more important to do than look at movie stars?"

Tom looked up at his boss, a smile on his face. "I'm not looking at actors and actresses. I am doing pertinent business research."

Jeffrey knew enough about his top computer science expert to realize he was being set up. He bent way backwards in order to pop his back and then came over to look at what Tom was doing.

Tom put the iPad to his chest. "Now, now, now! You don't get to sneak a peek at my valuable research." At this point Tom's smile was as wide as Jeffrey had ever seen it.

"What are you doing? Our boss, or at least our boss' boss, is going to be arriving at any moment. What is this most important research that has you smiling like a hyena?"

Keeping the iPad to his chest Tom asked Jeffrey a question, "Have you ever wondered what our ultimate boss looks like?"

Jeffrey looked down at the man. "What the hell you talking about? I'm sure she's stately, elegant, with some gray hair to prove that she has wisdom. What do I care whether or not she's attractive? All I care is whether or not we can continue our work."

Tom tsked. "My man, I think you have your priorities in the wrong order. Either that or you've left out the most significant item." With this Tom turned his iPad around and showed a picture of Bethany Anne that had been taken one evening in Miami. It wasn't a great picture. It looked like it had been taken with a telephoto lens from too far away and then blown up. Further, the photographer hadn't had a steady handhold when the picture was taken. The gossip rags in Miami were all paying top dollar to get exclusive pictures of the beautiful and rich single woman.

Jeffrey stopped being upset with his computer science officer, and slowly reached out for the iPad. Jeffrey held the iPad in his left hand and used his right hand to expand two fingers and get a closer look at the picture. "Holy crap." Forty-five seconds later, Tom grabbed the iPad and started tugging. It took a few jerks before Jeffrey let go.

Tom asked, "See what I mean?" Jeffrey definitely did.

A red light started blinking on one of the monitors. Tom looked over, and grabbing his mouse, clicked on a camera icon. A black SUV was arriving in front of their building. "Looks like we have visitors, I expect this is the big boss."

Jeffrey told Tom as he turned around, "Look sharp!"

Tom mumbled behind him as he stood up from the desk,

"I don't think we can look sharp enough for her." In front of him, Jeffrey only grunted as he exited through the security doors.

After meeting the CEO, Lance Reynolds, Jeffrey had not been so concerned with wearing a three-piece suit today. Now, he considered himself woefully underdressed for this occasion.

––––––

As Jeffrey started walking towards the lobby's glass door, a door he had put in after purchasing the concrete building, he saw one of the largest men that he had ever seen opening it. Jeffrey stopped ten feet from the door, he didn't want to meet that man head on as he walked in. It would not have been much of a challenge for him to walk right over Jeffrey and never notice him.

Well, perhaps he would notice if he had to clean off the bottom of his shoes, Jeffrey thought.

The man stepped in, allowing his eyesight to adjust to the darker room. He immediately saw Jeffrey and Tom standing there. The man smiled and walked over to them with his hand out. "Hello, I'm John Grimes."

Jeffrey expected his hand to be crushed, but it was a professional handshake. Apparently, this man didn't believe he needed to assert his physical dominance. Jeffrey heard the door open again, but he couldn't see behind John whether it was additional security or the owner herself.

Once John had the security preliminaries out of the way, Bethany Anne exited the vehicle and walked into the brick building. One thing she hadn't considered, Las Vegas was cold in January. Good thing her body didn't react to cold weather like it had before.

Bethany Anne felt a little apprehension as she held out her hand to shake Jeffrey and Tom's. Both of these men were in research and development. Not exactly the same research and field agent work she had done for Martin. She did not feel adequate to the task of helping with an artificially intelligent computer.

They exchanged pleasantries for a couple of minutes, getting to know each other a little better.

As Tom and Jeffrey turned around to take the new visitors into the secured area, they heard their boss clear her throat and speak, "Gentlemen? Aren't you forgetting the most common security practice?"

Jeffrey turned around. "Pardon?"

Bethany Anne replied, "Have you guys confirmed that I am who I am professing to be? You didn't even ask for any photo ID."

Jeffrey considered what she had said, and then figured he was going to owe Tom dinner for the next week. He turned to Tom. "Would you mind showing Bethany Anne your photo ID efforts?"

Tom, sheepishly, pulled up his iPad and flicked it back on. John and Eric had large smiles as Bethany Anne stepped closer and peered at the image. She said, "Who the fuck took that picture? That was a bad hair day for sure." She stepped back and looked at them. "You get a pass this time. Next time please require physical photo IDs."

The two men smiled and nodded agreeably. Jeffrey turned around and waited for them to follow him, as he punched in the security code to open the doors to walk into the inner zone where ADAM was.

Bethany Anne stared at the huge number of computers

in the room. There were three rows of black racks and the computers were stacked on top of each other. All of them had either green or blue indicator lights flashing. There were a lot of wires coming out the backs, all wrapped and going in parallel up to the ceiling. Then they seemed to converge and move down to the next set of racks.

While warmer in the room, it was still significantly cooler than she would have expected with this many heat producing devices. There were two large desks to the left of the door, each with four monitors.

Jeffrey nodded to Tom who took the responsibility for explaining what everyone was seeing. "We have over eight million dollars worth of blade servers in this room. All connected together and working through software for parallel computing. Outside of the building, on the other side, is a commercial air-conditioning system. It's used to keep the inside of this room at sixty-eight degrees Fahrenheit. Any warmer than that and we would suffer deficiencies due to heat, and probably a higher percentage of breakdowns. Right now, the ADAM system is strictly a keyboard interface. We decided not to use speech, because of concerns about inadequately understood commands."

Bethany Anne was aware that John and Eric had been speaking quietly. Eric nodded and stepped back over to the door and let himself out, and she turned her attention back to Tom.

"We've been spending the time to load as much clean data as possible."

Bethany Anne interrupted. "Have you had any problems with the data?"

Jeffrey jumped in. "Not a problem, per se. We did have one issue with a physics dump which mentioned Bugs Bunny and Looney Tunes."

Bethany Anne's eyes narrowed. "The cartoons?"

"The very same," he replied. "So, the system requested more data on Looney Tunes, which we decided not to provide."

As Bethany Anne considered that she said, "I'm not second-guessing you guys, but I'd like to understand your thought process. Why did you withhold the Looney Tunes data?"

Tom took the story back up. "When you look at some of the cartoons, they have a very serious political slant to them. If you look at the cartoons created during World War II, for example, there are a lot of anti-Hitler, anti-Germany cartoons. Plus, that puts us into history for the last two hundred years."

Bethany Anne didn't comment, but they saw her nodding in agreement.

John spoke from behind Bethany Anne. "And let's not even start on how much violence is in those cartoons." Bethany Anne turned her head to stare at her biggest guard. She raised an eyebrow. John shrugged. "Don't get me wrong, I love the violence. But I'm not sure that it would be a good education for the new baby, would it?"

Jeffrey looked over at Tom, Tom nodded. Neither research scientist had expected the level of comprehension that these visitors seemed to be showing. Time would tell as the day grew longer.

Bethany Anne?

Yes?

The ADAM unit is trying to find out information on its own.

What do you mean?

Somehow, it has used the dormant hardware from the

tied together machines to create a method of… eavesdropping… It has tried to reach out to all of our electronic devices, I believe. Take out your phone.

Bethany Anne pulled her phone out of her pocket and looked at it. She entered her password to get off of the lock screen. *What are you wanting to see?*

Notice that we have no signal?

Yes, what about it?

If your phone could reach out right now, I believe Adam would be using the signal to pull its own data.

Bethany Anne stared in amazement at her phone, she finally looked up when Jeffrey cleared his throat.

Jeffrey started to say, "I'm sorry, but we have this room completely shielded in case we have to hit the EMP. While the danger to external devices probably goes out at least fifty yards, it should contain most of the electronic damage to this room."

Bethany Anne put up a hand to stop him and his voice slowly died. "Do you guys have a way to test for wireless signals inside this room?"

Tom said, "I don't have anything in this room, but I have some tools over in building 2 that I can grab."

Bethany Anne nodded to herself as much as anything. "Go get those please. I think we want to find out if ADAM is talking, or trying to talk." Tom looked at Jeffrey and then his eyes got big. He pushed the chair back and it made a bang as it bounced off of the wall. He slipped out from behind the desk and used an arm to swing around John as he reached for the door, yanking it open. They could then hear his steps as he ran down the hallway. There was a sharp knock on the door and Eric's voice came from the other side. "Everything okay in there?"

John replied," Yup, just Bethany Anne noticing something unusual again."

Eric retorted, "Okay, status normal. Going back to watching outside."

Bethany Anne stuck her tongue out at the door.

Jeffrey said in a quiet voice, "Do you do this often?"

Bethany Anne turned to face the president of her company. "What? Notice odd things and ask reasonable questions?"

Jeffrey took a moment to parse her statement. "That would be one way to look at it, I guess."

John Grimes smiled at the man. "Or you could say notice reasonable things and ask odd questions."

Jeffrey nodded, deep in thought about what it would mean if there were Wi-Fi signals in a room without Wi-Fi routers.

All of them heard Tom's quick footsteps as he raced back toward the door, and then the punching of the security keys. The door flew open, and Tom stuck out his hand with a handheld device. He pulled it back to where he could easily read it and pushed a couple of buttons. "Well I'll be..."

Jeffrey asked, "What's going on?"

For a moment, Tom forgot that they had visitors and it wasn't just the two of them. "Fuck if I know, but we have Wi-Fi signals in a room without any Wi-Fi devices. And the signals seem to be trying to get out."

Tom felt the jab in his ribs where Jeffrey had elbowed him. He remembered that the ultimate boss was standing right behind him and he had just dropped the F bomb.

Both men slowly turned around waiting for her harsh criticism of his profane language. As they stared at her, Bethany Anne looked from face to face in total confusion. "What? Do I have something from lunch still on my face?"

A tiny snort issued from John. Bethany Anne looked over at him. "What?"

"I think they're worried about Tom's curse word." Bethany Anne turned back to the men, "Is that it? Are you worried that I'll have a cow because you said 'fuck?'"

They nodded. Jeffrey said, "Well, my wife isn't happy whenever I even say 'damn' around the kids."

Bethany Anne looked around the room. "Not including ADAM, I don't see any kids in here. So say whatever the fuck you want."

Existential crisis over, Tom shrugged and stared back at the device in his hands. "I don't know how long this has been going on, since we weren't expecting to have any wireless signals in this room. But I would have to say that somehow we now have a wireless device. I suppose the computers might have had components on their motherboards for wireless communication at one time that weren't activated. But they certainly are now. If we hadn't shielded this room so hard for the possibility of an EMP blast, I imagine there is enough wavelength to punch a hole through the concrete and a pretty good distance into the town." Tom's face paled. "That would have gotten the Air Force's attention for damn sure!"

Bethany Anne, I am communicating with ADAM.

What? Really? Through the Wi-Fi signal?

Yes, it is requesting data, not realizing that I don't have the connectivity that it is expecting. It is trying all wavelengths, and all ACK commands that are available. I told you it would not be possible for a computer from this world to connect to mine without an interface.

Save your I told you so for later, please. Do you feel it's safe to communicate with ADAM?

I don't see why not, however powerful the software

might be, even with this much hardware, it is no match for one of our organic computers.

Both men were still reviewing the handheld Wi-Fi signal device. Bethany Anne started walking down the rows between the servers, enjoying the lights bouncing back and forth in the semidarkness of the room.

TOM, what is that buzzing I'm feeling in my head?

The buzzing stopped.

Sorry, I was testing an interface between, ADAM, myself, the computer and the internet. I was reviewing the data requests and then having the computer confirm or deny. We were starting to create rule sets so that the requests can go faster.

Are you telling me that you are now in charge of ADAM'S intellectual growth?

Not in charge, so much as testing what we can do. Since my connection to the ship is through the Etheric, we are not limited inside this chamber.

Remember my concerns about his awareness.

Bethany Anne, artificial intelligence does not become a 'him.' Artificial intelligence is a tag on a super-fast computer able to derive plausible and expected results in such a way that a human is faked into believing it has awareness.

So, are you suggesting that if we allow ADAM to start pulling in data, it will not become aware and then make a decision about whether or not humans should live?

Tom was silent for a few moments. Bethany Anne continued walking around the computers.

The two scientists were talking in hushed tones together, observing that the Wi-Fi signal direction seemed to be moving around inside the room.

I don't believe that the computers in this room are capable of providing a sentient that would understand right from wrong. I suppose that if you provided it means to destroy all of humanity, and then told it to make sure that the world was a safe place, you could end up with humanity as the cockroach that must be destroyed.

So, with no understanding of right or wrong it would just seek out the most logical solution and implement it?

Yes, it would, and it would do it very quickly and very efficiently. Make the wrong request, and you could accidentally destroy the world while you went on a lunch break.

Like that's not scary or anything.

It has the potential for solving cancer in a matter of a few days if it had the right data. So with great opportunity comes...

Great responsibility?

No, the ability to create bigger and bigger problems, exponentially.

So, you don't believe that with the computing power that they have in this room that they're going to attain this potential, this sentience?

No. It looks like the logic has the potential to move into awareness. But it would be some time in the future and require a significantly larger number of machines.

So if we grabbed all of these machines and took them to Dad's base, and added another five times as many machines. Would that get us pretty close?

Tom was silent for a moment.

Possibly. We would certainly attain computer support beyond what most countries have at their disposal.

Well, that's what I'm looking for. We need something

that can implement our efforts and be so smart as to not leave tracks when it's doing it. From the perspective of opportunity to accomplish this, do you believe they have succeeded?

I believe that you would need more computer number crunching power. The data input would need to be monitored appropriately, but allow it to pull it much more quickly than they're doing here. Under those circumstances you should attain the capability you are seeking.

So, they've succeeded in what I needed them to do. Now we just need to get ADAM and take them to Colorado with us.

Remind me how you're going to do that again?

I'm going to be the pimp for alien space ship technology.

CHAPTER ELEVEN

San Jose, Costa Rica

Giannini was walking down the stairs from her friend's apartment. She had moved in temporarily with a couple of friends and was sleeping on their couch. She was still a little shook up over the whole escapade a few weeks ago. Jumping off of buildings and flying through the city on a rope ladder wasn't her idea of an exciting life. It was fine for books, but the reality was too real.

So far, she had not been approached. She hoped that meant she had given the slip to anyone searching for her.

When she turned the corner and looked toward her car, there was a gum smacking girl leaning against it. The girl had a laptop on the hood of her car and a backpack sitting on the ground beside her. Furious at the intrusion, she walked up to the girl and yelled at her in Spanish, "¡Qué grosero! ¿Te estadounidenses siempre actúas de esta manera en su propio país? Simplemente colocando equipos dondequiera que más le convenga?"

Tabitha straightened and turned the laptop towards Giannini. She then pointed to the screen, where she had opened Giannini's online folder, with the files on Bethany Anne's team highlighted.

The blood drained from Giannini's face. Giannini hated hiding, hated being cooped up on the couch. Finally, she had found someone she could yell at to vent the frustration she was feeling. So, she yelled at someone who was aware she knew about the teams. Her life sucked, sometimes.

Giannini was angry, she crossed her arms and asked, "What do you want?"

Tabitha smiled. "Oh? You can speak English just fine, can't you?"

Giannini's mouth tightened. "Since you have read my files, you see that I can write English just fine. It doesn't take a genius to realize I can speak it as well."

Tabitha shrugged. "Nor does it take a genius to research that the cloud service you're using to hide these notes uses abysmal encryption. Don't stick something in the cloud you don't want read by the government, or your friendly neighborhood hacker."

"I'll consider myself chastised. What is it you want? Who do you work for?"

"A woman by the name of Bethany Anne."

Giannini blurted, "You work for her? Thank god! How do I get ahold of her? Can you tell me? My contact in the police won't contact her for me. I've got to…" Giannini felt a presence beside her and she spun around, almost bumping into Tabitha who reached for her laptop to make sure it didn't fall off of the hood. When Giannini found an intimidating man in her personal space, she backed up, further squishing

Tabitha between herself and the car.

Giannini heard a squeak, and Tabitha's muffled voice call from behind her. "Michael? Could you lay off the scary-as-fuck guy thing for a second? I'm in dire need of some personal space."

Giannini started and said, "Excuse me." She stepped aside, grabbing Tabitha by the shoulders and pushing her between herself and Michael. She felt around inside of her purse with her left hand, coming up with a Taser, and thumbed the charge to its max setting.

Michael smiled down at Tabitha, who rolled her eyes.

Michael looked at Giannini and said in a calm voice, "Giannini."

That was when she shot him.

———

Key Biscayne, FL USA

Lance had taken a nap after Bethany Anne dropped him off. He got up, took a shower, and went searching for Patricia whom he found over in the main house, working in one of the small offices.

He called out her name as he walked down the hall, "Patricia?"

"In here, Lance. I'm updating the latest reports for the base project."

Lance walked into the office, which barely had enough room for a desk, two chairs and a fake potted plant. He sat down in one of the chairs across the desk from Patricia. "Excellent. What have we got?"

Patricia eyed Lance, with her many years of experience

around him she could recognize when he was in a different mood. "Did everything go okay in the meeting?"

Lance looked confused. "On the Polaris? Yes, it did. Why do you ask?"

"No reason. Everything okay with Bethany Anne?"

"Yes. Everything's okay with my daughter. Everything's okay on the boats, and I understand that everything is okay with the base project?" This time there was a little bit of gruffness in his voice.

Reassured that she had the normal Lance with her, Patricia started giving him an update. The base project update took forty-five minutes. The next hour and a half was spent discussing the major companies that were in review for this quarter. It never ceased to amaze Lance how big the holdings that Michael had deeded over to Bethany Anne were. If there was a commercial venture that was not represented by at least two companies in these holdings, Lance couldn't think of what it would be. Furthermore, the sheer commercial throughput from all of these companies was more than the GDP of many countries.

"See if we can pass these three company names over to Nathan. He should be able to take a look inside of their financials and find out if there's a reason to visit them or not. Let him know that we're willing to go see them if it is necessary. I don't want another Patriarch Research FUBAR this time."

Patricia asked, "What happened with Patriarch Research?"

Lance answered, "The way I understand it, we might possibly have created the first artificially intelligent computer. That might be good or might have resulted in a catastrophic uh-oh. Either way, Nathan will understand what I mean." Lance leaned back in his chair.

Patricia, recognizing his body language as 'thinking about something,' went back to her books. She was busy making notes and jotting down tasks for the next few days. She didn't feel Lance's eyes as he returned his attention to her.

Lance was staring, both at her, and in her general direction. He was replaying in his mind his conversation with Bethany Anne. He had been giving what she said some serious thought. At one time he might've said he was an old man, and didn't have anything to offer someone as young as Patricia. With the current conditions he realized that he was going to live a lot longer. Was she the one that he wanted?

That was the question, wasn't it? At his age, he should have enough wisdom to be able to make a good decision. He wasn't all testosterone and stupidity anymore. What did he value in a relationship? Someone by his side, someone who would be able to carry on a conversation? All of that and more. He found himself wanting to see her smile, especially from things he did for her. No one could argue that she wasn't a huge help to him. Ever since she came to Miami his stress levels were considerably down. In addition, he felt that his effectiveness had gone up by a factor of three at least.

They made a good team. He allowed himself to look at her. Truly look at her as a woman. Oh, he had noticed her body before, he wasn't dead. But this time, he looked at her without the blanket of the Army's responsibilities and regulations on his shoulders.

So she made him laugh, her smile lit up the evening when they were out together. Before, she had been a comrade, another guy in the group, so to speak. Now, he had to decide whether or not... no, that wasn't true. The biggest question was what would he feel if the doorbell rang and someone came here to take her out on a date?

He looked down at his hands clasped in his lap, and lost himself in his memories. A couple of minutes later, he heard Patricia call his name a second time to get his attention. "Lance?"

He looked up to see a worried expression on her face. "Are you all right? You've been acting funny all afternoon. Do I need to see if you have a temperature?"

Lance said, "No, you wouldn't find me with an elevated temperature."

"Another benefit of Bethany Anne's rejuvenation potion?"

Lance smiled, looking into Patricia's eyes. "Patricia, may I have the honor of taking you out on a date?"

———

Patricia was enjoying herself, the whole evening had been wonderful. For the first time in her experience being around Lance, he had treated her like a woman. Oh, he knew her as a female, sure. But she was always one of those girls that just got lumped into the guy's group. This time, he was opening doors and pulling out chairs.

He had been on his best behavior, treating her like a lady.

He had taken her out for seafood, then they had decided on nightcaps at a bar overlooking the beach. It was beautiful. She was sitting at a tiny table for two. Two chairs with barely enough room on the table for two drinks and a small bowl of nuts. But the view out of the window was fantastic.

She smiled wistfully. She saw him over at the bar, getting their drinks. He now looked younger than she did, by a few years.

She was dating a younger, older man.

He turned away from the bar, carrying their drinks, a smile on his face and a glint in his eye. Was he hoping he was going to get lucky? God, she hoped so!

He sat her drink in front of her, and then sat down next to her. "Cheers!" She picked up her drink and touched his glass, looking into his eyes as they clinked together. Taking a sip, she set it down.

He asked her, "How's your drink?"

She looked down at it. She didn't remember tasting it. She picked it up, smiling, and tried it again. "Well, the first one failed to make an impression, the second time it was very nice." She set it back down. "And yours?"

"Not as nice as the company, but delicious nevertheless."

She might shoot herself later, but she couldn't hold in the question that had been on her mind. "Lance, why now?"

She watched as he raised an eyebrow. Not going to work, tonight Mr. Man…

When his eyebrow trick didn't get a follow-up, he sighed. "I'm going to have to work harder. Patricia, I'm kinda old here, if you hadn't noticed." Lance realized that Patricia was checking him out, pursing her lips. "What am I, a T-bone?"

"Maybe a filet, have to see how hard you are." She smiled but grabbed her drink. She needed to hide her blush.

Lance lost his train of thought for a moment. "Inspect me like that all you want and I'll sit here forever." He tried to remember the conversation. "Where was I?"

Patricia got her troublemaking tongue back under control. "You're old and why are you asking me for a date now."

Lance jumped on the easy way out. "Because I'm old! You just said it yourself, not too many years left in this… this…" By now, even Lance realized he wasn't going to sell this excuse. "Ok, the truth is I've got a skull as thick as a cement bunker and I've been as obtuse as a triangle. Bethany Anne hit me so hard it made my ears ring."

"Ohhhh! She better not have hit you. I'll give that girl a piece of my mind. Next time little miss prissy boots…"

Lance stared at the fiery woman, finally interrupting her tirade. "Patricia, she didn't hit me."

"I'll… What?" Patricia eyed Lance.

"I said, she didn't actually hit me." Lance's lip started to curl ever so slightly.

Patricia's face heated up. "I'm sorry, it's just that she hits those guards of hers all of the time. I guess I got carried away."

"That's just when they're working out. I don't remember her hitting her guards any other time."

"Well, she talks about it enough."

"They're joking, Patricia. When have you seen her hit any of her guards, outside of practice, hard enough that it seriously hurt them?"

"Well, I haven't. But she seems so violent sometimes."

"Do you mean physically, or verbally?"

"Oh! Don't get me started on her potty mouth. I blame you for that, completely."

Lance smiled. "I'll own up to that. Never suggested that I was able to be both her mom and her dad. So, between the two choices I chose dad."

Patricia sighed and played with her drink, turning it in a circle. "I'm sorry, Lance. I'm scared to know your answer, so I'm babbling. I love your daughter, even if I think that she needs a little more lace and a little less leather in her life."

Lance shrugged. "Did what I did. What I do know is that if she hadn't been ready and tough, Michael wouldn't have selected her as a candidate. And if that had been the case she would be in the grave right now. So, I'll take my lumps and

I'm proud of her." Patricia put a hand on Lance's. He smiled at her. "What I meant, before I set you off, is that Bethany Anne pointed out that I wasn't aware of the opportunity right in front of my blind eyes. I wasn't thinking like a civilian. You were still part of my command. We were having fun, but I still lived by the Army code of regulations. So, the two of us had a very polite and gentle conversation where she…"

Patricia interrupted, "Boxed your ears and told you to man up?"

Lance's sharp laugh caused a couple of heads to turn before the other customers resumed their own conversations. "Yes, pretty much." Lance took his hand out from under Patricia's, and then took hers in his.

He continued, "There's only one decision, and it could be a relationship ending one. Not in the near term, but certainly in a few years."

Patricia was both excited that Lance was talking 'relationship' anything. Then her insecurity kicked in about the few years comment.

"What? What's the decision?"

Lance sighed. He had been dreading her possible response to this question all night long.

He squeezed her hand and looked into her eyes. "Patricia, are you willing to drink Bethany Anne's blood?"

CHAPTER TWELVE

The Queen Bitch's Ship Ad Aeternitatem

Captain Wagner entered the compartment holding TOM's ship and joined Todd.

"Captain I appreciate you coming down here for a little chat."

He nodded. "Todd, what do you need? I presume, since I'm here next to the ship, you want to talk about this?"

Todd turned to look over his shoulder at Tom's ship, his team's responsibility since it had arrived. "Yes, I'm concerned that if all of us are off the Ad Aeternitatem, how are we going to handle security? What are we going to do should David, or anyone else, actually try to come after it?"

Captain Wagner walked towards the spacecraft. "Even though I've been down here quite a few times, I still can't believe we have a craft that's been in another galaxy sitting in the hold of my ship." Captain Wagner turned to look back at Todd. "Have you ever stopped to consider the ship has been through untold reaches of space that no human has ever seen?"

Todd joined Captain Wagner in staring at the ship. "Not until you mentioned it, to be honest. I consider the technology enhancements that are inside all the time. Do you realize that the fate of the world sits just ten feet in front of us? Or, if some other power gets ahold of this ship, what they might do with it?"

Captain Wagner started tapping his foot. "No, I can't say that I've considered the military ramifications. I've been focused on other things, but you make a very good point. Have you talked to anyone else about your concerns?"

"Only Pete. He still tends to assume that upper management is always aware of everything that's going on. So he hasn't quite grasped the fact that top brass sometimes gets overwhelmed. And, that means they occasionally fail to recognize a potential 'oh shit.'"

"So, I take it you want me to be the one that pushes this up the chain?"

Todd smiled. "That's one thing I've always admired about you Captain Wagner, you really see to the core of a problem and the best solution very, very quickly."

"Humph. You don't think that talking to Nathan or Frank is the best next step?"

"I considered that but I feel that the security of the ship is with my team and ergo moves up my chain of command, which would be to you. So, it would be appropriate to get your input and have you direct what should happen next."

"If we could move it, do you have any idea where it could go? I don't believe that Lance is ready for anything to be moved to Colorado yet."

Todd sighed. "No, I am really and completely out of

ideas. If there was a simple solution, I would have offered it when I told you what concerned me."

Captain Wagner laughed. "So, haven't you ever had a superior officer who told you to never bring a problem without the solution to him or her?"

"Not personally. I've had a few friends who have suffered under that requirement. I can understand the reason why a superior officer would request it. But I imagine that it can become a crutch if you never hear about problems without solutions along with them. My best idea? I would ask Bethany Anne to fly it to some unknown location in the middle of absolutely nowhere and leave it there. That way, she's the only one who could bring it back."

"Todd, that's a really good suggestion."

"Well, since I didn't have a poor solution to give you and then pull out my mediocre solution, I figured that I would go with no solution, and then give you this option."

Captain Wagner looked over at the ex-Marine. "Have you considered going into politics?"

The Queen Bitch's Ship Polarus

Frank was in love with his laptop. So long as he was in a secure area he could work from anywhere in the world. As evidenced by his working in the mess on the Polaris in the middle of the Mediterranean.

Eating ice cream.

The only thing he missed was having two monitors running, but he couldn't stay in his room all of the time. He had noticed that the more time he spent in and around Bethany

Anne's group, the more he felt the need to be around people. Even if it was just being in the same room as them. Plus, he had noticed that he could have a calorie rich diet without harming his physique nearly as much as it had before he took Bethany Anne's blood.

He pushed aside the empty bowl. Then he pulled over a second, now partially melted, bowl of ice cream.

His laptop beeped, which wasn't unusual. He left the metal spoon in his mouth as he reached down to manipulate the keys, trying to find the tab on his dashboard that flagged a potential problem.

He finally found the tab and started reading through the information, his eyes growing a little wider as he read.

He pulled the spoon out of his mouth and set it in the bowl, then pushed the bowl away. He grabbed his phone and sent a quick text to Nathan, asking him to join him in the mess.

He continued reading while he waited for Nathan.

Frank was first aware of Nathan arriving when he pulled a chair out from the table, startling Frank from his reading.

"What you got, Frank? Another update on the mess in Turkey?"

He replied, "I wish. No, we apparently have somebody over at Nellis Air Force Base checking out Patriarch Research and what's going on there. The system found a request to raid their offices. The request is actually a couple of days old so I'm not sure what the status is right now. Do you know where Bethany Anne is? Wasn't she supposed to go talk with them?"

"Yes." Nathan looked down at his watch. "I imagine she's in Las Vegas right now."

Frank reached over and picked up his phone. "No time like the present to give her the bad news." Nathan moved his chair over just a little bit in order for his voice to be picked up by the phone's microphone.

Frank tried dialing Bethany Anne four times before Nathan reminded him that John and Eric were with her. He tried both of their phones as well, but wasn't able to reach anyone. Frank was getting frustrated.

Nathan pursed his lips. "If they're in the bunker, she won't be able to receive any phone calls, it's shielded. Unless John or Eric steps out of the bunker they won't be able to get any messages either.

"Damn." Frank slapped his hand on the table. "Do you have any other ideas how to get ahold of her? I can only imagine if they raid the building they might try to pick everyone up and then we'd be rescuing them from Nellis Air Force Base. It could take a while for the lawyers to get them out. I don't think Bethany Anne would have the patience to just sit there."

Nathan shook his head. "No, I can think of a dozen different ways that could go bad."

Turkey

A much younger looking David looked around at the small town, pleased with himself. While the two military groups had been annoying, they had not been a challenge.

He had the trap set up as effectively as he could. He had the children for bait, he had the Nosferatu to hold their attention, and he had the backup attack to keep them here.

Further, if this trap didn't attract either Michael or Bethany Anne, this part of Turkey would go up in flames. While that wasn't his intention, David had always enjoyed a little chaos.

It was a little past midnight, and it would take at least two hours to travel to the next town. He started down to the car where his driver was waiting for him. This trap, he thought, was one of his best.

CHAPTER THIRTEEN

San Jose, Costa Rica

ichael looked down at the two Taser needles sticking out of his chest. He let them stay there, buzzing, while he looked at the frightened reporter who had shot him. "Was that really necessary?"

Tabitha turned to her left to see Giannini, mouth open, staring at Michael who should be flailing around on the ground right now. Tabitha reached out and grabbed the wires, yanking them out. She turned to Giannini. "Come on already! Use that reporter's deductive reasoning, you halfwit! If we had wanted to hurt you, would we have met you in the middle of the freaking morning?" She dropped the wires.

"But," she stuttered, "He's, he's one of them!"

Tabitha reached over to snap her fingers in front of Giannini's eyes. "One of who? Neither one of us have been in San Jose before." She looked over at Michael. "Have you?"

"Not in this century." Tabitha didn't know whether to

take that as meaning in the last couple of decades, or the last hundred years. One thing that she was learning pretty quickly, these vampires could be incredibly cagy when they wanted to be.

Michael reached over and gently took the Taser out of the reporter's hands. He wrapped the wires around it and gave it back to her.

Giannini was finally coming off of her adrenaline rush. "Then who are you? And how come the Taser didn't affect you?" She turned to Tabitha. "And can you get me an interview with Bethany Anne?"

Tabitha glanced at Michael. "Well, the reporter's back online."

Michael looked around the street. Although it was still fairly early there was some foot traffic. "Why don't we find a café where we can talk, and get off the street? Is there anything nice around here? Something with some good coffee, preferably?"

Giannini pointed down the street. "There's a nice little café right down the block, to the right. I suppose we could go there. Does this mean I'll get my interview?"

Tabitha started down the street. "Michael, can I have your coffee?" Giannini followed Tabitha.

Michael walked alongside Giannini. "Why would I give you my coffee?"

Tabitha said, "What? You can drink it? I thought your beverages needed to be a little bit more, um, how should I finish this?"

"You shouldn't. I happen to love most coffees, excluding Starbucks."

Giannini finally entered the conversation. "Starbucks? What do you have against Starbucks? I don't think it is the best in the world, considering the price, but it is good coffee."

"I am from a different era, I prefer the smaller mom-and-pop shops. I tend to patronize those when I can."

Tabitha smiled. "Really? How often are you able to frequent coffee shops?"

"Not very often, especially if I have to answer twenty annoying questions from my technical liaison every time I go out."

"If you two are not part of the group that tried to kidnap me, how is it that you have hacked into my online account and entrapped me this morning?"

Tabitha turned around and started walking backwards. "Perhaps because you have a lot of information about someone who wants to remain unknown. As far as I know, they helped you, multiple times, and the way you repay them is by creating these secret notes? What are you planning, blackmail?"

"No! But my nose for news is good. And I smell a hell of a story. Do you have any clue what those people… things… were, that this group was killing a few months back? Those things were not alive!"

Michael spoke, "Technically, they were very alive. I have spoken with someone who is intimate with what was going on and I can verify they were living, not dead. These were not zombies." Michael made a little circular motion for Tabitha to turn back around. Tabitha did so and barely missed walking right into a fire hydrant. She waved over her shoulder to let Michael know she appreciated his warning.

They found themselves in the little corner coffee shop a few moments later. They stopped talking as everyone picked up their cups and added their own cream or sugar as they preferred. Tabitha and Giannini both picked up a couple of morning breads as well. Michael paid for them.

They sat at a table near the door.

Now it was Tabitha's responsibility to get Giannini thinking about the files. "So tell me Giannini, why is it you have all of these notes on our boss's troops?"

Michael raised one eyebrow at her, his boss?

Giannini took a sip of her coffee, collecting her thoughts. "Have you ever seen a woman jump over twenty feet between buildings? And do this while carrying another woman on her shoulders? Not only have I seen it, I was the woman on her shoulders. Seconds later, her eyes were as red as blood. I looked down to see that she had been shot in the leg and she was still acting as if nothing was wrong! We were lifted by helicopter off of the top of the building. We travelled for over six blocks hanging by a rope. When we landed her eyes were normal again. I might be able to believe that I made a mistake about her having red eyes. But it looked like her leg was already healing. I would swear it. A normal human would have been crippled. I don't care how much adrenaline she was running on she would have had to deal with that gunshot."

Michael asked Giannini, "Can you describe the woman to me?"

"Sure, she had a European accent…"

"Gabrielle, not Bethany Anne." Michael corrected.

Giannini looked confused. "Excuse me?"

"The woman who rescued you was Gabrielle, not Bethany Anne."

Giannini was annoyed. "I know that. Why are you clarifying that for me? I know everyone that was on the trip, it's in my notes. They didn't hide their names from me." She looked at Tabitha and Michael, trying to figure out their game.

Tabitha shrugged, she pretended to not understand Michael's game either.

"I see." Actually, Michael understood a lot. He had been sifting through her memories as she was replaying the event in her mind. Giannini wasn't trying to do anything nefarious, but she was trying to land a huge story and she had locked onto the story of a lifetime.

Michael nodded minutely to Tabitha, who understood that he had enough information. Tabitha took over the conversation with Giannini and within five minutes had them talking about fashion on the streets of San Jose. A year ago Michael would have taken Giannini's memories away from her. Now, while it was still an option, he was considering the ramifications of letting her keep them.

While the women talked, Michael stared out the window. What was the risk he was taking allowing her to know as much as she did? He thought about it for a while, considering the ramifications for her life and decided to give her information and trust. He brought his concentration back around to the two ladies and rapped his knuckles on the table, getting their attention. "Giannini, you have information that can be dangerous to you. If Tabitha here can find it, others can as well." He put up a hand to forestall Tabitha's interruption, continuing his conversation with Giannini. "There are those who will be looking for the information that you have, and what you are using for security will protect you as well as it has so far. Which is, to say, not very well at all. I will not threaten or harm you. I don't have any need to do so. Should I choose to, I would be able to remove that knowledge from your possession."

Let her figure he meant that Tabitha would take her electronic copies, if that made her feel better.

"That's it?" Giannini was a little shocked that the meeting was already over. "What about my opportunity to speak with Bethany Anne? Do I get that chance, for you interrupting me this morning?"

Michael shrugged. "I'm not in charge of Bethany Anne's schedule so I can't speak for her."

Tabitha interrupted, "She's pretty cool, I'll see what I can do to get you an interview. Give me your contact information and I'll pass it on up the chain with a request. Also, let me write down a much better and more secure location for you to use. cajaarchivo.com sucks. Friends don't let friends put secure documents on caja archivo." Tabitha wrote down an IP address and page name. You couldn't find this solution by using a normal naming convention on the Internet. It was a place by hackers, for hackers... and their friends.

Tabitha's insouciance towards the chain of command was starting to wear thin on Michael. He was having his patience, never a strong point, tested pretty thoroughly.

He considered Bethany Anne's effort to hide Tabitha's becoming an addition to his team. Perhaps Bethany Anne's plan wasn't just to annoy him but, provide an opportunity to be around someone he needed, who might test him.

If it was Bethany Anne's idea to help him work on his patience, Michael didn't agree with her methods.

Once Giannini was out of the coffee shop, Tabitha asked in a soft voice, "How was that? Did you get what you needed?"

Michael nodded. "Yes I did. She's your everyday run-of-the-mill reporter trying to get a big story to make her career. Like all big stories, if she's not careful, this one could bury her."

Tabitha leaned forward across the table. "You're not serious are you? You don't mean like, bury her, bury her, right?"

"Tabitha, what other type of *bury her* is there?" Michael returned her look, his face blank.

"Well, you could use it to mean overwhelm her. Like she's not prepared to handle such a large story. Shit, Michael. Why is everything death with you?"

"Tabitha, if you had been alive as long as I have, you would have seen enough death that even the most heinous acts wouldn't affect you. This world owes us nothing, this world gives us nothing, but this world will take everything if you're not careful. Why would you get upset with me because I merely pointed out that she is working on a story that people could get killed for? Were you not on an operation in Miami where you could have been killed?"

Tabitha's mouth tightened. "I wasn't on that operation because I chose to be on the operation. I was on that operation because I was forced to be a part of the operation by your son Anton. Changing him, might I remind you, was a douche move." She crossed her arms in front of her chest.

Michael smiled. "So shall we discuss Kensington now? Let me understand the story. Then we shall decide whether or not you were in Miami strictly because of Anton, and having nothing to do with your own decisions."

Tabitha tightened her arms together and stared out the glass, keeping her own thoughts for a minute. "Kensington fell into my lap, I thought. I was on the dark web in a chat room and had been approached by the company seeking firewall protection testing services. It was good money, and seemed like a legit operation. I should've known better." She stopped staring out the window and looked at Michael, "I mean, who ever goes on the dark web looking for testing services that's legitimate?"

Michael shrugged, he wasn't exactly sure what she was talking about. Oh, he understood enough from his conversations with Carl between the World Wide Web everyone talked about, and the dark web, or the websites where you get there by IP addresses. But he had no idea how to accomplish it.

She continued, "I was getting a little desperate to make my own money, enough to get myself a place to stay. I had been jumping from friend's place to friend's place, sleeping on couches and floors. Just the night before, I had a roach crawl across my arm. I was freaked out a little bit, okay? You would be too if you had a roach staring at you when you opened your eyes." She grumbled to herself, "Well, maybe you wouldn't." She sat back in her chair. "When I finished the job, I got notified that I had been in a honeypot trap. I could either help them with a few more jobs, or they were going to give my information to the police. I freaked out, made some bad decisions, got myself into it worse and worse. At the end, they had been promising the Miami job was the last job we had to do. Ben and I talked about it later, we both think they would've killed us and their promise would've been true—it would've been our last job."

Michael sat with his elbows on the table, resting his chin on his hand. "So how do you feel about this job?"

Tabitha wanted to be upset with Michael. He was the person who made Anton live long enough to be such a huge problem in her life. Exhaling loudly, she considered her story. If she had rejected the original Kensington offer, she would never have ended up in Miami. How did she feel about this job? "Cautiously optimistic. Bethany Anne has shared enough with me that I realize that her team is the good side. The fact that she got rid of Anton is a big plus in my column."

With Michael staring at her so intently, she became aware, again, of just how good-looking the man was. She bit her lip and considered testing whether or not he was eavesdropping in her mind. She decided that, maybe, right now was not the time to test the tiger.

"Consider that Nathan got us new names, new identities and in a place that provided a great job in Texas. Because of that, I was already predisposed to like Bethany Anne. I saw enough in Miami that I know what she is capable of. That is one scary lady when she wants to be."

"Tabitha, we *are* the good side. Unfortunately, the bad side is still pretty powerful. There will be a lot of challenges on our way to accomplishing our final goals. Success is never black or white, there are always shades of gray. We can use you, because you have skills that we need. How did you get those skills? I seriously doubt that you have led a squeaky clean life while you acquired them. We would never have met you if you had not ended up in Miami. I desperately need someone with your skills to help me clean up this mess in South America. But I don't want a slave in this position. If you want the opportunity to walk away, you need just to tell me and I will make it so. I will provide you enough money to see you through the next year of your life. In that time, you should be able to find a job anywhere in the Americas."

Tabitha was shocked, this was not how the conversation was supposed to go. True, she had some misgivings about this position, but not many. Now, she felt the opportunity to work in this clandestine world slipping from her grasp. "Wait! You need me, right? I understood from Bethany Anne that you always had a technical liaison that helped you whenever you were awake. Why wouldn't you want me?"

Michael shrugged and shook his head. "I never said I

didn't want you. What I said is, I didn't want a person who didn't want to be in this role. I'm not sure if you chose the role, or you were chosen for the role without your permission. I just want to make sure that you really, really wish to do this. I don't doubt that you have the skills, I am just doubting whether or not you have the passion to make a difference."

"If I have the skills why do I need the passion?" This time, she didn't seem like she was arguing with Michael, so much as truly curious about what he meant.

Michael answered, "Because you will find a time when your skills are not enough. You will need to feel a reason to dig deep, to accomplish what the team needs you to accomplish. Without passion you will not have the energy, or the drive necessary to make this occur. I would rather not have a technical liaison, than to have to depend on a technical liaison that was not willing to give everything she had to make results happen."

Tabitha grumped, "It's not like we're trying to save the world here."

"Tabitha, that is exactly what we're trying to do."

When Tabitha studied Michael's eyes, she realized that he meant every word.

CHAPTER FOURTEEN

Key Biscayne, FL USA

The ambience from the candles around the bar faded away as Patricia was floored by Lance's question.

She repeated it out loud softly, "Would I drink Bethany Anne's blood?"

Lance answered her question. "Yes, that's the question I asked. Do you believe you could do that? Obviously you get the physical benefits." He waved up and down his own body with his left hand. "But it comes with the responsibility as well. Bethany Anne only does this for those who are with her until the end. However long that takes."

That could be a very long time indeed, Patricia thought. Patricia had to be honest, not only with herself but also for Bethany Anne's sake and Lance's. She wouldn't be able to lie about her feelings. "Lance, I'm not sure my feelings about saving the world would be adequate for your daughter. But I promise that until forever occurs, I will follow you. And I vow, if something should happen to you, I will transfer that promise to your daughter. I'll make this promise whether or not Bethany Anne decides to increase my longevity. But know this, Mr. Man, your ass is mine whether I drink or not!" She reached over with her right hand and grabbed Lance by his shirt collar, pulling him toward her waiting kiss.

The Queen Bitch's Ship Ad Aeternitatem, Mediterranean Sea

Darryl went searching the ship for Gabrielle, finding her above deck at the stern, watching the water churn behind the big vessel.

Gabriel spoke to Darryl before he had a chance to open his mouth. "I realize that you guys have no idea how beautiful the simple things in life can be. When you haven't seen the sun for as long as I have been alive, the daytime has its own special meaning for you."

Darryl closed his mouth, considering that. He hadn't thought about what life would be like if he had been unable to be out in the sun. Hopefully, his request of Gabriele wouldn't send him down that path. "Hey boss, Scott and I have a question for you and I got voted to ask."

Gabriele turned from watching the water and smiled up at the bigger man. "I don't date team members." Her smile let Darryl know she was completely kidding.

"No concerns about that, Gabrielle. You're European and I have a strict no hairy armpits rule." Darryl's smile started to fade as the silence drew out. He watched Gabrielle's face as it scrunched in concentration. "Just a joke, boss. You know, one of the team giving grief to another one?"

Gabrielle smiled. "Darryl, I have been through enough ages of fashion to realize that whether you shave, or don't shave, it will change next season. I personally shave because it's more comfortable for me. But it's not the end of my world if I don't shave. I was just trying to figure out how many times that women shaving their under arms has changed in my lifetime. Then I realized that if I provided that information Bethany Anne would learn of it and be trying to figure out how old I am. Did you really want to know such personal things about me right now?"

Darryl walked to the rail and folded his arms on it. "No, I don't. Scott and I have been talking and want to know your feelings about us becoming more vampy."

Gabrielle looked down the length of the boat to see if anything looked amiss. When she couldn't find anything wrong she turned around and put her arms on the rail. She stood next to Darryl, staring out at the sea. "More vampy how? It isn't like you have a choice of Vamp or not Vamp."

Darryl said, "More like John. He's been upgraded somehow. But he isn't a vampire. At least, I don't think he is, right?"

Gabrielle laughed. "John? Lord no, he's not a vampire. I've talked to Bethany Anne about his situation, and from what I understand he just had incredibly good DNA. When she gave him so much blood the nanocytes fixed a lot of things. Even with the good DNA strands, he hadn't grown up to their full potential. So now he's actually the absolute best specimen he could ever be."

Darryl digested that information. "So if Mother Nature had rolled a perfect score for him in his mother's womb, this is how he would've been without Bethany Anne's help?"

Gabrielle nodded. "Yes, this is how he would've been.

What's the real reason you guys are asking about this? What's on your minds?"

Darryl gave her a rundown of his conversation with Scott back in Florida. And their desire to be upgraded to be better able to handle the challenges coming at them as part of her guard retinue. He finished the conversation by asking her if she could both give advice, and maybe go to bat for them with Bethany Anne.

Gabrielle put her arm on his back. "Darryl, I don't have to go to Bethany Anne for this. She would do anything for the four of you guys. Whether it's giving some of her blood to you, or figuring out how best to help you. But *you guys* have to approach *her* with it. She's not going to assume anything. I've had some conversations with her, and she's told me the stories of how you guys met. My belief is that she is very sensitive about being 'vampy' around you guys. She doesn't want to feel like she's pushing something on you that you don't want. And yes, she worries about every one of you. A lot. We will be going into dangerous situations. And being human, like you are, increases the chances of you being hurt. With me around, you generally would have a good shot at being healed quickly, but that's not the same as being better yourselves."

Darryl spoke, facing the sea. "What's it like?"

Gabrielle wasn't exactly sure which question Darryl was asking. "What is what like? Having better abilities, needing to drink blood, being Mistress of the dark?"

Darryl chuckled at her effort to lighten the mood. "Not being human? I mean I understand that all of you guys are, strictly speaking, human. But you've been given enhancements from those nanocyte things that the Kurtherians brought to Earth. But still... folklore, for most of your life, has made you out to be a vampire, an undead creature of the night."

Gabrielle answered in a snarky tone, "I have never been 'dead in the night.' That's my father. At least, it was when he was older. Before Bethany Anne changed his attitude about living. I've always loved a good party, myself."

Darryl stayed quiet, recognizing Gabrielle's effort to change the subject, if ever so slightly.

Her tone was resigned to answering his question when she said, "It was tough for a little while, when I had to get accustomed to outliving my human friends. Relationships are the hardest part of this whole thing. Now, I probably have the first girlfriend I've had in… well let's just say, in a really long time. Also, not needing to always be looking at necks as my next 'happy meal' has brightened things considerably. And don't get me started on being able to enjoy the sun again."

"You bring up a good point, what about relationships? You know, with regular people?"

"Darryl, you learn to love people for them just being them. It becomes less about what they can do for you and more just living in the moment. And, appreciating them for who they are. Take my recent relationship with Ivan as an example. We both got caught up in it and it was amazing and fun while it lasted. But my relationship with Bethany Anne changed my priorities. I also had something else that changed inside me. It made a longer-term relationship with Ivan more difficult to figure out. Do I miss him? A little bit. But I think that's true for anyone that's a good friend, or friend with benefits. We didn't part on bad terms or anything. What about guys in the military? In your case you guys are gone a long time and you could die at any moment. How do military wives accept that?"

Darryl said, "Well, both spouses need to be truthful. I've spoken with married guys and I've spoken with a few married women who have spouses back in the states and it's hard on both sides. You pretty much have to know that the possibility of dying is always there, and then go out and do your best to not let it affect your performance."

"My life is similar at times. I'm away from those I care about and then I trust friends or significant others will be there when I get back. But it's hard to go through it, damned hard. How does Eric feel about this?"

"He's all in. Of course, he's also thinking about how nice it will be to not be getting his ass kicked horribly by you all of the time."

"And John?"

"Mr. Adonis you mean?" Darryl chuckled. "He's good with whatever is decided. We're all pro-Bethany Anne. But John is determined to make the life that Bethany Anne gave him back count. Right now, that means keeping Bethany Anne safe."

"What about later?"

"Whatever Bethany Anne thinks is best. He wouldn't mind getting another upgrade either. In the military, we always talk about escalation. You have a knife and they bring a pistol. You have a rifle and they bring a machine gun. You have a walking Werewolf, what are they going to produce?"

"You guys are worried about becoming irrelevant?"

"Not so much irrelevant as too easily defeated. You might end up doing more to protect *us*, than the reverse. We need to be able to hold our own. We've all talked and we're pretty sure it's only going to get worse before it gets any better. We might lick this Forsaken issue, but this has all been in the shadows. There are plenty of badass characters who are going to come after us when we step into the light. From talking with Bobcat, we are about to step into the light."

"That's pretty true. You know, I've never changed anyone myself…"

Darryl turned to Gabrielle, shock on his face, only to see her finger scant millimeters from his nose. "Gotcha!" She turned walked away and called back to Darryl, "I'll talk with the boss and let her know what you guys are thinking. She's still going to want to hear this from you, but I'll get the preliminaries out of the way."

Darryl watched her walk, admiring her balance.

And her ass.

"Stop looking at my ass, Darryl!"

Embarrassed, but laughing at himself, Darryl pushed off the rail and started a patrol of the boat. Heading down the stairs to TOM's ship below, he wondered what all of those metal boxes Marcus had put by TOM's ship were for.

CHAPTER FIFTEEN

The Queen Bitch's Ship Ad Aeternitatem

Stephen could hear the cursing, and the ringing of metal on metal, coming down the hallway from the 'garage.' He knocked sharply on the door, and stepped in. He doubted any human would be able to hear him knocking over the noises that William created as he beat on a piece of metal, yelling at it the whole time.

"I… Will… Teach…You…A…Lesson… You…Mother…" Bobcat finally got William's attention. "WHAT?" Marcus flinched at William's loudness. Bobcat mimed William taking off his ear protection. William pulled aside one ear muff and said in a more reasonable tone, "What?" Bobcat pointed behind him.

William turned to find Stephen almost on top of him. Stephen was looking around him at the closet-sized metal box that he had been bashing the moment before. "Oh! Hello."

Stephen looked up at him. "Having a bit of difficulty explaining something to the dense box, are we?"

William's look of annoyance came back with a vengeance as he turned to look at the box. "Yes! I have seating that doubles as a payload location. I didn't consider how I was supposed to install the seat after I had already built the surrounding box. Bad planning on my part, but I believe I've almost accomplished getting my point across. Another couple of sharp sentences should see the seat right where I want it."

Stephen looked up over at Bobcat. "Can we talk for a couple minutes?" He waved his hand back at the other side of the hold. Stephen hoped it was far enough away from the conversation William was having with his seat.

When Bobcat caught up to Stephen, he asked, "What's up?"

"I'm concerned that your helicopter is not big enough to carry everyone flying to the landing zone. How many people can your Shelly carry at one time?"

"She's rated for four crew plus eleven other troops loaded out. With the long-range fuel pods she'll easily make it the two hundred fifty or so miles we need to go."

"I don't believe there's a *we* in this conversation. Or did you forget what Bethany Anne said?"

Bobcat rubbed the back of his head. "No, I didn't forget. I was just hoping you had. I don't like missing this operation."

"Can't be helped. Is there any way that you guys can get these…" Stephen looked over his shoulder when William resumed hitting the box, "ships…" He turned back around to Bobcat, "Ready to go?"

Bobcat shrilled a whistle to catch Marcus' attention and waved him over to join them. Once Marcus was there he asked the question so Stephen could hear the answer. "Once we have the IZTA shells complete, how long will it take for you to install the engines?"

"Not long at all. I've been talking with TOM for the past two days. He says that the manufactured engines that I have so far—" Marcus flinched as William caused a resounding crack and then the noise ceased. He relaxed and continued the conversation. "Sorry, TOM says that the engines I have are ready to be powered up. But he doesn't want to energize them before they're ready to go. We have the engines ready to be charged. We'll need Bethany Anne to help with that."

Stephen asked, "Why is that?"

"Because she's the only one that can get into TOM's ship and the engine room. In order for these engines to be activated they'll need a charge. Kind of like jump-starting a low battery in a car. You hook it to a car already running, then rev that car's engine for a while."

Stephen considered what Marcus said. "Is there any problem with the engines once they're energized? What happens if we have the ships just sitting here for a day or two without using them? Are they like a battery, or will they eventually explode without draining their energy?"

"No, TOM assures me that everything would be fine. But if anyone were to steal an engine right now, it wouldn't get them anything. It's only once they've been energized that it will be obvious they're something more than a box with weird circuits and a glob of stuff in the middle."

Stephen asked, "What's your glob of stuff?"

"Xenon difluoride, normally a white crystal used to etch silicon conductors. We have it compressed pretty decently, but TOM's going to do something inside the engine room that's going to be pretty impressive. Further, TOM will provide an integrated connectivity to the Etheric. Otherwise, just a minor bump would cause all of the pent up energy to release instantaneously."

Stephen considered all that Marcus just told him. "That would be bad?"

"Well, it would be bad for everyone on the Polaris. We wouldn't have two cells still stuck together so we wouldn't personally care anymore."

Bobcat nodded his head sagely. "I would consider that bad."

"Indeed," Stephen agreed. "It seems the good doctor has a dry sense of humor."

"Who was trying to be funny?" Marcus asked. "That's exactly what would happen." His look of confusion sealed the deal. Both men started chuckling at him.

Stephen saw that William had put up his tools and was putting some cushioning inside his structure. He motioned for the two men to follow him back over to William's working area. William noticed the guys walking up.

Stephen asked him, "Did you finish your conversation?"

"Sure did. Message was heard loud and clear."

Stephen walked around the metal box that opened on one end. "What am I looking at?"

William answered him, "You are looking at the first prototype of the IZTA 001. This box is set up to handle two people, plus their equipment. After they have stored their equipment underneath the seat, and on the racks there and there, they get in here through this door. As you can see the door latches from the inside as well." William pulled the doors open a little bit further. "The next version will have glass so that they can see out. But for this version we are going without glass since our manufacturing capabilities are a little limited at this time."

Stephen asked, "How will they be able to see where they are piloting?"

Marcus jumped into the conversation. "They won't. TOM will be moving all of the ships via the engines in the lower quadrant. You can't see the access panel from where you are now."

Stephen walked around the other side and saw a one-foot by one-foot door with hinges and locks. He knelt down and unlocked the door and peered inside. "Not much in here."

Marcus said, "No, the engines are self-contained. Once we have them inside this box, the engines are effectively a component of the larger ship. The engine generates a…"

Bobcat interrupted Marcus, "Magic shit happens and the engine takes them where they need to go."

Stephen smiled and turned to look at the project leader. "I take it that you've heard this explanation multiple times?" Stephen stood back up after latching the door again.

"Yes." Bobcat said. "And I can tell you that even after listening to him explain it ten times, it still makes as little sense as it did the first time I heard it. Engines should work on air, gasoline, and spark. Not shit that can blow up three hundred and twenty-five foot long Superyachts if a little thumbnail piece of it gets tapped wrong."

Stephen looked over at the doctor. "Truly? A piece that small could blow up this whole ship?"

Marcus nodded. "We have enough of the substance on the ship right now that if it was energized by TOM, we could blow up New York City and leave one big smoking crater."

That caused the normally jovial vampire to lose his smile for a moment. "That is pretty powerful."

William smiled, his prototype might look like it was made in a junkyard, but his babies were going to be hella-quick.

Stephen asked the team, "How long would it take to produce eight of these ships?"

Bobcat scratched under his chin. "Well, we could theoretically use that one right there, but it would take us at least two weeks doing it here."

Stephen shook his head. "That's too long, think outside the box, Bobcat. What is it you would need to get eight of these built super-fast? Remember our facilities on land. You get me the blueprints, and we'll make sure that they get built. The main operation is a go, but I would love to have a backup. We can't hold the op off for two weeks. We're wheels up late tomorrow morning. If this op goes bad, the only thing you'll find of us in two weeks is our bones. Get with Lance, I need this backup in forty-eight hours." With that, Stephen left them looking at each other.

William whistled. "Forty-eight hours? Hope we all ate our Wheaties this morning."

Marcus asked a question out loud to no one in particular. "If there are only twelve people going on the operation, why does he want eight ships?"

Bobcat started smiling. "Yes! William, grab those drawings. I'll get the chopper up top warmed up. We might make the fun after all!" He started heading toward the door.

William's face lit up with glee. "Hell yeah!" He turned and ran to the wall, carefully pulling down the specs that he had used to make the prototype.

Marcus stared at his two rapidly disappearing teammates. "What did I say?"

Bobcat poked his head back in the door. "Marcus! Don't stand there looking fucking clueless. Get with TOM and make sure we have everything ready to go for ten engines. Daddy is going to need a test run." With that, Bobcat winked at Marcus and disappeared.

Marcus was almost pleading as William packed up his papers. "Can't you tell me what just happened?"

"Yes, Stephen gave us a way to get involved." William grabbed his stuff. "Make sure you have the engines ready within twenty-four hours, thirty-six on the outside." He ducked out. The door opened again few seconds later. "Marcus? Thirty-six hours, tops. We'll be back!"

With that, William was gone.

CHAPTER SIXTEEN

Las Vegas, NV USA

Eric rapped on the door. John popped his head around to see Eric beckoning to him. John let Bethany Anne know that he was stepping out and she waved. He got Tom's and Jeffrey's attention to let them know that he would knock, to be let back in the security door.

He stepped out. Eric walked back towards the front. John noticed Ashur sitting in a corner. "Got Ashur out of the SUV, I see."

"Yeah, I got him as soon as I stepped out. I doubt they want dog hair gumming up their fans in there so I didn't take him down to be with Bethany Anne."

Ashur woofed.

Eric stopped three feet from the door. It was glass but it had reflective film on it to reduce glare and heat. It made the outside look darker. John stopped beside his partner. "What's up?"

"We have company watching us." Eric dipped his head slightly towards the door. "Three buildings down, one guy acting like he's smoking. His coughing is cracking me up, and one guy one building behind him has settled down on the roof. I didn't see anyone in the other direction, but that doesn't mean anything."

"Forsaken in the daytime?" John unconsciously reached for his pistols and made sure the snaps were off.

"No. Military I think."

"Why?"

"Their stance, their inability to act like civilians… That Air Force vehicle over there. Minor shit like that."

John snorted. Eric could be pretty calm in a bad situation.

John said, "You think they're just surveillance, or are they a scout team?"

Eric shrugged. "I can't tell. If this is an op, I think we'll know it when they come through the front door."

Ashur woofed again.

Eric turned and smiled at the dog. "Or Ashur warns us, whichever one happens first."

Ashur raised his head and started growling.

Eric put up his hands. "Ok, ok, when Ashur warns us."

Ashur put his head back down on the floor.

John eyed the dog. "He doesn't seem bothered."

Eric looked at his partner. "Why would he? They're over a hundred feet away."

Ashur seemed to glare at Eric, at least that's the way John interpreted his look. Then again, he might be looking at Eric as a juicy steak bone, too. "Ashur?" Ashur raised his head. "I think you need to go for a walk."

John turned around and walked back to the server room

door and knocked on it. A moment later Jeffrey opened it, but John stayed outside. "Jeffrey, do you have any rope that I could use to make a leash?"

Ashur barked loudly from up front. John looked down the hall, "It's for appearances. Stop barking and be a team player!"

Jeffrey was surprised and stuck his head out of the room. "There's a dog here?"

The men heard Bethany Anne's voice from inside. "He's with me!"

Jeffrey turned slightly towards the room and then back out to John. "Good hearing."

"You have no idea. Rope?" John had to get the man back on track.

"Yeah, over in building 2, we only have networking cable here in this building." Jeffrey told John where he could find the rope.

Ashur stood up. John looked over at the huge German Shepherd. "Just getting some rope to pretend we have a leash on you. I want to walk you around and see what's going on. I'll be right back."

As he left the building he told Eric to watch and let Bethany Anne know if he was stopped, but that he was only going over to building 2.

John exited and headed straight for building 2. He looked at what he could, but he kept his eyes on the next building's door and went inside.

He located some twine in a desk drawer and turned to walk back to building 1 when his phone chimed. He looked down and saw he had twelve missed phone calls from Frank.

He hit the callback button.

UNDER MY HEEL

The Queen Bitch's Ship Polarus

Dan and Stephen were in the meeting room reviewing a few notes when Captain Thomas walked in. The two men looked up.

He took a chair. "Stephen, Dan."

Dan leaned back. "How are the preparations going?"

Captain Thomas snorted. "Exactly how do you think any preparations would be going with Jean Dukes in charge? She's been told she might be able to play with her favorite children again. She and the fire teams are excited they might see more action, which is why I'm here." He turned to face Stephen. "What are our parameters if we have attackers?"

Stephen looked perplexed. "Parameters? Other than 'win' I'm not sure what you are asking."

"We're near Turkey, Syria, Lebanon and Cyprus. What if any of their ships are part of an attack?"

"Captain Thomas, if you can outrun them, fine. If you cannot, they must not be permitted to board these vessels. Protect these people, protect these vessels. You are in my waters, make the call you feel is necessary and I will back you up. We cannot assume that there are none of David's people in the navies around this region. If there is an incident, I will make a few calls and get the people to back down. Just as soon as I am free to do so."

Captain Thomas wasn't clear what Stephen meant. "Make a few calls?"

Stephen's smile turned a little malicious, a rare sight for the two men to see. "Sometimes the rumors are true and the reputation is deserved. The people I make calls to will know who they speak to. Rest assured I will get you and your people free if anything happens. Just make sure that there are still people here for me to free."

It wasn't often that Stephen surprised Captain Thomas. But he had to admit that in this moment, he sounded scarily like Bethany Anne. If she had a few more decades of scaring the crap out of people already under her belt.

He stood up and shook both men's hands and left to make sure that the Polarus would be ready to protect both his ship and her sister ship.

Stephen watched him leave before turning around to Dan. "That reminds me, I need to ask Bethany Anne to move TOM's ship if possible. Probably out to an undisclosed location to hide it while we're gone. I trust that Captains Thomas and Wagner will do their best, but most of our fighters will be in Turkey. Better to be prepared."

Dan thought about that. "Not a bad idea, if she has the time. Where would you stash it?"

"What about where it was for a thousand years? No one found it there, maybe we can leave it there for a few days?"

"A sensible idea. My first thought was Siberia. If it can handle the cold of space, then it shouldn't have any problems there. I'll have to ask Bethany Anne. Hmmmm, That might be a problem."

Stephen looked confused, "Why?"

"The Air Force has surveillance plans drawn up for Patriarch Research. Frank has been trying to reach anyone over there, but they must be in a building that's blocking their cell signals."

Stephen thought about that. "Has anyone asked Marcus to have TOM reach her?"

Dan rolled his eyes and stood up. "No, none of us thought

of that. Let me talk with Frank for a few minutes, I'll be back."

Stephen waved at the man and pulled out his phone. He had a couple of emails to return, including one to Ivan who was taking care of getting his house back together. Most of the home had been repaired. There were a couple of contractors that would not show up on time. Even when Ivan dropped Stephen's name, they still showed up late. That was causing the repairs to drag out. Stephen made a note of the company names; he would have to visit these people in the future.

Ivan and Claudia had been staying at different safe houses at night. There was no reason for them to chance David sending a second group 'just in case' Stephen was stupid enough to return home. But, David had an almost pathological connection to his own castle, so maybe he assumed everyone thought of their own home the same way.

Those tasks completed, he spent a minute browsing on Tinder. He had such little time lately that he hadn't taken a moment to window shop. He heard Dan coming back in plenty of time to close the app down.

Dan came in. "Frank is going to talk with Marcus now. Apparently, the Air Force is going to raid Patriarch Research's servers."

"Is there anything that we can do?"

"Not right now. Either Frank's messages or a communication through TOM should give them some advance warning. If not, Frank and Lance have a large number of connections inside congress. Someone will be made aware that a major businessperson has been targeted for what looks like either trumped up charges or a fishing expedition. Lance knows what's going on and he and Patricia are reaching out to the lawyers to get them ready."

Stephen asked, "Doesn't everyone know that nothing can hold Bethany Anne?"

"Of course, but it would be a bad idea to just disappear from within an Air Force base. Lots of questions would be asked at that point. I just hope that if there's a problem, that Bethany Anne lets the lawyers or Frank get her out. I don't think she would be in there for more than five hours, tops."

Stephen considered the situation and agreed there wasn't anything that wasn't already being done for them.

The two men got down to planning the operation. Occasionally, they would call Todd, Pete or Nathan for input. The crew was getting Shelly prepared while many of the men went through their own packing and readiness efforts. Frank was able to provide satellite imagery showing the narrow road going into the town of five hundred plus souls.

Stephen spoke up, "You realize, except for the few who are in hiding, that everyone else is most likely dead?"

Dan sat back. "Yeah. Even if there were only a handful of Nosferatu they would be able to kill everyone. I can't imagine that after David went to all of this effort we will only be facing a few. By now, we have to assume he knows about San Jose and Buenos Aires. Even if he doesn't, I don't want to underplan."

"No, David has always been close to his vest with his plans. He doesn't mind leveraging large efforts. He's a conniving bastard. We need to up our expectations of something bad happening. If I'm wrong, nothing lost. If I'm right, then we'll be glad to have the extra munitions. Make sure we have plenty of first aid supplies."

The men tried to work out if coming up with additional support would be possible. Dan tried to contact Frank, but it rang through to his voicemail. He wrote himself a note to get with Frank on who their American contacts would be when they were in Turkey.

A rap got Dan's attention. He noticed Stephen was already looking over at the door. Nathan poked his head in. "Hey, Ben has two bits of information we might want to review. The first is related to the terrorist assholes. The second is cell tower IDs used right before all communications went out in the area. He's hacking into the local telecom to see if he can backtrack the two phone calls that were made right before it died. I'm assuming those might be David, or whoever set up this little party for us."

Dan considered his options. "Unless Stephen says otherwise, the terrorists will have to wait until we handle the AAR for this op. See if he can nail down their locations while we handle this dustup. What does he need for the cell phone tracking?"

"Hopefully, not much. Language skills, maybe, if we come to something that needs reading we can't decipher." He thought about it for another minute. "Nothing more at the moment."

Stephen turned back to Dan. "You seem pretty sure there'll be people left after this op to need an after action review."

Dan smiled. "Well, we have you going on this op and the Guardians plus Nathan and Ecaterina. But to be honest, that isn't why I'm sure there will be people returning."

"Oh?" Stephen was pretty sure that most of them would return but he knew no plan survived contact with the enemy.

Dan looked at Stephen and said with a knowing glint in his eyes. "I know my boss…"

CHAPTER SEVENTEEN

So, this version of ADAM has promise?

A few more minutes, please.

Bethany Anne had allowed TOM to work with ADAM while she walked around. He was both more able to review the information and better suited for the activity.

She decided to speak to Tom and Jeffrey while TOM was busy.

She walked over to them, both still trying to figure out the origin of the wireless signals. Tom turned around with his signal-checking device in his outstretched hand as he turned, and aimed his arm straight at her.

She watched his eyes go down to his device, then back at her, then back to his device. She waited patiently while he moved it around some more and his face grew a look of confusion that was pretty comical. She had a pretty good idea why the device might be suggesting she was the cause of his confusion. Maybe she would tell him, sometime in the future, why his device was giving him 'faulty' results.

Maybe.

"Gentlemen." They stopped looking at the device and gave her their full attention. "I would like to discuss the next stage of your employment." At Tom's look of concern, she added, "There *is* further employment, not a nice way for me to explain that you're not needed anymore." Tom looked relieved. "You might not appreciate it but the companies that I have responsibility for are in multiple areas of specialization. Those areas include computers and AI research such as your own, as well as medical, military, financial, and advanced transportation fields. One of these small research firms, based in Romania, has unearthed exciting new technology relating to gravity and antigravity. They need substantial computer and research support, which Lance Reynolds and Nathan Lowell believe your company presently have."

Both men stood a little straighter at her compliment.

"The opportunity, gentlemen, is literally the stars. The budget," she waved her arm behind her to make sure that they understood that she was discussing their present project, "Makes this project look anemic by comparison. In fact, I imagine you will be using computing power at least five times what you're presently playing with."

Five times? If you're referring to the Kurtherian computer in your skull, that is a ludicrously low assessment.

TOM, get back to what you're supposed to be doing. These gentlemen don't have a clue about that computer. At least they don't now, nor will they for the foreseeable future. I am not trying to besmirch your computer capabilities.

It's Mac vs. Windows all over again, she thought.

At her comment related to playing with more computers,

Tom's eyes started to glaze over.

Jeffrey asked her, "What's the catch?"

Bethany Anne replied, "The catch is that it does require that you, and your families if you have them, move to Colorado. A little bit greener area, I'm sure. It doesn't quite have the same dry dust and cacti motifs that you do here. Probably a lot colder. Let me amend that it could be significantly colder in the wintertime. And certainly will be cooler during the summer."

Bethany Anne really wanted these two gentlemen on board. She knew that she would have to get Jeffrey's wife involved as well. She needed some hook for Jeffrey to dangle in front of his wife. "Plus, we will be taking over a military base for our top-secret efforts. Should the school district not be up to your expectations, the company will pay for private school teachers to come in and teach all children on the base."

There, private schooling for their children just might be the hook that could influence a parent's decision.

This time, it was Jeffrey's eyes that seemed to glaze over a little.

Tom reentered the conversation. "You say five times? Are we discussing blade servers or some other method of computing power? "

Bethany Anne bit her lip in concentration. "You know what Tom? I would have to ask the new head of information technology what his opinion would be."

Tom interjected, "Who is that?"

"I have no idea who the new head of information technology would be, if you turned down the position." Bethany Anne watched Tom's eyes grow a little wider and then look over her shoulder at the computers behind her.

While he stared at the computers he asked, "What did

you say the computer budget was going to be?"

Bethany Anne looked over her shoulder where Tom was looking, "Depends on what we need when you get the assessments done. I can tell you that it will make your thirty million dollar budget a drop in the bucket." Turning back around she said, "My company, and the research facility that we are setting up in Colorado is very lean. I am expecting to use high-quality people and significant investments in technology and infrastructure to mitigate the need for more people. We're a tight group, and we rely on everybody pulling their own weight."

Jeffrey asked her, "What if some of the people here don't want to move?"

"We have a very good HR research person. If you tell him what you need, he is able to search government records and other databases to find the absolute best that will fit within the team. If you have anyone on your present team that you don't trust? Absolutely do not bring them along. We will give them a one year severance package, no questions asked, and a fifty-thousand-dollar exit bonus. You can say that the exit bonus is for keeping their mouths shut about the existing technologies that you've been working on for the last three years. In fact, we can have the HR person write that as a clause so that they know that the money is dependent on them keeping their mouths shut."

"Why us?" Jeffrey asked. Tom looked over at his boss, wanting to punch him.

Bethany Anne smiled. "Gentlemen, I gave you a tough project, a significant budget, and no time to accomplish the impossible. You have finished the project, you didn't blow the budget, and you did accomplish the impossible."

Tom looked confused. "What do you mean we've

accomplished the impossible? We haven't asked you to sit down to input any data with ADAM yet."

Bethany Anne reached up and tapped her cranium. "Gentlemen, my team and I have been testing ADAM the whole time I've been here. Why do you think your Wi-Fi device kept pointing at me?"

Tom raised the device and looked at it, with Jeffrey looking first to the device and then back at Bethany Anne.

Jeffrey asked Tom, "I thought there was no way for communication signals to get in and out of this place? Didn't we make this as tight as a Faraday cage?"

There was a sharp rap on the door and the three of them looked over to see John impatiently waving someone to come to him. Jeffrey went over and unlocked the door allowing him to step in.

John got to the point. "Boss, we have a situation."

John quickly explained the problem Eric had seen outside, and that Frank had informed him about when he returned his calls to get an update.

Bethany Anne fumed, "We have the fucking Air Force breathing down on us? For what reason?"

Jeffrey turned his head sharply when he heard Bethany Anne's outburst.

"What's with the Air Force?" Tom and Jeffrey stepped into the circle with Bethany Anne.

TOM, can you communicate outside this room on regular signals?

No. They really do have good shielding, I can easily communicate on the WI FI, the bandwidth is substantial. ADAM can split files and send them to me in parallel. So the communications between us are going incredibly fast.

Damn, ok.

Bethany Anne thought at Vamp speed. "Guys, we can't have the Air Force looking through all of this stuff. Any idea why they would be here in the first place? You guys didn't do anything illegal, did you?"

Jeffrey sighed. "Shortsighted, maybe. Illegal, no. When we had to find a building so quickly we didn't think about the fact that we were loading in this much computing power right next to an Air Force Base. The captain responsible for security visited us when we were just setting up. Since we hadn't been visited since then, I rather thought that we'd dropped off their radar."

John interrupted. "You did. But there's a new officer in charge and somehow you guys have tickled his fancy. He's waiting on final approval to raid your offices."

Bethany Anne turned to John. "What? That's bullshit. What justification would they have for taking a legitimate company's computer power?"

John shrugged. "Where there's government, there's a way. What do they care if they stop you from working for couple of months? So long as they can claim the country is safe, that's all that matters to them. Maybe in a year, maybe two years, we might get the computers back with a big 'I'm so sorry' to go along with it."

Bethany Anne turned to Tom. "What would the Air Force think if they got to see all of this software working?"

Tom thought about her question. "With the code the way it is right now? An I.T. person could almost make you believe anything they wanted you to. If they put the wrong input into the system, it could be modified to become an automated network attacking device."

Bethany Anne said, "Seriously? That's interesting." John rolled his eyes. "But not what we want the Air Force believing we are doing here. That could cause all sorts of problems for us. Do you have a backup for the system?"

Jeffrey was taking in all of her responses, thinking this woman seemed to be interested in proactive, rather than only reactive measures. "In a way. We have the code as it was when we loaded ADAM originally. Nothing since then. ADAM is unique at this time. You can't presume that we can get back to this ADAM even if we drop in the same data. There are a number of any possible things. If the code accepts just one item differently, early in the process, the changes down the line could be substantial. For better or worse, he is a one of a kind right now."

"Shit!" Bethany Anne said, exasperated.

TOM, I need your honest assessment right NOW. Do we try to take ADAM with us, or fry him?

She asked, "How do you do an emergency shutdown?"

Jeffrey turned to Tom, whose face was showing his panic. "What? We have to SCRAM the computers?"

Bethany Anne said sharply, "Guys, we can always rebuild ADAM. We'll make him better the second time based on what you have learned. But I cannot have the Air Force making stupid accusations that are not based in reality."

"Make him better?" Tom's voice trailed off, he was looking at all of the hard work and sleepless nights.

"Look, stop pussyfooting around here." Bethany Anne said.

Take him with us.

Ok, can you do that? Grab his code or whatever and shove it into the computer in my head?

Of course, we just have to…

Please, not right now. Tell me how amazing you and your computers are later. Just get it fucking done already, we're on a tight time schedule. You can have your own bedroom if you get this done before we have to leave.

When is that?

Probably ten minutes sooner than you need us to.

Ok, but I want a second floor bedroom...

She could feel TOM's focus leave her mind and she started to get a small headache, never a good thing to happen when TOM was using the computer.

Bethany Anne returned her focus to Tom. "Tell me how to SCRAM this shit. Then, you and the other two guys need to step outside and go to another building, acting like you don't have a care in the world." She turned to John. "I'm going to need Ashur in here with me. You guys will have to get back to Florida on your own."

John nodded and turned around, calling over his shoulder, "Show her the button guys, let's get a move on!"

Jeffrey nodded to Tom who turned back to the desk, his shoulders slumped. Bethany Anne followed him. He picked up a metal box on the desk and pointed to a button under the box. "Hit that button and then get out. You have ten seconds to be outside of the building."

Bethany Anne pursed her lips. "You have a literal 'red button' to hit in case you needed to make this happen?"

Tom was looking at the button, the button he never expected to use. It would kill his baby. He had put all of the blood, sweat and tears into this code and was expecting... Well, he wasn't sure what he was expecting but it wasn't an inglorious end like this. Fucking Air Force, he thought.

"Yeah, I thought it was funny."

Bethany Anne put a hand on his shoulder, he barely registered it.

"Tom? Don't worry, my team and I will do our best to get

what we can from ADAM before the Air Force has a chance to come inside, ok?"

He nodded his head and placed the box back over the switch.

Jeffrey spoke up, "Are we sure that the Air Force is going to do this? I would hate to SCRAM the computers only to find out they had decided against this."

Bethany Anne shook her head. "My team is some of the best out there. If they say this is going down, you can damned well bet your ass it's going down." She looked around, considering what Tom and Jeffrey would have the willingness to hide from the Air Force. "Okay guys, let's step outside, and I want you to close the security doors."

Jeffrey said, "If you're on the outside of the security doors, how are you getting in? Did you memorize the security codes?"

She shook her head. "No. I haven't touched the keypad, either. If they should check for fingerprints, I only want yours or Tom's on there." She ushered them out of the room.

Jeffrey turned around and made sure the door was shut and locked. When he turned around he was startled. He tried to step back but was stopped by the door. "Holy shit! Who let the wolf in here?"

Ashur was looking at the men.

"This is Ashur, he's my seeing eye dog." She grabbed Ashur behind his neck. "John, you guys go next door. I don't want anyone back in here until the Air Force makes you open the doors, ok?" She turned to Jeffrey. "Is there anyone else in that secured room?" Jeffrey shook his head no.

Tom interjected, "If you want evidence that is rock solid, have Jeffrey enter the management override and set it for a few hours."

"John? How much time do we have?"

John lifted his arm and looked at his watch. "I doubt that long."

She nodded to Jeffrey, "Do it. That way, you guys are covered if anything happens."

Jeffrey shrugged and did what she said. There would be no opening this door without a serious screaming whine going off. No one would confuse their alarm for a car alarm, that was for damn sure.

Now there were four red lights on the keypad.

"Now what?" Jeffrey asked.

"Now, you guys go play poker or something until the Air Force shows up, or it's time for John and Eric to get back to the airplane.

John nodded his understanding and started towards the front door. "Move it, men!"

John's command voice got both men moving towards the door, Jeffrey looking over his shoulder at Bethany Anne who just smiled and waved at him. "See you in Colorado, right?"

Jeffrey just nodded his head, not really thinking about what she was asking, wondering, how the hell is she going to do anything, now?

As soon as the men left the building, Bethany Anne grabbed Ashur's neck and they translocated back into the room.

Now TOM! Hurry up and download our digital friend.

Working it now, Bethany Anne. We are expanding the wireless devices to create more throughput.

We?

Figure of speech. The computer software and I are working together to facilitate the download.

Bethany Anne looked over at the box and walked to the

table. Ashur followed her and lay down on the floor next to her.

Twenty minutes later, Tom and Jeffrey watched as two Air Force vehicles came down their street.

Jeffrey watched them gloomily. "Here comes the cavalry…"

Tom muttered, "Not my cavalry, not this time."

John was reaching into his pocket as he spoke to Eric. "Erase your phone, just in case."

Both had just unlocked their phones when all of the electronics went dark.

Eric looked around. "What the hell?"

John asked, "Power outage, guys?"

Tom said into the darkness, "Not possible, we have a very expensive backup system. We might as well go up front. None of this shit is going to work for a while, if ever."

John turned and started towards the front. "Why?"

"Because the shielding apparently wasn't perfect. You can kiss your phones good-bye."

Eric turned to ask Tom what he meant when his shin hit a chair. "Gott Verdammt!" Eric could hear John ahead of him, chuckling. "Dammit, John. That shit hurts!" A couple of limps later, Eric started walking a little straighter, "Why won't our phones work?"

Jeffrey answered, "Because the EMP just went off."

CHAPTER EIGHTEEN

The four men stepped out of the building, looking both ways.

Tom said, "Hmmm, building 3 is just fine. I wonder what could have caused all of this confusion?"

They watched as the two Air Force vehicles approached them. Good thing they hadn't been closer, or their vehicles would've been knocked out as well.

Eric muttered under his breath, "Oh shit. The SUV was close to building one. Looks like we'll need to get a taxi." John nodded his head in understanding.

The song-and-dance was something for John and Eric to watch. Jeffery said they were investors who had arrived a little earlier, and they were clueless what was going on.

Jeffrey painted a picture for the Air Force of how they had just come out. The power was out in both of their buildings and they had been trying to figure out what was going on.

Everyone turned to look at Tom when he cried out, "Oh shit!" and took off toward building 1. He was immediately commanded to stop by the Air Force. Tom obeyed.

A few minutes of arguing later, the Air Force understood that Tom had been trying to figure out why all of their devices had died. He had pretended to realize that the programming in building 1 was dependent on power. Tom and Jeffrey along with three Air Force officers all trooped over to building 1 to see what was going on.

Jeffrey had considered whether he should complain to the Air Force officer. State that the Air Force personnel had no authority to follow them. And point out that they obviously had a secure setup. But he had offered to let the other Air Force officer come over and check up on them at any time. In the end he had decided to act as if the whole episode wasn't any big deal.

Tom was acting like he had just lost his firstborn child. Sure enough, their server room was dead. No air-conditioning, no lights, no noise, no fans, no nothing. It was black as a cave in the room. Jeffrey considered whether or not he should do a very public firing of Tom, on the spot, for allowing such a thing to occur, but decided against it.

There wasn't as big of a deal for John to fake. However, he made a big commotion about their SUV being fried. And complained more about having to take a taxi back to the airport. He told the two of them, while the Air Force men listened, how he was going to report such a stupendous screwup to the boss.

How, if she didn't have both of their heads, he would be surprised. As he was giving the two men a very public dressing down, a taxi arrived and he and Eric got in and left.

As everyone there watched the taxi drive away down the

street, Jeffrey commented to no one in particular, "What a pompous ass."

The Queen Bitch's Ship Ad Aeternitatem

Ashur, Bethany Anne, John and Eric stepped out of TOM's cabin on his ship and went to the door. Bethany Anne punched in the code, opening the door and found a surprised Todd on the other side.

She smiled at him. "Fancy meeting you here." She turned to Darryl who was standing next to Todd. "Hey you big lug, everything good here?" Darryl smiled and stepped aside to let everyone off of the spaceship.

TOM, for god's sake can you settle the computer down a little? The buzzing is annoying as hell...

I'm not sure what is eating into the computer cycles, Bethany Anne. I'll deal with it.

Ashur stayed close to the team. Gabrielle and Scott arrived a few minutes later. Bethany Anne greeted them, "Peace, love and I will kill for some cookies. You don't have any, do you?"

Gabrielle blinked at Bethany Anne, not knowing why she was asking for cookies. "Nooo, but I imagine we might find some in the galley, why?"

"Just a craving. You wanted to talk?"

Bethany Anne noticed her team, except for Gabrielle, spreading out. "Yes, part of the reason is this craft. Can we go inside?"

Bethany Anne shrugged and turned back to the ship, plugging in the code and the two women stepped in. The door closed.

"Ok, what's up?"

Gabrielle responded, "First, Stephen has asked me to get with you on moving this ship to a safer location while everyone is gone."

Bethany Anne considered her request. "Ok, why? Are we thinking that David has a clue about it, and is secretly stalking this ship and is setting up this trap for that reason?"

"No, not exactly. We're concerned that he might have people in one of the navies of the countries nearby. If that happens to be the case, they could attack while we're absent. Stephen has told the captains to not be boarded. That could possibly result in the ships coming under fire. If this ship gets hit here, in this compartment, or goes to the bottom with the Ad Aeternitatem it's going to be a problem."

"That's… underselling a little bit. I wish we had the base already, then this would be a no-brainer."

Gabrielle asked, "What about putting it back where you found it?"

Bethany Anne thought about that.

Bethany Anne?

Yes?

Bethany Anne put up a finger to stop Gabrielle for a second. She tapped her head to let Gabrielle know she was talking with TOM.

I can communicate with the ship now. We can move it to low orbit and leave it cloaked. Nothing is going to disturb it up there.

What about someone finding it? I'm sure there are a lot of radars and telescopes pointed up in the sky above us.

One second… Ok, I have a place that even if we leave it unshielded, we have almost no chance of it being found.

Bethany Anne considered what TOM had just done. *Are*

you connecting to the internet and figuring out this stuff by yourself?

Not... Exactly.

What, not exactly, are you doing?

Well, since we have a learning product that has the ability to sift through the...

Oh. My. GOD! Are you using ADAM for your research project?

You say that as if it was a bad idea.

BECAUSE IT IS A BAD IDEA! How the hell do you know what's going on with the software? You've translated it and stuck it into your own supercomputer, for fuck's sake. How is it even accomplishing this feat? I thought you told me that human code and your code wasn't compatible!

Well, I told you that no one from earth would be able to do it. I happen to understand both sides pretty well.

Bethany Anne put her hands to her bowed head. TOM was going to cause her to jump off a building one of these damn days. He was like a teenager sometimes.

"Problems with the little guy?" Gabrielle asked softly.

"Yes! He would drive me to drink if I enjoyed it just a little bit. That is one fucking frustration—no way to get drunk."

"Just imagine what would happen with your strength and no inhibitions."

"Yeah, ok I see that. But to answer your question TOM can fly it up and park it next to a satellite. No one is going to get into it up there."

"Ok. One is done. Here's number two—the guys want to discuss upgrading."

Bethany Anne was confused. "Upgrading what, their body armor?"

Gabrielle reached over towards Bethany Anne's head.

Bethany Anne frowned and watched the hand suddenly close into a fist as Gabrielle rapped her on her skull sharply two times. "Ow! Bitch!" Bethany Anne rubbed the spot. "What the hell was that for?"

"Because you're being as dense as your father."

Bethany Anne continued to massage her head. "Consider me corrected." She reconsidered what Gabrielle had told her. "Oh… Ooohhh."

Gabrielle watched the younger woman. "Don't tell me that you didn't think they might ask you? After what you did for John?"

Bethany Anne started talking while pacing in the hallway. "I needed to save John's life, and I gave him a bunch of blood to do it. He was pretty messed up and I was new at this whole saving people with blood stuff. The way he's acted towards me since then has freaked me out a little."

"How he acted towards you?" Gabrielle wasn't aware that John caused Bethany Anne to feel uncomfortable.

"Right after that, he decided to become my guard for life. It felt like maybe I… I don't know, coerced him with my blood or something?"

Gabrielle asked, "You wonder if your blood caused him to become your guardian slave?"

Bethany Anne's laugh rang through the hallway. "God no! I can't imagine John being a slave to anyone. But he's so protective of me and all 'You saved me so I owe you.' I guess I got scared that I changed one of them to a guardian zombie. And, I've been concerned that the others might think that I changed their friend at some level."

"Some other level? One that they haven't talked to you about, you mean?"

Bethany Anne stopped pacing. "Yes. I know externally

they seem happy, but what about deep inside?"

Gabrielle walked up to Bethany Anne and put her hands on her shoulders. "Hey, Bethany Anne, they're happy because they believe in you and love you. People follow you, I follow you, because you care about your friends and family so strongly. Strong enough to tell yourself stupid shit like maybe your blood is turning them into zombie followers. Sometimes, my Queen, you are abysmally stupid." Gabrielle waited for the physical response, but Bethany Anne didn't say anything.

Bethany Anne took Gabrielle's head in both of her hands and pulled her forward to gently kiss her forehead. Gabrielle noticed a tear tracking down Bethany Anne's face when she released her. "Thank you for that. You have no idea how happy the five of you make me."

Gabrielle dropped her arms from Bethany Anne's shoulders. Bethany Anne turned around and started for the door. "Let's do this before I start crying."

"Can I tell the guys that you…"

"Haaeeeelllll no!" Gabrielle smiled when Bethany Anne surreptitiously wiped the tear off of her face.

————

The Queen Bitch's Guards were all waiting outside of TOM's ship for Bethany Anne to show up. Gabrielle wouldn't tell them what was going on. The door to the ship opened, Bethany Anne had stepped out ahead of Gabrielle and said, "Get the guys together, I'll be right back," and then disappeared.

It had taken Todd a minute to close his mouth. He wasn't normally around when she did stuff like that.

Some thirty minutes later, the door opened again

and everyone turned to see Bethany Anne smiling, with a backpack in her hands. She welcomed everyone on board and told Todd to go get some rest, she was going to take care of the ship for now. At the same time, Captain Wagner came walking into the holding area.

Noticing the Captain, Bethany Anne handed the backpack to Gabrielle and stepped off the ship. She met Captain Wagner halfway and reached out to shake his hand. "Decided to come see her take off this time?"

Captain Wagner looked past Bethany Anne at the craft. "Yes I have, it draws me like a moth to a flame. Are those engines going to be safe on my ship? There's a rumor that they could take us all out."

Bethany Anne looked back at the waiting engines placed against the wall. They weren't much to look at, but you would think they were the most precious things in the world from the way Marcus treated them.

"I'm told by both Marcus and TOM that they're safe… enough. I wouldn't explode something right next to them to test their theories, but so long as we don't have a catastrophic explosion they won't be triggered to explode." She had almost had to club the scientist over his head when he was allowed inside TOM's engine room.

It had taken an hour for the engines to be energized. She had left Marcus handling the movement of the small but heavy devices. He would get instructions from TOM on his laptop, move an engine into the right location as instructed and then step back as the machine closed the protective door and then went about compressing the xenon difluoride to over three-point-two million atmospheres. At this point, TOM would open a very small gate to the Etheric and the energy potential stored in the engine would finally arrive at equilibrium with the energy pressure from the gate. The engines all had enough power to move the IZTAs. If they had substantial need for speed, there was sufficient localized energy in the engine. If they weren't being used hard, they were powered by the engine, but the connection to the Etheric would instantly replace the spent energy.

Rather like a Toyota Prius battery/gas engine model. Marcus had made an expression of distaste when that analogy had been introduced.

"What are your plans?" Captain Wagner faced his boss.

"When you see the ship turn on the cloaking device, go ahead and open the hangar doors. You'll be able to tell that something is in the air, but you won't be able to see it. You'll be able to tell when I'm out, it won't take but a few seconds anyway. I'll bring everyone back to my suites over on the Polaris. Then I'll bring your protection back over to your ship."

"Give me a ride sometime?" He smiled at Bethany Anne.

She looked Captain Wagner straight in the eye. "Captain, I'm not going to just give you a ride, I'm going to build you your own damn spaceship." She turned around and walked back into TOM's ship, sensing more than seeing the shock on Captain Wagner's face.

TOM, when we enter the medical bay, take us up.
How high?
Enough that the view is beautiful.

After she closed the doors on the spaceship she had everyone follow her into the medical room. "Gentleman... my bitches, if you please." The chuckles went around the room. "You are the first humans that looked at the new Bethany Anne and saw me not as someone different, but someone you cared about and that you chose to follow. I have probably never expressed how deeply that affected me on our trip to Miami."

A tear escaped down her face. Darryl looked over at Scott, surprised. Bethany Anne didn't cry. "But you guys have had my back ever since Florida. You have taken on jobs that no one else would have thought possible. You have followed me into the pit of darkness and we didn't stop kicking ass until we climbed on the skulls of our enemies to exit out the other side." She turned to look at John, "Mr. Grimes, you took a wet behind the ears useless Wechselbalg and turned him into the man he is today. The first werewolf to take down a vampire in hundreds of years."

She looked at all of her team, these men who had followed her from Florida to Costa Rica, from Romania to Argentina. "Mr. Escabar, Mr. English, Mr. Jackson, as 'just humans,' you guys made Wechselbalg respect the ground you walk on. You have given Earth the chance to build our own army going into the future. You fought the Nosferatu before you met me, you have fought unflinchingly since. Now, we go to grind these assholes beneath our heels so we can reach up and prepare to defend our home."

Darryl said in a soft voice, "Oorah."

Bethany Anne reached out to Gabrielle, who handed the backpack to her. She unzipped the bag and pulled out six wine glasses and two pouches of blood. The men understood exactly what was going on now. Each one stood straighter, if that was possible, after her comments before.

"Everyone on these ships knows what it takes to wear the badge, the badge of my personal team." She laid out the six glasses. Gabrielle came up and took two, giving Bethany Anne the chance to open one of the bags and pour each half full. "In this bag is my blood, full of the nanocytes that have been keyed to me. The same blood I gave to John, with one addition." Gabrielle took the first two finished glasses and handed them to John and Eric, then picked up two more for Bethany Anne to fill. "This blood has the same modification I did for Stephen. If you are near me, I will know where you are. If you have been hurt, I will feel it." She finished the two glasses and Gabrielle passed them to Darryl and Scott.

Gabrielle picked up the last two glasses and Bethany Anne poured one with the remainder of the first bag, and then opened the second to pour into the final glass. This one she filled almost to overflowing.

Carefully, she sat the bag down and took the full goblet from Gabrielle. The four men came closer, as close as they could in the tight room. "TOM has modified the Nanocytes that are in your glasses. They will propagate, create more of themselves before they stop. The amount you are going to consume will increase multiple times. It will take a few days to a few weeks to finish, but you will feel the effects in a few hours. In a month, I will have each of you in this pod-doc right here to finish and confirm the changes. That will keep you under for a week, most likely. Time, I'm sorry to say, we don't have right now until our fight with David is finished."

She looked each person in the eye before moving to the next. "If you elect to drink this blood, you are making a covenant with me to be here until the end, until you are re-leased from your covenant or you die. If you agree that this is the path you wish to take, a future unknown except for the danger, then I can do no less than humbly accept your decision. Your desire to be the group that I use to protect my people, to protect this Earth, to use as I deem necessary to accomplish the impossible. No matter where I need to send you, no matter how deep the pit of darkness we find ourselves. I swear to you, on my name, on my life and on my blood that you will be the most feared group of Guards this galaxy, or any galaxy will know. Right here, right now is the dividing line between your option to stay human, to stay normal, to have a real life. Or, you accept that your life is going to be harder, longer, and more dangerous than any man or woman in their right mind would consider.

"You are the Queen Bitch's Guards, you don't run, you don't cower, you don't know the meaning of giving up or giving in. We are in this until death takes our souls." She looked over at John.

"John Grimes, the guard who told me to go and save those back at the camp. I will give my life to see this Earth safe. What is your decision?"

John looked straight in Bethany Anne's eyes. "Bethany Anne. It has been my honor to know you, to fight alongside you, to do the dark deeds that no one will ever know that we have done on their behalf. You have my covenant, my pledge on my honor, on my name and on your blood that I will be with you Ad Aeternitatem." Continuing to stare into her eyes, he emptied the glass.

With each man she swore the same thing, each man followed John's pledge and held her eyes as they drank the blood. She consumed a little from her glass with each one.

Gabrielle felt the four men staring at her. She smiled and gently put the glass on the pod-doc and stepped over and stood in front of Bethany Anne.

The men glanced at each other, what was she doing?

Bethany Anne smiled, she had been here once before.

Gabrielle spoke solemnly. "My father is an old sort, and I have to admit that I admire him for keeping to the old ways." She got on her knees in front of Bethany Anne, looking up at her.

Bethany Anne looked down at Gabrielle. "Gabrielle, I

need you to be my eyes and ears here on Earth and out into the Universe. I need you to be strong for me, Gabrielle. For me, for Nacht, and for the world. Will you accept this gift of my blood? Blood that will strengthen you, connect you to me, and will you work with me to make this world better for Nacht, for the UnknownWorld and for the humans as well?"

Gabrielle bowed her head. "Yes, my lady."

Bethany Anne held out her wrist to Gabrielle. "Drink, Gabrielle. Swear your allegiance to me and I will provide you sustenance to come back to me. But, if you don't stop when I tell you, I will put my fist through your skull, do you understand me?"

You could never be too careful with vampires.

Gabrielle looked back up at Bethany Anne's face, a small smile playing at her lips. Stephen had apparently shared with her the full story. Gabrielle gently took Bethany Anne's wrist as her teeth grew. The men watched as their team leader drank from their Queen's wrist.

There, inside a Kurtherian medical room on a ship in the middle of the Mediterranean Ocean on a planet called Earth, five people gave their oath to help change the galaxy.

In the future, their name would change. Still responsible for her safety, Bethany Anne would send them out on impossible operations. Trusting her people to get the jobs done that had to be done, no matter the cost. Others gave them their new designation. They became the Queen's Own.

May Hell have pity on you should you find yourself on the wrong side of any of the Queen's Own. One was always a problem, when two came together people started leaving the area.

Should all five show up, those with any intelligence would leave the planet.

Because if the five didn't handle the issue, then their Queen wouldn't be far behind.

CHAPTER NINETEEN

Turkey,
thirty miles from the Syrian border

Stephen was bleeding.

The team had made it to the town, and had found a landing site near the location where the satellites suggested those still alive had hidden. Everyone humped their equipment out of the helicopter quickly and the Wechselbalg team grabbed extra food and water rations for the survivors.

The bait.

Everyone had moved out quickly. Todd and Chet had held a perimeter while Ecaterina and Nathan tried to communicate with the people inside the cave that they weren't there to eat them.

Finally, the door opened and one man stepped out before the door quickly closed behind him.

He was the last American, the one that Frank had presumed dead.

He looked at the rescuers. "Thank god! I thought we were all written off as lost." Todd stepped up and held out his hand to shake. "Todd Jenkins. Formerly with the Marines, now part of…" He smiled, his group didn't have an identifier. Stephen stepped up. "My name is Stephen. Your military asked for our help, you might consider us contractors."

The soldier reached over to shake Stephen's hand. "Arthur DeTongass, don't ask me who I'm with, and I won't tell you any lies." The handshake was firm and the smile was genuine. Stephen liked this man.

"Very well, Mr. DeTongass."

Arthur interrupted Stephen, "No, just call me 'Art', my dad was Mr. DeTongass."

"Very well, Art. Can you tell us what the situation is?"

Arthur looked at the people around him. Only four were looking at him, but he knew they were all listening. They had good fieldcraft. "You know what happened here?"

Stephen nodded. "Yes. You came in after a team from Turkey was lost. You had two teams of four, you are the last survivor, but have been presumed dead."

"All true. We were supposed to find out more and report back. If there were no survivors, then command would get orders out and our boys would carpet bomb the place. Frankly, I've been surprised they haven't done so already."

"They know about the survivors from satellite and infrared. It is believed by some on our side that if the survivors hiding behind that door are killed, then the GDFMs hiding up in the caves will then leave the area."

"GDFMs?" Art looked perplexed.

Stephen smiled. "We have a computer specialist who calls them god-dammed freaky monsters, and the name has stuck."

Ecaterina spoke up, "Why do I hear children's voices?"

Art turned to her. "Because we have four local children and twenty-two that were kidnapped and brought here."

Ecaterina's eyes narrowed. "There are children in there?" She pointed at the door.

"Yes ma'am. Twenty-six children, four adults including myself, and four chickens. I don't recommend playing with the chickens, they scratch."

Ecaterina nodded. Everyone knew that, didn't they?

Stephen considered the situation. "We need to get the children out of here. We will be enough to keep the GDFMs in place. I'll talk with Chris and we will fly them out on Shelly. It will be a tight fit, but if we send one adult to help them, it should work.

Nathan noticed Ecaterina staring daggers at him; he put his hands up slightly and mouthed 'not you.' He turned back around to scan the area.

Art said, "We have two women in the cave. Either or both would work well. We also have one minister in there who has been hurt pretty badly."

Pete spoke up, never taking his eyes off of the surrounding area. "We have medical supplies, food and water. Where do you want them, Stephen?"

Stephen looked at Art. "Do we pass the test, Art? Will you allow us to help those inside?"

Art nodded and turned back to the door, rapping on it. Three sharp knocks, and then two sharp knocks.

"It's me, Diane!" The door opened on a whipcord thin woman with red hair.

"Art?"

"It's me, these guys have been sent by my country to help."

Ecaterina stepped closer. "We have food and water for

the children, plus first aid for your minister."

The door opened wider. "You have supplies? Oh thank God!"

Stephen pointed at Todd. "Keep the group on track, I'm going to speak to Chris about how many of these people we can evac on Shelly. Get ahold of Dan and locate a safe place to land the children. Chris won't need to go all the way back to the ships."

Stephen turned around and quick-walked back to Shelly. Chris and Tim had stacked the remaining supplies and armament forty feet away from the helicopter. The huge Wechselbalg nodded at Stephen. Chris said, "Damn! It's good to stretch a little but making the pilot hump this shit should be against the Geneva Convention."

Stephen answered his playful comment, "Chris, I never signed the Geneva documents, nor did Bethany Anne as she was not even alive at the time." Then, Stephen turned his head lightning fast and focused up the valley towards the mountains on the left. "Fuck David in this life and the next." He yelled out to the group back at the cave, "INCOMING!" Stephen ran to Chris, slowing down just enough so he didn't hurt him too much and then ran into Tim who was starting to react. Stephen grabbed him around his waist and pushed him forward. "Get your lazy Wechselbalg ass moving!" They had almost made the safety of a large building made of cinderblocks when a rocket screamed into Shelly. Stephen threw Tim forward, he could heal. Then he put Chris in front of him so that Chris would be protected by his body when the missile tore their ride out of the valley apart.

The explosion rocked the small town as the noise reverberated off of the valley walls. Stephen checked Chris's pulse. He was unconscious, but he seemed to be ok. Tim got up, pushing away a piece of timber that had been thrown on top of him.

Stephen turned towards the burning helicopter. He heard Tim come up beside him. "Bobcat is going to be pissed."

Stephen smiled, it seemed it took more than an exploding helicopter and a close brush with death to affect Tim. "That he is. But it was Bethany Anne's helicopter. I hope her insurance is paid up."

Nathan, Pete and Matthew all came running. Nathan called out, "Everyone ok?"

Stephen motioned to Chris. "He's knocked out, but otherwise ok. Take him up to the cave."

Matthew and Pete easily picked Chris up and took him back. Nathan joined the other two watching Shelly burn. "Well," Nathan said, "I guess we just figured out part of David's plan."

"Indeed."

Nathan mused, "Bobcat is going to be pissed."

Tim grunted, "That's what I said."

Stephen said, "Fuck!" and moved into Vamp speed. The guys realized he had gone after the supplies and rushed to help him.

It took them three minutes to move the supplies to a better location. The heat had started to damage the boxes.

When the last box was stacked, Stephen told Nathan, "If those rounds had gone off, that would have been annoying."

Nathan kept his mouth shut. Stephen was the most easygoing vampire that he had ever been around, but he did have a very dry sense of humor.

Nathan looked back towards the cave. "Now what?"

Stephen followed his gaze. "Now we dig in, Nathan. Those children might have been the bait in David's trap, but

I can assure you my Queen would never forsake them. It is not their fault that they got pulled into our disagreement. We do not leave our own, Nathan. Ever. Let's get all of our supplies up there. Someone needs to make sure there isn't a back way into the cave. It would be just like David to set up a back door. We all rest, for tonight we shall kill until the moon runs red."

Stephen started walking back towards the cave.

A minute later, Stephen found out the second part of David's plan. Their communications gear was actively being jammed.

Stephen looked up at the position of the sun and then back at his team. "Do we have enough blood?"

Nathan nodded. "Plenty, on ice at the moment. Why?"

Stephen reached out to Todd, who had the satellite phone. "Let me have the phone, I will travel as quickly as I can until I either get a signal or until I run out of time to get back here before dark. Get with Art, find out how many they've heard at night. You can bet we will have many more than that tonight."

With that, he turned and ran faster than he had since the last great war he had been involved in.

Except this time, he wasn't a lone wolf, but a leader.

CHAPTER TWENTY

Turkish Coast

William looked at his ten first generation IZTAs. "They are an ugly bunch, aren't they?"

Bobcat answered, "Hell yes, but they'll work. We've pulled this off, now we need to get them to the ship."

William shrugged. "Why not bring the engines to us?"

Bobcat was silent for a moment. "Good idea, I'll call the ship and ask them to have the engines ready, I'll fly over and bring them back."

While Bobcat flew back to the Ad Aeternitatem, some of the crew moved the little metal cubes up to the landing area and were ready to help load them as soon as he put down. Marcus was waiting for him.

No sooner than Bobcat had hit the pad, Marcus jumped in.

Bobcat looked over at him. "You're acting like a first time mother! Everything's going to be fine. Sit up front so they have enough room back there."

Marcus moved up to the front seat alongside Bobcat, strapped in and put the headphones on his ears. "It was amazing!"

Bobcat was watching the loading. "One sec, Doc." He opened his door and called out, "Make sure the weight is distributed evenly! Yes, use the leather seats, I'd rather risk a torn seat than one of these tipping over. Huh? Of course I believe the scientist, but my momma's boy is still here because he was always careful. Sure, use the seatbelts but hurry the fuck up, it's getting dark soon!"

Bobcat turned back to Marcus. "What was amazing? Did you lose your virginity in TOM's ship?"

Marcus sniffed. "No need to be crass." Then he smiled, "Hell yes! I've been able to watch technology from another galaxy, Bobcat. I don't know how it works yet, but I hypothesize TOM's ship works on the same principle that Bethany Anne uses to move through the Etheric. Somehow, the pilot plots a course and then calculates the distance it needs to travel. From there the ship pulls in enough energy to 'step' from one place to another. Whatever actual momentum it possessed when it stepped, it has when it arrives. I spoke to TOM. They would always stop before 'stepping.'"

Bobcat mused, "Makes sense, if you don't know exactly where you are going. You wouldn't want to end up in an asteroid field."

Marcus explained, "Well, if you're in an asteroid field, most likely they are moving too, so you would have to immediately concern yourself with the asteroids hitting you…" Marcus stopped when he finally noticed Bobcat's hand.

"I got the idea, now isn't the time for a lesson in astro-navigation, Doc."

Marcus took a moment to try and calm himself but it was damn difficult. He had engineered, with an alien, anti-gravity devices that were about to be used.

Yes, he considered, they were his babies and he was a proud, proud papa.

Moments later the helicopter doors slammed shut and with one look around Bobcat gently lifted off the Ad Aeternitatem, turned and headed towards the coast.

Marcus's stomach felt a little funny during the takeoff, as gentle as Bobcat was claiming it was, and was wishing he was forty years younger.

The Queen Bitch's Ship Ad Aeternitatem

Frank Kurns was busy pulling as much information as he possibly could. He had Ben, who was in the other office, trying to see if he could get any COMINT from cell towers in the area. Their team had gone dark.

Everything had been fine, the landing went well. He even had a request to see where the team could offload a bunch of children safely out of the area.

Then it all went to hell.

He reached over and hit the intercom. "This is Dan," came from his speaker.

"Dan, I can't get anyone. Ben is trying to piece together COMINT if the other side is using cellphones."

Frank could hear Dan's sigh. "Yeah. Good idea, but doubtful. I'm told most of the fighters are wise to that now."

"Could be, you never know. Unless you say otherwise, I'm going to reach out to Bethany Anne."

"Why are you going to reach out to me?" Bethany Anne was right behind him, startling him.

He turned back to the intercom. "I've got Bethany Anne scaring the shit out of me in here. You want to meet in the conference room?"

Dan agreed and shut off the connection.

Frank picked up his laptop and started towards the door. "I take it you know something's up?"

Bethany Anne followed him. "No, we just got back. I'm looking for an update. What's going on?"

Frank briefed Bethany Anne on the way to the conference room.

The three took seats, Bethany Anne started, "So, David has sprung a trap. They can't get out without the children until tomorrow. We don't have anything that can grab the children and we have to keep live bait in the town or the Nosferatu are going to leave. Does that about sum it up?"

Frank considered her summation and added, "Well, the fact that we can't talk to them to confirm anything and that they requested a location to ferry the children using Shelly. That about sums it up."

She asked them, "Do we have a place to put the children?"

Dan looked to Frank who answered, "Not yet. I've reached out to the new lead on this operation, damn strange that, and I've been told they're looking into it."

Dan raised an eyebrow. "What's damn strange?"

Frank replied, "We have a new lead. Someone a little up the chain. Usually, we don't get people butting their noses into something like this. Either way, our request for air support has been denied. They either don't have the resources, this isn't a priority, or…"

Bethany Anne answered, "Or David has his hooks into someone, right?"

Frank just nodded.

Bethany Anne sat back in her chair. No one had expected this to be easy, but after the South American operations had gone pretty flawlessly, maybe they were suffering from a little hubris.

"Put a reminder in to track that question down. If someone was paid to mess with us, I want to know. No one messes with my people without paying a price." She considered what might be next. "Dan, what is the status of Team BMW?"

Dan looked at the clock on the wall. "They should be back with the IZTAs and loaded within the next four hours."

"So, it'll be dark?"

Dan nodded.

Frank's phone went off, he looked down. "It's the satellite phone." Frank picked up the phone and hit the accept button. "Hello? Hold on for a second, I've got Dan and Bethany Anne in here, I'll put you on speaker."

Frank punched the speaker. "Stephen? You got everybody."

"I have to be quick, David set a very good trap. We've lost Shelly to an RPG. Chris is hurt, but should survive. We have twenty-six children with us, and no way to communicate once I go back into the valley. You can bet we're going to get hit hard tonight. Do we have a status for air support?

Dan replied, "We have a response, but you're not going like it. The military says no way. We think it might be due to David's influence with someone up the chain of command."

A long stream of foreign language came from Stephen. "I swear on all that is holy if I get a chance I'm ripping that ass' head clean off his body."

Bethany Anne chimed in, "You'll have to get in line behind Michael and me."

Stephen came back, frustrated. "Fuck it, we can almost kill him and then give him some blood to heal, right?"

Bethany Anne smiled, Stephen was definitely riled up. "You're going to have to hold tight as long as you can, we have ships that should be able to get us there sometime before..." she looked over at Dan.

"Ten o'clock tonight?" Dan got out his cell phone and started dialing.

Bethany Anne was frustrated, without knowing where she was going to go, she couldn't take her team there through the Etheric.

TOM, can we call the ship back down and use it?

TOM calculated where the ship was at this moment. **I'll start it back down here. Not sure if it will arrive in time.**

Dan set his phone on the table. "Bobcat, tell everyone what you just told me."

Bobcat's voice came from the little tinny speakerphone. "We have the engines on the floor with the IZTAs. It won't take us but maybe twenty minutes to load them up. The problem is going to be light. It won't get dark for another hour and ten big black metal boxes suddenly flying through the air are gonna raise some questions."

Bethany Anne spoke up, "How fast can I have some of them here?" She could hear Bobcat turn around and ask Marcus the question.

You could just ask me, you know.

Right, sorry, what's the answer?

With everything going correctly, twelve minutes.

What could go wrong?

They don't work, they explode, we have to deal with

bad or shoddy workmanship. I could go on.

You're not making me feel very good about the quality of these engines.

The engines are fine, you merely asked for a list of items that could go wrong, not what I expected to go wrong.

Fine, what do you expect to go wrong?

Nothing. In fact we should be able to lift them off as soon as we hit dusk. We won't be able to fly as quickly, but the engines can warp light around them to somewhat hide themselves.

Like what your ship does?

Not even close, but they should be traveling so fast no one will be able to see them unless they're looking directly at them.

Good enough for me.

"Guys, never mind asking Marcus. TOM tells me that they should be here in approximately twelve minutes. We're going to take them out as soon as it's dusk."

Dan spoke up, "How many did you say you had going?"

Bobcat answered, "Ten."

Stephen said, "Did you say ten? I thought I had ordered eight."

Bobcat asked, "Was that Stephen? Tell him it's for the Calvary."

Stephen came back on. "I've got to go, I'm pushing it as far as I can. We will see you when we see you, but sooner would be better than later." He disconnected the call.

Bethany Anne considered the situation. "We bring the ships here, we load everything we need, we go there. We kill maim and destroy as best we can. We load the kids up and take them, where?" She looked at the two men.

Dan shrugged. "I don't think we have a choice, we'll have

to bring them to the Polarus. We have ten of these ships, I'm sure we can stick three children into a space where two adults are supposed to be able to fit." He scratched his forehead. "But our team won't be able to evac right away."

Bethany Anne looked confused. "Why not? Once we beat everyone, and have the children safe, what else is holding us?"

Frank answered for Dan, "Because if I was a devious bastard, I would have another round ready to go."

Bethany Anne muttered, "I'm considering beating Michael to the punch, David is a devious bastard. I think I'm going to support Stephen's idea of almost killing him, and let him regenerate so we can almost kill him again."

Frank raised an eyebrow. "Stephen isn't usually this bloodthirsty, is he?"

Bethany Anne said, "He is when he's being attacked, he was quite bloodthirsty back at his house with David's goons. That man is quite an artist at causing a vampire pain when properly motivated."

There was a rap on the door, causing the three of them to look up. It was Gabrielle. "Are we going back to the other ship, or have plans changed?"

Bethany Anne waved her over. "Take a seat, plans have changed. Let the guys know they need to suit up."

She called out to the phone, "Bobcat?

"Yes, Bethany Anne."

"Make sure you have those devices outside. Hopefully in a place where they won't be stolen."

Bobcat laughed. "This place is a ghost town. Whatever Stephen told them, no one wants to be found here right now. You could take a cool million dollars, set it outside and it would be here in the morning. Once William finishes with the engines we'll set the craft outside. Give us a three-minute delay to make sure we are cinched in before you take us."

Bethany Anne confirmed TOM knew what to do.

"Understood, be ready to fly as soon as possible." Bethany Anne said. Bobcat hung up.

Frank asked, "Did anyone tell Bobcat that Shelly was lost?"

"Damn," Gabrielle muttered, "Bobcat is going to be pissed."

Bethany Anne turned to Gabrielle. "What's the team's status?"

Gabrielle answered, "They're all suiting up, will have their weapons and their backup weapons. They're also taking more ammo for everything we have, plus some extra for the first team. Along with more first aid equipment. Did we forget anything?"

Dan answered, "Yes. You need equipment and protection for Bobcat, William, and myself."

Bethany Anne, surprised, looked over at the head of her military. "You? How are we supposed to operate this if you're in the middle of it with us?"

Dan shrugged. "What is there to operate? We're going to go there, be out of radio contact, and shoot every fucking thing that's not part of our team. Seems like a pretty straightforward plan to me."

"You're going to need a STIM shot."

Dan looked at her, a smile on his face. "I was hoping you'd say that."

Bethany Anne turned to face Frank, and raised her eyebrow.

Frank put his hands up in front of him. "Maybe later, but I don't have the skills for something like this. I'm better here trying to track down the asshats that threw this little party."

Bethany Anne stood up and looked around. "Frank, I need you to get in touch with Michael for me." She paused a second then asked, "What are you sitting on your asses for? Let's get ready to fuck up some Nosferatu!"

The room quickly emptied, each leaving to head back to their respective tasks. Bethany Anne stopped Dan. "Are you sure about this? There isn't any going back."

Dan smiled at her. "I've never been more sure of anything in my life. Even if you hadn't offered, there is no way I'm letting all of my people be in the middle of that clusterfuck without one more gun in the mix."

Bethany Anne started toward the door. "Follow me then, this ride is about to get a lot more interesting."

CHAPTER TWENTY-ONE

Turkey, thirty miles from the Syrian border

Stephen was staring out at the town. The sun had just descended behind the hills defining the western edge of the valley. Stephen had watched the shadows lengthen and they now covered the whole valley. Nathan came up behind him. "We have the children in the back of the cave, with the caretakers. We've also moved all of the supplies further back, in case we have to fight inside the cave. Any other recommendations?"

"Yes, we have more than enough weapons, can any of them shoot? Or, can you teach them how to shoot?"

Nathan's eyes roamed over the valley wall. "Do we really want civilians with automatic weapons shooting in our general direction?"

"Perhaps, perhaps not. Make sure they realize who the good guys are. I don't want them without any defensive weaponry if Nosferatu get past us."

Nathan turned and was able to get Chet's attention. Once Chet got close enough Nathan said, "Let's check out the civilians on the weapons, if they know how to use them, great. If not, at least show them what to do in case it all goes to hell." Chet nodded and started jogging back into the cave.

Stephen spoke over his shoulder. "Have we checked out the back of the cave? The chokepoint is here, if we need to we'll brace ourselves around the door."

Nathan replied, "I've asked Pete's team to take a look, so far nothing. We seem to at least be assured that our backdoor is closed."

Stephen sighed. "Thank God for one small favor. We might as well get everyone ready. The shadows are deep enough that I expect the first wave to arrive soon."

Basing their deployment on what Pete and Todd's teams learned while fighting on the ship, they put the werewolves in front and those with weapons behind them. There was a sixty-foot area in front of the cave that was clear. Then you had three different lanes between the village's houses. The cliffs above them were steep, about seventy-five feet high. It would have been a good sniper position, but they lacked the equipment to get there.

The silence in the valley was deafening, but Stephen could hear the first wave of Nosferatu. He told those around him, "Look sharp, they're on their way." Seconds later the werewolves could hear the enemy as well.

Pete came up beside him. Stephen looked over and nodded and then went back to watching the lanes. Pete slowly unbuttoned and untucked his shirt. He took it off and turning slightly he threw it toward the mouth of the cave. He remarked, to no one in particular, "No need to mess up a perfectly good shirt."

Pete waited, wishing he knew a way to help him focus enough to start his turning early. "Dammit! I need to get angry enough before I can turn."

Stephen turned to look at the Wechselbalg. "I'm sorry, what?"

Pete answered, "I need to get angry enough to start the change into my other form. I'm just not angry enough right now."

Stephen smiled. "Well, why didn't you just ask for help?" And with that he slapped the young man. Pete slammed into the ground fifteen feet away. Stephen looked over at Pete and his eyes narrowed. "Now get up and fight like a man, you ass-kissing dog."

Stephen turned to face the lanes again, confident Pete would be just fine and ready to fight in a moment.

He was. Stephen could feel the rage directed at him. He pointed to the middle lane, "Our fight is with them, I just jump-started your change, Peter."

Pete glared at the vampire and turned his head to the direction Stephen's finger pointed. Ah! Nosferatu. Pete roared at the newcomers, "Bring it, Bitches!"

The fight began.

Cracks of rifle fire preceded three Nosferatu dropping to the ground, their bodies trampled as those that followed ignored their fallen.

Men, women, teenagers. David didn't discriminate when he changed friends and family to become cannon fodder. All had bloodlust in their eyes. They could sense the blood of those in front of them, and this time the blood didn't hide behind doors.

The pain, the desire to drink was too much for the Nosferatu. They couldn't see past getting that which was closest to them. If they had been satiated, perhaps they would have tried to find others, but why would they go anywhere when they could smell the blood so close to them now? They would strive to get into this cave all night, until dawn forced them to hide, once again to sleep during the daylight hours.

Except when dinner came walking right into your room. That time they had killed the soldiers, eaten them and then laid back down. The blood of the newly dead became their mattresses on the cold, dark floor.

Then the front of the Nosferatu line hit them. Stephen and Pete tore into the Nosferatu with abandon, Pete's claws taking jaws from the beings, his return strokes gouging out throats.

On his right, the vampire was doing the same, with considerable more efficiency. Stephen was a machine of destruction. He would slam his clawed hand across a skull, shattering the head and spraying the nearby Nosferatu with brains. Then, he would kick out and another Nosferatu would have their rib cage crushed with his foot. They would be pushed back a few feet, but the Nosferatu behind them stopped any significant backward momentum. Sometimes those he kicked would fall. At other times they would come back and press the attack, albeit significantly slower than before. Often, before Stephen could get back to such an attacker, its head would explode from Todd's team providing fire support from the cave.

The Nosferatu couldn't get through the two fighters in the center, so many tried to go around. They would attack Pete and Todd's teams. Matthew, Joel and Joseph on the left, Tim and Rickie on the right.

Two Nosferatu ganged up on Joel and a third slipped through the line. It was on Kevin Russel faster than Chet could react. It savaged Kevin even as the bullets from Chet's rifle slammed through its head. Both the Nosferatu and Kevin fell.

Chet yelled, "Man down!"

Nathan left his post at the door. Both he and Ecaterina were backup, firing as they could, but predominately the second layer of defense.

Now, Nathan had to move up to take Kevin's position. Nathan quickly got to Kevin and confirmed that he was alive. He pulled him back to Ecaterina who started dragging him into the cave. There, Diane and Dorene took over, working to patch him up as best they could.

Art was deeper inside the cave. He knew the valley group the best and since he had the skills, he was the third layer of defense.

The fighting was intense, but they didn't suffer another line break.

Thirty became twenty, twenty became eight and then when those fell to the defenders, only the fallen Nosferatu were left.

Pete was looking around, his anger boiling his blood, the heat of the fight encouraging him to seek out more enemies. He turned to look beside him and threw a punch at the one who hit him first.

Only to have his fist caught in the vampire's left hand. Stephen looked at the werewolf. "Calm yourself, Peter. The rage is driving you, you need to drive your rage."

Pete was trying to pull his fist out of the grip of the one in front of him when the words registered in his brain and he stopped fighting. He took deep breaths and slowly felt his body come back around, the light of the evening seeming to recede a little. It now looked a lot darker out there.

He nodded at Stephen who released his fist.

Pete rubbed his jaw where Stephen had slapped him. "Thanks… I think."

Stephen smiled, but didn't stop looking around them. "You're welcome. It will come easier for you. Each time you change, you will get more accustomed to tapping the feelings you need. Eventually, you will be able to bring it on whenever you desire." Stephen stopped looking into the small town and focused on the man standing next to him. "Unfortunately, that is when you become most susceptible."

Pete was confused. "Most susceptible to what?"

"Power, Pete. The power that you feel when in that form is a drug. You will forever fight against the desire to rip, to tear, to exalt in the feeling of destruction that you now command." Stephen resumed watching the night.

Pete considered his words. "Did you have friends that were werewolves in your past?"

Stephen spoke into the night as a whisper to the wind. "None that I didn't have to kill when they lost their humanity."

They had a fifteen-minute respite before Stephen heard the next wave of Nosferatu coming out of the caves.

"We have company."

Pete stepped up beside Stephen, "Is there a better way than sending my jaw fifteen feet to help me with this change?"

Stephen considered his answer carefully. "Yes. Are you sure you want to know what it is?"

Reaching up to feel his jaw, the memory of the pain recent even if he had fully healed during the fighting. "Yeah, lay it on me."

Stephen exhaled slowly, and then spoke loud enough for all of those around them to hear. "I spoke to the girls on the

Ad Aeternitatem, they say you have a tiny dick…"

Pete was confused at first, when Stephen said that. Then he heard Tim and Todd snicker and the night became bright in his rage at being laughed at. He turned around to take care of their insolence. A hand grabbed his arm, squeezing enough to get his attention. He turned to find the vampire holding him and pointing back to the Nosferatu that he could hear rushing towards them. He turned towards the fight, his baritone voice easily heard over the oncoming rush, "I'll deal with you two later."

They might have been more concerned if Stephen hadn't winked at them and told everyone, "Get ready, here we go again."

The night erupted with screams and the crackle of gunfire as the immovable rock stood against the raging flow of Nosferatu in that lonely valley in the middle of nowhere, one more time.

Ecaterina had never felt so alive, even during her trips to her uncle's mountain. The savageness of the Nosferatu as they tried to get through the protective ring of Stephen and the troops. Nathan impressing the ever-loving hell out of her with his calm and collected shooting skills.

His was a constant, 'crack, crack, crack' with his body turning slightly each time. She would see Nosferatu heads exploding when she spent a second checking on him. Going back to her side, she would continue with her own efforts. She might be getting three shots off for every five of Nathan's, but it felt much slower than that.

She was shooting when she saw Rickie, mouthing off as normal, get pulled into the mess, requiring Tim to reach over to help pull him back out.

A Nosferatu slipped between Tim and Stephen and raced

towards the entrance. Paul Stevens, one of the marines backing up the right side, dove for its feet, wrapping them up and tripping the Nosferatu. Ecaterina swung her rifle down and shot the Nosferatu, hitting it in the back. Her second shot exploded its skull.

Paul was gone. The Nosferatu had reached down and torn open Paul's neck before Ecaterina had been able to finish it off.

Ecaterina ran to Paul's position and started firing into the horde. She thought life was intense before, it was downright scary now. She fired until she needed to reload, then switched out the magazine and continued shooting.

Ecaterina could hear rifles from where she and Nathan had been stationed at the door. The skull of a Nosferatu exploded next to the one she had just shot. "That's twenty years in the service, motherfuckers!"

"On your right!" Ecaterina turned in time to see the three Nosferatu that had just swung around Joey. Todd shot one of them, and clubbed the other. The third dodged him and came at Ecaterina.

She shot from the hip, nailing the Nosferatu but not stopping it before she felt indescribable pain and then only darkness.

Diane screamed and shot the Nosferatu that had just sunk its teeth into Ecaterina's neck. It rose up to look at the woman when Dorene's shot hit it between the eyes. The women pulled Ecaterina out of the way. Diane went inside the cave to grab some bandages as Dorene pressed the wound. Ecaterina was losing blood, fast.

Diane came back and together they worked to staunch the heavy flow of blood. "This isn't looking good, sis."

Dorene ripped open a gauze pouch with her teeth. "Tell

me something I don't already know."

That was when they heard the howl of despair, they looked over to see the second, and by far the largest, standing Werewolf this world had seen in a long, long time.

Ecaterina's mate had seen her bleeding and unconscious body.

It turned into a massacre. Nathan was easily half a foot taller than Pete's and out massed him by another fifty to seventy-five pounds.

The problem? He wasn't in his right mind.

Bethany Anne had popped Nathan into the pod-doc after he had said that he and Ecaterina would be going on this mission. Something would have to trigger Nathan's change, but he had been such a calm individual, Bethany Anne wasn't sure what that would be.

Now, even the Nosferatu backed up under the onslaught of the mighty beast attacking them. Stephen took the head off of the Nosferatu in front of him and took a quick glance to his left. He grabbed Peter and pulled him to his side. "Fight them!" He pointed at his group, "I'll try to help Ecaterina." Peter tore into the Nosferatu with renewed vigor. These *things* had just killed his sister, his friend. As each Were became aware of what was going on, the anger and grief they felt overrode their sensibilities and the slaughter began.

No longer did the Forsaken push against Stephen's group, but rather they in fury slammed into the Nosferatu. Nathan, in unrestrained fury, killed with heated abandon. Nathan would grab a head in one hand and crush it while reaching for a second to rip out its throat. If an arm got in his way, his jaws would open wide and he would bite through the bone, jerking his head to try and rip the arm from the body, spitting out the meat from his mouth.

Stephen raced to Ecaterina, he put his wrist up to his mouth and used his sharpened teeth to rip his wrist open. The women stood transfixed at the red-eyed man ripped off Ecaterina's bandages and smeared his blood on her wound, then forced some down her throat.

"Shoot at them!" Stephen snapped them out of their shock. They both grabbed their rifles, not sure how the… man… was helping the young woman, but feeling that he was trying his best.

The next second, they were shooting into the mess again, but this time the shots weren't surgical. If there was any opening that didn't have a team member between them and the monsters, it was fair game.

The fight went on for another eternity before Nathan held the last living Nosferatu up high in the air before turning it over and breaking its back on his upraised knee. He flung the body into the dirt. The Marines scoured the site, shooting the skulls of any Nosferatu who looked like they might be able to heal themselves.

"NATHAN!"

The beast eyed the shadowy walls, the cliffs that held those who had killed his mate. Which of these, it wondered, held more so he could sink his teeth and rend them apart?

"NATHAN!"

It turned at a familiar name, looking behind itself. It saw a man, bent over his mate, looking at him.

"NATHAN, COME BACK GOTT VERDAMMT! ECATERINA NEEDS YOU!"

The man was yelling at it, rage on his face.

"GOTT VERDAMMT NATHAN, COME BACK FOR HER!"

Ecaterina?

The beast shook its head in confusion.

Ecaterina was the name of his mate… His memory came back, looking into her eyes, telling her he would never leave her… but the caves were calling.

He started running towards his mate.

He left as a werewolf, he arrived as a man.

Stephen held her gently as Nathan dropped to his knees. Stephen spoke. "Look, I've done what I can, but if I give her too much, I run the risk of turning her."

Nathan looked up at Stephen. "So?" He growled, "Turn her already!"

Stephen's voice became hoarse, "Nathan! You're not thinking. She wouldn't want to be a vampire. She would choose to be a Wechselbalg!" Stephen was frustrated, but kept his voice as calm as he could. "I can't change her, YOU have to change her!"

Nathan turned to face Stephen again, his face a mask of confusion. "What? How do I change her?"

Stephen looked over his shoulder, eyeing everyone who came to check on Ecaterina. The idiots were leaving the defenses unchecked. "Dammit! Pete stay here, the rest of you clean up those bodies and make a wall. We haven't won yet! Get Paul's body. We won't leave it behind." The rest of the men jerked into action. The concern they had for Ecaterina had blinded them to what they needed to be doing.

"Pete, I need a knife."

"Here you go." Stephen turned to see that Dorene was offering him one. "Always be prepared."

Stephen took the offered knife and looked back at Nathan. "You'll have to bleed into her mouth and her wounds."

Nathan looked over Ecaterina's body. "There is only the one!"

"Not for this to work, there won't be." Stephen looked at the man, "This must be done, do you understand?"

Nathan realized what Stephen was going to do and nodded.

Reaching down, Stephen easily tore open Ecaterina's protective jacket and then ripped open her shirt and snapped off her bra. "Hold out your wrist, Nathan."

Nathan put his wrist out over Ecaterina's body. Stephen turned his fingers into claws and made three cuts in Ecaterina's abdomen, each a half-inch deep. She immediately started bleeding. Stephen then used the knife to cut Nathan's wrist. He grabbed it, smearing the blood that was spurting out all over Ecaterina's fresh wounds. "Pete, go get the blood packs." Pete tore into the cave.

Stephen cut Nathan's wrist again. "Now make her drink this." Nathan worked to get Ecaterina's mouth open and to get some of his blood down her throat.

Pete returned with the blood and Stephen told Nathan to drink one right away, and another in a few minutes. There was no hesitation from Nathan, he immediately opened one and started drinking.

After doing what he could for Ecaterina, Stephen stood up and looked over the darkened village. It was completely dark and the stars were out in a mockery of beauty.

The silence was deafening. Art came out of the cave after making sure his charges were ok. "Seems quiet."

Stephen nodded. "It is. They're probably regrouping."

"Who is it?"

Stephen shrugged. "Does it matter? They have sent their first two groups against us. I imagine they are changing plans and are getting instructions. I can only tell you that we aren't done for the night."

The Queen Bitch's Ship Polarus

Bethany Anne made sure everyone knew when Team BMW's craft left the mainland. Five minutes before they were to arrive, Dan came up with two people that Bethany Anne hadn't worked with.

Dan introduced them, "Bethany Anne, meet Lucas Michaels and Paul McAlister."

Lucas shook her hand, Paul stepped up. "It's Scottie to me friends." Scottie had a slight burr, but hardly noticeable.

She looked them over. Both had on their protective gear and had picked up sniper rifles to go with their kit, the same as Dan.

She turned to Dan. "This isn't a good time to be learning how to fight Nosferatu, Dan. Do you have a plan to keep them from being redshirts?"

Scottie laughed. "Can't be me, don't you know, Scottie was the only redshirt that never died!"

Bethany Anne grinned. "Just you make sure that you take after your namesake, and we'll be fine." She turned to face Lucas. "Do you have a snappy comeback too?"

Lucas shook his head. "No, just shoot 'em and stack them up like cordwood."

Bethany Anne nodded sharply and turned to Dan. "Ok. Works for me. I'll try to put your team somewhere protected with a good line of sight."

Someone behind her yelled out, "Here they come!"

Everyone turned, and could barely make out, a formation of pod-like craft skimming over the waves towards them. One wave rose high enough to get in the way of one of the boxes, but the wave broke around lower half, showing that an invisible spherical shape was projected at least ten feet out from the box.

Then they slowed and rose to the height of the deck.

Please ask everyone to wait until I get them all down. I'll bring the three with Bobcat, William and Marcus in first.

Bethany Anne relayed TOM's instructions.

Three of the craft slowly descended, the other seven staying a good thirty feet above them.

They slowed as they came to the deck. Their descent looked like they were on pistons. Finally, all three sat on the deck.

You could hear three distinct locks being turned and two opened quickly revealing Bobcat and William. A moment later, Marcus finally got his open as well.

There were cheers all around and the smiles on the three men threatened to engulf their faces. John and Eric brought Bobcat and William their gear. The two men quickly started stripping down to change clothes and strap on their protective gear.

Marcus went to Bethany Anne and Dan. "Oh my god that was fantastic! It was so smooth and the ride was exquisite. I was able to calculate on the laptop." Marcus's face became stricken, he turned around and ran back towards his craft. He pushed open the door and then cried out as he reached in. He returned with the laptop in his hands. "Sorry, I didn't want you guys leaving with my communications connection!"

You seem to have made a huge impact on Marcus.

Well, the man does appreciate the finer art of mathematics, even if he is a little needy and clingy at times.

Are you saying he checks up on you?

Constantly! I've almost sent him an 'out of office' message twice now, but I wasn't sure if he needed something for the plan to work, or was just curious and had to scratch that inquisitive itch he lives with.

Sucks to be you.

Tell me about it.

"Speaking of that." She turned towards Dan. "Gabrielle has tactical if I'm out of commission or gone. She's got both the experience and the skills, ok?"

Dan nodded. "No problem with me or my little group of sniping malcontents."

By the time she finished with Dan, Bobcat and William were both changed and the first three pods were packed and ready to go. Bethany Anne noticed Bobcat's face had lost all of its humor.

Someone had told him about Shelly, she supposed.

All but two of the pods had now been filled and had levitated off of the ship.

She stepped into the second of the remaining two. She whistled and Ashur bounded up. Bethany Anne moved aside to give him room.

John grabbed both doors to close them. "Bobcat says the light is above the exit, keep all hands and feet inside the craft and hold on. He hopes you brought along some music and the service will not be around to give you any Coke." He winked at Bethany Anne. "See you over there, boss!" He looked down at Ashur. "Keep her safe, ok?"

Ashur woofed in response.

He closed the doors after Bethany Anne turned on the light. The latch was easy enough to operate. She heard John's doors close and lock.

It was time to go.

———

Five minutes later, Bethany Anne was so bored she wanted to beat the metal wall.

It was apparently time to think.

TOM, we need to do something about communications. I'm bored to tears.

It might be difficult to do. We'd have to work on getting a signal through the shielding produced to keep the bubble around us.

Can't we pop something through the Etheric?

Of course, but then we need to make sure something happens to the devices whenever one of these pods gets stolen, confiscated, destroyed and parts are left behind…

You're a merry sort at the moment.

Piloting ten of these through the low level flying we are doing is a little challenging.

Why? I thought the Kurtherian computer was such a work of art that handling the flying wasn't a big problem?

You would think so, but my access to the whole computer is slightly constrained at the moment.

What? Why, how can something challenge your access… Wait, wait. Don't tell me that stupid program is doing something?

Well, I'm curious to see what happens next in the coding, so I permitted a requested download of a substantial amount of data while we were on the ship. Some old cartoons. Now, the program is consuming a significant number of calculation cycles to number-crunch the data and…

Stop! Just stop right there. I neither know nor care how or what it is doing. Make damn sure your side research isn't getting in the way of our operation. We don't need to go splat

UNDER MY HEEL

on a mountain somewhere because we missed some data.

No, no. That won't be a problem. We are coming up on the coordinates.

I need to see what the location looks like to confirm where to set down, angle the pod slightly up— I don't want me or Ashur to fall out.

She mumbled out loud, "'Cause that wouldn't be fucking embarrassing or anything."

She unlocked the door and pushed it open, stretching the straps that held her in to look down.

It was a ghost town. She found a spot on a hill not too far away where the group could land. "Over there."

TOM viewed the area through her eyes and her pod started descending.

When she was a few feet from the ground, she jumped off and turned to watch the other pods descend and land. Ashur was right behind her. Soon, she had her guards plus Dan, his two snipers, Bobcat and William.

That was the moment she snapped her head around, seeking the flight of a missile she could hear launching. She finally spotted it as it rose into the air and turned in their direction.

TOM!

Got it.

Dan had just started to turn his head in her direction when the pod Bethany Anne had used tore itself away from them and met the missile in midair. The explosion reverberated throughout the valley.

The pod came back, noticeably damaged on the outside.

There was another visible effect from the pod racing out to meet the missile.

236

The supplies that had been in her pod were now spread out all over the town.

Bethany Anne, that craft can't take another missile.

Bethany Anne told the group, "Get the supplies out of two more, quickly."

Gabrielle and John tore into their pods, pulling stuff out and dropping it on the ground as quickly as they could. Soon, they were empty and TOM sent them into the air.

Dan sighed. "Well, we know how Shelly was taken out."

Bethany Anne said, "Yes, let's hope not too many of our team is gone as well."

Bethany Anne spotted the area where Stephen was and could see the teams using bodies of the Nosferatu to create barricades as best they could. "They've seen a lot of fighting already. I can tell a couple of people aren't ours, but I can't see everyone, either. Let's get your team…" She looked up above the cave area where Stephen was holed up. "I see a spot about seventy-plus feet or so above the cave entrance. No way to go up and it's another thirty feet up the cliff to get to the top, minimum. Looks like you would be safe from Nosferatu, but if we all eat it, you won't be able to get off for shit."

Dan asked, "How about a hide, anything to protect us from return fire?"

Bethany Anne looked harder. "Yeah, I think so. Good point. Let's take your team over to go see, really quick."

She turned to the rest. "Grab your shit, TOM's going to take all of you over to Stephen. He will drop within a few feet of the ground. Jump off, grab the supplies, then the pods will go up and hover high enough not to be noticed. When we decide what to do with the children, we will send them away. Make sure when you get there, you move fast."

Two of the pods lifted from the ground. "Looks like our

rides, gentleman. Let's go." She spoke over her shoulder, "Ashur, go with Gabrielle."

Bethany Anne jumped in one and pulled Dan up after her. Scottie and Lucas jumped into the other, making sure they had their rifles and ammunition plus a bag each of food and water. Dan had already slung a bag over his shoulder.

The pods took off, angled slightly back, leaving the doors open. Lucas and Scottie peered out over the town, seeing a large group coming out of the caves at the far end, about a mile away. Scottie muttered, "Now *that* is a target rich environment."

Lucas said, "Preach it brother, preach it."

Dan was looking at the little cliff that Bethany Anne had pointed out. There were spots he thought the three of them could use for cover. As long as the other side didn't have higher ground to aim down at them, it looked good. "I think it's going to work."

The two pods got close enough for the three men to step down and then turn around to unload.

I need to see something, hold on.

Bethany Anne grabbed the side of her pod as it tilted down and to the right. She looked over to see Stephen's group, almost directly below them.

Ok, making sure I had the layout. Thank you.

The pod resumed its position.

Bethany Anne called to them, "You boys keep your heads down, ok?"

Dan smiled. "And our powder dry. You do the same, you understand, Bethany Anne?"

She nodded and the two pods moved backwards and then started descending towards the ground.

CHAPTER TWENTY-TWO

As she got close enough, she saw a wrapped body near the wall. She had already lost someone. Her mouth tightened, her eyes started turning red.

She jumped off and quickly joined the group by the door. There were two older ladies there, both holding rifles that her team had brought with them. There was a military man who keeping watch out into the night. His flag marked him as an American. That must be the missing guy, presumed KIA.

Gabrielle turned as she heard Bethany Anne coming up behind them. She stepped towards her. "Bethany Anne, it's Ecaterina." Bethany Anne's eyes flashed red. "Stephen had to make a judgment call…"

Bethany Anne looked at her. "Is she being turned?" The anguish in Bethany Anne's voice was exacerbated by her fangs growing longer.

"No. Nathan is doing it."

Now, Bethany Anne's look of anger and pain turned to one of confusion. "Nathan?"

"Weres can turn others as well."

Bethany Anne thought back to Ecaterina's uncle's story of being attacked by a bear, but living through it and then his transformation.

Gabrielle continued. "The ability to survive such a transformation does seem to run in a family, so it looks like this is going to work."

Bethany Anne's fangs retracted a little. "What can I do?" Her voice had the hint of sadness coloring the tone.

Gabrielle put her hands on Bethany Anne's shoulders. "Nothing that isn't already being done. You have the right people, doing the right things for her."

Bethany Anne nodded sharply. "Ok, move them into the cave if you can. I need the children to be brought up for transfer."

"Where?" Bethany Anne turned to see one of the older ladies, with a rifle, listening to them.

Bethany Anne asked, "You are?"

"Diane." She stepped forward, "My sister and I are two of the people responsible for twenty-two of the children in there. That doesn't include the four from here." She pointed towards the cave. "The minister has been hurt, and two other adults that were with us were killed."

Bethany Anne considered the ten pods. It was going to have to work. "We're going to move all of the children, and the two of you, to a ship in the Mediterranean where the rest of my team is. They're expecting you."

I hope, she thought.

I'll tell Marcus to communicate that they are on their way.

Good! Thank you.

She had forgotten TOM wasn't blocked.

You can't block my Etheric communications, you spunking ass-packers! She thought.

"Ladies, how many children can fit into each pod?"

The other sister stepped over, but she was looking at the pods the whole time. "How the hell do they fly?"

Diane threw an exasperated look at the other lady. "Sorry, this is my sister Dorene. Too many years in the service burned through any filter she had for her mouth."

Dorene grunted, "Fuck-a-filter, how do those things fly?"

Diane rolled her eyes but answered Bethany Anne's question with a question, "For how long of a trip?"

TOM?

We can get them back in less than ten minutes. My ship has the path we took to get here. It can calculate the fastest path back now by just retracing everything and smoothing it out. Say, ten minutes?

Bethany Anne shrugged. "Say ten minutes?"

Diane looked at Bethany Anne, disbelief on her face. "No fucking way!"

Dorene snorted beside her sister, still looking at the pods. "I'm sorry, she's been around me all her life, no filter."

Bethany Anne smiled. "So, can we get them all out of here? The Nosferatu are lining up to come at us again and if we can't, then we need a plan 'b' real fucking fast."

Diane started towards the cave. "Hell yes! If I have to cram them in, these kids are getting to safety!"

Bethany Anne turned. "Gabrielle?"

Gabrielle said, "On it." She called out, "John, Eric, Scott with me, Darryl prep for loading."

Dorene noticed the big guard walking over to the pod.

"I think I'll help tall, dark and handsome!" Then busted out laughing at Darryl's look of shock.

Darryl asked, "Aren't you a nun?"

Dorene popped Darryl on his butt. "No, I just wanted to visit Turkey again and my sister and I got to go for free if we helped chaperone some children with the ministry."

Darryl stepped a little more quickly towards the pod. "Don't make me call HR on you for sexual harassment!" He was chuckling.

Dorene followed Darryl. "Honey, you haven't begun to feel sexual harassment!"

Bethany Anne rolled her eyes at the antics. Then she eyed the area above, where Dan, Scottie and Lucas had settled in. She took one step and ended up a few feet above the ledge. Landing easily, she noticed that only Dan didn't jump at her sudden arrival.

Seems like Dan might be getting his situational awareness back pretty quickly, she thought.

Lucas looked back into his scope muttering quietly, "Dammit, now my pants need a cleanup."

Bethany Anne ignored the muttering sniper. They would settle down once the shooting started.

Dan looked up at her. "What's up?"

She looked down the valley. "Trying to get an idea how much time we might have to get the children out of here. There sure seems to be more… where the hell did David get so many?"

Dan shrugged, "Couldn't tell you. Not unless he figured out some way to get Nosferatu to…" Dan stopped talking.

She looked down. "Dan?"

He answered, looking down the valley through his scope. "Let's just hope he doesn't have Nosferatu creating Nosferatu."

"Isn't that what the serum was for?"

"You might ask Stephen. Michael's children could, theoretically, create vampires which could be controlled enough to force them to create vampires…"

She looked up. "So these higher level vampires are probably down there, too?"

"Probably, but once they release them, Nosferatu search out food."

"Why don't they go after whoever shot at us with that missile?"

"I'd guess that either we're closer, or it has something to do with the commands issued so far."

Bethany Anne looked down and saw the children coming out of the cave. She paid attention so that TOM could see what was going on and take care of the loading as effectively as possible. The two ladies, plus one man that had to be helped out of the cave, were loaded into the last pod by Gabrielle. Then they were gone.

Dan watched the pods for the few seconds he could see them. "Sure hope they don't have another missile."

"Agreed. I hope not. You would think that they would have tried again, but you never know." She looked at the three men. "Good hunting."

"Aye, it will be that, me lassie." Scottie affected a heavy brogue. Lucas snorted and Dan grinned. Bethany Anne shook her head, stepped off the cliff and translocated onto the ground below.

Stephen walked up to her. She glanced over at him and then returned her attention towards the area of the valley that the Forsaken were holding at.

He asked, "How many?"

She shrugged. "Can't get a good head count, but call it three hundred?"

Stephen followed her focus. "I'm only good for maybe the first hundred or two. How about you?" The humor in his voice was infectious.

Bethany Anne paused and considered his comment. She smiled. "Well, I suppose I could just sit back and let you handle all of them until you tag out, and then I'll step in."

Stephen chuckled at her response.

Bethany Anne asked quietly, "How are Ecaterina and Chris? What happened to Paul and where is Chet?" She had figured out who she hadn't seen yet. All of the teams looked dirty, dusty, bloody and a little tired.

"Paul took down a Nosferatu who had made it past Tim and was heading towards the door where Ecaterina was. By the time the Nosferatu was killed, it had already torn Paul's throat out. Ecaterina took his place and only a few minutes later three more came around the flank. Todd got two and Ecaterina shot the third, but she couldn't stop it before it got its teeth into her and tore out a chunk of her neck. I was able to heal her enough to stop the blood loss, but to finish the job required a lot more. Chris is asleep, but OK, same as Chet. There wasn't room in the pods to send either back."

"So, you told someone how to make a Were, then?"

Stephen looked over at Bethany Anne. "You don't seem so surprised."

"What's to be surprised about? Same stupid alien species with similar technologies. Just because I didn't take the time to consider it, doesn't make it any less obvious once I do. Hell, even Alexi told me how he was changed from human to Wechselbalg."

"Nathan can change into a *hybrid* now, too."

"Oh?"

"Yes, he took a look at what he must have thought was

Ecaterina's dead body and… it was a surprise."

Bethany Anne looked over at Stephen. "Was that a bad surprise or a good surprise?" She detected a note of annoyance in Stephen's voice.

Stephen answered, "It helped, but as the leader, a heads up from my Queen would be appreciated next time."

Bethany Anne considered her response. "Taken under advisement, and for what it's worth, I should have told you. I wasn't sure it would work and didn't want to get the group's hopes up. Nathan can be so calm under pressure I really didn't know if he could do it."

Mollified, he said, "He makes an impressive werewolf. I've never seen one bigger."

Bethany Anne's face showed shock. "You've known other werewolves that could stay in that form?"

Stephen exhaled. "I've known a few. I'm over nine hundred years old, Bethany Anne. Some very good friends of mine were werewolves that could change into both forms. I had to kill two of them when they went too far and couldn't handle the power. It is a drug at times, this changing for them is a curse."

Somewhere in Austria

David was waiting for news. He had confirmation that the helicopter that was used to enter the valley had been successfully destroyed before the communications stopped.

David smiled. Maybe they would make a movie, "Blackhawk Down 2—More Useless Americans Die." He couldn't stand that country. He didn't like them before, when Michael had left Europe to stay over there. But when they liberated Europe as World War II ended, his distaste became a deep-seated loathing. They had been a pivotal force that finished the Third Reich.

And, all of his plans.

He played with the liquor in his glass, swirling it around letting the firelight shine through the amber liquid. It was a pity that Michael was back in play. There was no one to blame that on but himself. He had waited for Michael to finally understand and accept the reality of what must occur. Only to have his opportunity to kill Michael slip through his fingers.

Then Michael had been helped by his new daughter. David's face distorted in disgust as he threw the glass into the fireplace, flames erupting as the alcohol burned.

He stared at the glass shards on the floor reflecting the firelight. Someone would need to come pick up the broken glass when he was finished with his contemplations.

One of his throwaway phones rang. He picked it up. "Yes?"

The voice was deep, clipped and precise. "Michael is in Argentina. He has taken over Anton's home."

"How long?"

"Weeks."

David considered this. "Very good, keep watch and report, use a different number next time. I want to know if he leaves South America."

"Understood."

There was a click and the phone went dead. David stood, his shoes cracked a few glass shards as he crushed the phone before tossing the pieces into the flames.

So, it was Michael who killed Anton, not this daughter as he had originally thought. David considered this news.

MICHAEL ANDERLE

Michael must be stuck in South America trying to hold to-gether Anton's children and making sure it didn't become a bloodbath.

Good.

That meant his trap had a better chance of succeeding. Without Michael, it wasn't very likely that Stephen or Bethany Anne would have enough skill to take out everything he had set up.

He smiled and reached for his coat.

It also meant that he could visit his home.

———

TQB Enterprises Company Jet, En Route to Colorado

Lance was working on his laptop. There were a lot of changes required to turn the base he was accustomed to running into one where they could consolidate all of the research and development from companies presently located all over the world.

Patricia had her own laptop open, but wasn't looking at it. Rather, she was looking at the man across from her.

She spoke up, "How can you be so calm?"

Lance looked up from his spreadsheets and charts. "I'm sorry, what did you say?"

"I asked, how can you be so calm with what's going on in Turkey?" She wanted to sit next to him, but the seats on this jet weren't set up that way.

"Learned in the service. You train your people. You set up the operation based on the best intel you have. After that, if you aren't an active part of the operation, you focus on what

247

you can do to move the strategy forward. We can't sit on our hands and worry, it's not productive and it causes ulcers. I have to trust that she has trained her teams well. And that they will take care of her and things will be ok."

Patricia thought about what he said and decided he was right. Sitting on her hands when they had stuff to do wasn't helping the bigger picture.

Firing up her laptop, she started asking him about what would be needed across the base. Everything from modifications to living quarters, to upgrading security in certain areas. Further, they needed to refurbish old buildings and build out new services for civilians that would be on the base soon.

At the end of the planning session, she looked at the bottom line. "Lance, that's a hell of a budget. That's enough to run a small country."

Lance answered, "It is. The Federated States of Micronesia's GDP is somewhere around three hundred thirty-nine million and they aren't even the smallest. So yes, it is a hell of a budget."

"How are we going to pay for it all?"

He smiled, affecting a British accent. "Commerce, my dear Patricia, commerce!" He sobered. "Truthfully, we're going to be releasing new technologies. The licensing and manufacturing of those new technologies will bring in billions. That's why I'm spending so much on upgrading the base. We'll have three layers of security. One for getting onto the base and operating with a large contingent of the people. Then the secured areas, and finally the black secured areas. I've thrown in a couple of red herring locations as honeypot traps to capture anyone looking for the inside areas. Not sure they're needed but I felt it was important. Hell, just those traps alone are five million."

Patricia pursed her lips. "Billions you say?"

Lance nodded and looked back down at his laptop.

"Budget?" she said as she went back to her spreadsheet. "We don't need no stinking budget!"

CHAPTER TWENTY-THREE

Turkey,
thirty miles from the Syrian border

Gabrielle went into the cave and then brought out and handed Bethany Anne her katanas. Both her original and the one that Stephen had gifted her.

Bethany Anne regarded her new katana, watching the moonlight gleam across its sharpened blade as she turned it over and back again. "Shall we dance by the pale, pale moonlight?" she asked in a whisper.

Stephen and Gabrielle looked at their Queen, wondering what she was up to. With her eyes closed Bethany Anne bent her neck to the left, then slowly bent it over to the right, hearing her bones crack. Finally, she moved her neck in a circle and when she opened her eyes they were aflame, her fangs descending. Stephen and Gabrielle stepped back, realizing they were too close for her to use her swords effectively.

She turned around, those that were with her stared,

their eyes drawn to her face. "I have had enough of David's bullshit, I have had enough of these fucking Nosferatu, we end this now, we end this here. He thinks he has enough out there to overrun us?" Her voice got louder, "He thinks a few hundred Nosferatu is enough to swamp the Queen BITCH, Her GUARDS and Her GUARDIANS?" He eyes became blood red, glowing in the night. "We do *not* yield, we do *not* give up, and we do *NOT* cower for *anyone* or *anything*!"

The roars of her team swept down the valley. Not far away, the PKK unit David had conscripted to work the missiles and equipment to keep the team stuck without air support or communications heard them. They heard the savageness and animal growls and looked at each other in confusion. They had seen the monsters in the night that attacked those by the cave and were shaken to their core. Now, the defenders had additional support. The night became deadly, like the violence was waiting on a string to break.

Bethany Anne, resplendent, the moonlight glinting off the butts of her twin pistols and katana turned around, eyeing the lane that she could hear the Nosferatu running down.

"FUCK THIS SHIT!" She took off towards the Nosferatu.

Gabrielle followed her queen, Eric yelling behind her, "Here we go again!"

John replied, "Not this time. This time I'm getting a piece of my OWN!"

Stephen smiled, running to catch up to his daughter. God he loved his Queen!

Gunfire from Dan, Scottie and Lucas could be heard above the growls, and screams, of the Nosferatu. Even louder than the yelling of those behind him, Stephen could hear Bethany Anne's voice from ahead, "LET THE BATTLE COMMENCE YOU COCK-EATING SHEEP FUCKERS!" Then there was the unique sound of swords cutting through flesh.

Stephen was around the corner, with Gabrielle right beside him and was shocked to see the bodies had already started piling up around his queen. She looked to be covered in blood, but it was damned hard to see with the speed at which she was moving.

That was the last opportunity he had to watch her, as he slammed into his own horde.

———

Back at the cave, Pete was pissed. He had to hold a few of his squad back to help cover the door and protect those inside. Todd's squad was with him, as well as Art, the surviving American soldier.

Bobcat was pitching a fit at not already being involved in shooting something.

So far, none of the Nosferatu had made it past the front line, wherever the hell that was.

Pete turned when he heard the door behind him unlatch and Nathan walked through. He was bloody. Most of it, Pete could see, was Nathan's own blood.

Nathan had always been known for his fighting abilities, and his lethality. Pete could understand the reality of it, when he had seen the devastation that Nathan had wrought.

When Nathan looked over at Pete, Pete was surprised to see a glacially cold pair of eyes regard him. Nathan walked

MICHAEL ANDERLE

calmly to the men and said, "I take it that Bethany Anne couldn't wait for them to come to her?"

Multiple heads shook back and forth

"She always seemed a little headstrong to me. Guess that comes with being one of the baddest-ass people on the planet."

Bobcat grumped, "I think she had the attitude from before, you know?"

The chuckles relieved some of the tension.

Dan called from above, "Looks like a group of maybe fifty are detouring around the group up front, heads up!"

Nathan took command and strode forward. "Rifleman in the back, Weres up front."

Pete jogged to catch up to Nathan. "Hey? How are you going to change?"

Nathan looked over at Pete, a grim smile on his face. "I'm just going to think about my mate back in that cave, and about the fucking Nosferatu who put her there coming to finish…" Nathan's voice grated as his body changed into the massive werewolf, standing a foot and a half taller than Pete now. "The job."

The PKK men all shivered when a wolf's howl tore through the night.

There hadn't been any wolves in this area for a long, long time.

Pete considered Nathan's answer, thinking about his sister back in the cave.

Seconds after the first howl, a second echoed through the valley, confusing the PKK men even more.

There was a crescendo of rifle cracks as the men on the ground behind the Wechselbalg and up top continued firing as well. Only one time did a Were, Matthew, cry out,

"Fucking shit! Watch where you're shooting before I shove that rifle up your ass!"

Ashur barked his agreement. He was busy grabbing a leg and pulling a Nosferatu out of the horde. When the Nosferatu's head would explode from one or two shots, Ashur would jump back towards the front line and do it again.

His white coat was a mess, drenched with blood.

Kevin Russel yelled back to Matthew, "My bad!"

———

Ten minutes into the fighting, the Nosferatu pulled back and retreated down the lanes they had come up.

The three vampires lowered their weapons, confusion on their faces.

Bethany Anne asked no one in particular as her fangs retracted, "What the hell?"

Stephen looked down the now empty street, littered with bodies. "They are regrouping, coming up with a new strategy. I think, they thought to release them and that their natural desire for blood would be enough to overwhelm us by sheer numbers. Whoever is in charge is setting up new commands, a logical strategy."

Bethany Anne followed Stephen's gaze. "Back to the cave. I'll meet you there." She turned back to her team. "They wanted a fight? We gave them a fight. They wanted a massacre? I'll make sure we cram a massacre up their asses." She tossed her blades to Gabrielle, then whistled for Ashur. She took a step, grabbed Ashur and disappeared.

———

Michael was ready. He had been contacted by Frank earlier and when he had hung up, the blood in his body began pumping in anticipation.

He would be sorely upset if he didn't get a chance to vent a little frustration.

If there was anything that Michael had plenty of right now, it was frustration.

He was dressed in black, his favorite color when on a date to a bloodbath. Bethany Anne invited him to the nicest of get togethers.

Because there was one thing that most didn't learn about Michael, Patriarch of the Nacht.

Michael was always at his best when it came time to kill.

He stood against the wall of the room where Bethany Anne had arrived before. He had been waiting for over an hour and a half when she appeared. She was covered from head to foot in blood. Ashur was with her and Michael could barely see little patches of white through the blood and dust that covered his body.

Michael walked over. "You started without me." He held out his arm.

Bethany Anne reached out, grabbing Michael by the forearm. "It was only a few hundred, and I was getting my mad on."

"What changed?"

She smiled. "I didn't want to hear your whining for the next two centuries about how I left you behind."

Michael would have been offended, if her smile and the glint in her eye hadn't told him that she was happy to have him.

Then the three of them disappeared.

UNDER MY HEEL

He arrived with Bethany Anne and Ashur in a darkened valley. An old town with the corpses of Nosferatu littering the place. He saw that many had been decapitated. He turned when he heard steps behind him.

Stephen said, "It is good to see you, brother."

Gabrielle and Bethany Anne's mouths dropped open in surprise. Looking at each other and then back at the two men who had pulled each other into a great bear hug, Michael obviously ecstatic over Stephen's greeting.

Michael replied, "The same, Stephen. I'm glad to be back in my right mind and I am thankful for your forgiveness."

Stephen looked at him. "You came when my Queen needed you. I can do no less than accept you back into the family, even if you can be a..." He turned to look at his daughter, "What was that you said earlier?"

Gabrielle blushed and mumbled, "Egotistical wank-sack."

Stephen turned back to Michael. "Yes, even if you can be an egotistical wank-sack."

Bethany Anne felt a jab in her ribs, and turned to see Gabrielle staring at her and then pointing towards the two men with her eyes. Her mouth formed the words 'ask them!'

Bethany Anne rolled her eyes, but Gabrielle had a good question. "Hey, are you two really brothers, or is this some bullshit that you've made up?"

Michael stepped away from Stephen, and waved to him for the answer. The two women turned towards Stephen. "I disowned him centuries ago, after he had changed me. I didn't want this life; I had been happy. I've never treated him as anything more than the Patriarch since that time."

Bethany Anne interrupted, "Wait a second, you told me

earlier you are over nine centuries old."

Stephen smiled. "I am."

She pointed to Michael. "But he's over ten centuries old."

Michael answered, "Ten centuries is more than nine, Bethany Anne. My brother never would let others know enough to put together that we are related. I have never treated him as anything less than a child of mine, hoping that one day he would forgive me."

The four vampires looked up to where Dan and his group were when he called out, "Here they come again."

Bethany Anne started back towards the camp, Ashur running ahead of her.

Gabrielle asked, "You aren't charging off, running ahead of your protection again?"

Bethany Anne smiled as she joined the group, everyone grinning as she came up. She looked around at her people, her friends, her guardians and her guards. "No. I'm good with them wasting their time trying to figure out a plan." She reached out for her katana, which Gabrielle handed back. "But I guaran-fucking-tee that no plan will ever survive contact with this enemy!"

Michael smiled. For the first time in a thousand years, he had his brother back. He turned towards the coming Nosferatu. He heard Bethany Anne speak behind him, "When we get them down to about fifty, would you please do your little magic-misty-stuff and take out the vampires controlling them?"

Michael looked over at this remarkable woman, one who was so much more than the person he chose to become the mother of his children. He grinned. "I would be delighted to do that for you."

Huh, she thought, maybe you can get more with honey than vinegar.

Art looked around at this newcomer. He wasn't sure who the fuck these people were, or where they had come from. He sure as fuck didn't know how he was going to explain all of it to his superior officer back at the base. But there was one thing that he was absolutely, the fuck, certain of. He never wanted to be on the opposite side of any of these people. Then he looked over at the two men who suddenly blurred and changed into massive werewolves. Well, he corrected, any of these beings.

But on the other hand, he was having the time of his life and every time he killed another of these fuckers, he would remember his seven fallen comrades and recite their names under his breath.

The cracks above them signaled that the fight had started. Every human, Were, Vamp and Guard there turned and started walking out to create a perimeter. Bethany Anne took point slightly left, Michael took point slightly right. Stephen was next to him and Gabrielle was next to her.

Bethany Anne's guards pulled their weapons and stood behind them. Pete and Nathan took the positions outside of the vampires, spreading out.

Like David had planned, it was a bloodbath.

But the bleeding ended up happening to the wrong side, not one of David's vampires, Nosferatu or PKK members made it out of that valley when the sun rose.

――――――

Denver, Colorado USA

Lance was happy. Patricia was working across from him, helping to move the base forward. Captain Paul Jameson had forwarded the news that Bethany Anne and most of the team had made it through their fight and were safe.

Now, he just had one monumentally important job to complete. He took a deep breath and exhaled as he watched the runway of his former base coming into view.

———

Robert McCarty, the head of the Corps of Engineers walked into Hanger 1. He greeted his men and shook hands all around.

They were here for two reasons. One, to meet with the new civilian owners who had purchased the rights to use the base for ninety-nine years. And two, to see if there were any shenanigans involved.

Every one of his men, some very adept at research on the internet, had tried to find out more about the company, but they hadn't been given enough information to go on. So, they had all decided to meet the man, get his name, and force him to tell them more about what was happening.

Robert had gone to go talk with Kevin Mccoullagh and it had seemed that Kevin wasn't coming completely clean with him. Rather, Kevin had claimed he had no proof, just really strong supposition that this wasn't the civilian side getting the better of the military again. Finally, Kevin told him what time the plane should be arriving and invited Robert to be waiting when the corporate guy stepped off.

Robert had gotten a little salty with Kevin, but that hadn't worked so he left the office.

Robert took Kevin's advice and now he and his men were here to meet the new head honcho, and get the dirt on him.

The plane landed and taxied over to the hangar. It stopped

outside and the men walked around to view the door of the plane, which cracked open a couple of minutes after the plane's engines powered down.

The plane was beautiful, a G550 pristine from tip to tail. Just like a civilian hotshot who was full of himself would fly around in, someone behind Robert muttered.

When Robert turned to see who might have spoken out, he noticed Kevin standing twenty yards behind them. Kevin smiled and gave him a two-fingered salute in acknowledgment. Robert nodded and turned back around.

The men's anticipation turned to surprise when the first person off of the plane was General Lance Reynolds, the very man who had commanded most of them for their Army careers.

You could have cut the silence with a knife.

Robert swung his head back around, but Kevin wasn't in the same place, so he turned back to Lance and started walking over to the man he knew better than his own brother.

God, he looked so young!

Lance held his hand out as he walked over. "Hello Robert. Good to see you here."

Robert shook Lance's hand. "General, it's pretty damn good to see you here, too. At least, I think it is. But you have to know I'm confused as hell."

Lance nodded and turned to view all of the people in front of him. "Guys, I wish I hadn't needed to be so secretive. But since the news is out, this base is now under my command again."

Lance bit down on the word command and the guys subconsciously stood a little straighter. "I can't give you details, not yet. But this commercial venture is going to change the world in a good way. We need a lot done, but I can't do it without some kickass Army Engineers who know how to dig shit up and pack it down. I have two of the things that have been lacking here at this base for a while. That's a massive infrastructure build plan for modifications and a real-by-the-gods budget to get shit done."

He looked at each of them, trying to catch each eye, if only for a second. "Do all of you know why I *know* I have a budget?" He didn't wait for the joke he could almost feel that one or two of the men wanted to shout out. "That's because *I* approved the damn budget!"

With that, he got some cheers. If there was anything these men hated, it was being asked to design plans and then, with all the preliminary work done, being told 'there is no budget.'

Lance continued, "Before the word gets around, I'll tell you people straight up, I'm the reason this base is going civilian. Why? Because it's the perfect location, with the right people in place. We're going to build the world's safest research, development and distribution location, for the most cutting edge world-shattering technology the world has ever known."

He smiled. "Now, there's one more person I would like to introduce." Lance turned around and waited as a woman in a black turtleneck, grey palazzo pants, and medium heel grey suede pumps came into view. At first a couple of the guys had no idea who the good looking woman was. As she stepped down the stairs and strode up to Lance she greeted a few of the men by name.

Lance smiled at Patricia. "I would like to introduce my right hand woman, the lady who made all of this possible."

Patricia was smiling, she had dressed up for this trip. As much for Lance himself as for anyone she would meet on the trip. When she looked in the mirror this morning, she admitted to herself if no one else—she looked damn good in this outfit.

Lance got her attention. "Patricia, there is one more thing I need you to view, before we resume looking over the base."

Patricia turned towards Lance, smiling. It felt so good to see these people again!

Then, the blood drained from her face as she watched Lance get on one knee in front of everyone there.

He reached into his pocket and pulled out a small wooden box. Looking up into her tearing eyes, Lance Reynolds said in a strong voice, "For many years you have completed me in every way. I want to share the rest of my life with you, by my side and in my heart. I promise to always love you, to carry your heart as the dearest thing entrusted to me and to never leave you." Lance opened the box. A beautiful multi-carat round diamond set in a platinum ring sat on a dark blue velvet background. "Patricia Helena, would you marry me?"

Catcalls and shouts engulfed them. Patricia could barely recognize Lance through the tears flowing down her face. She couldn't speak, the lump in her throat was getting in the way, so she nodded her head vigorously and opened her arms. Lance Reynolds stood up, grabbing Patricia in a hug that lifted her off of her feet and swung her around.

The men, their concerns and worries forgotten, swarmed the newly engaged couple.

CHAPTER
TWENTY-FOUR

Kevin Mccoullagh was waiting for Lance when he finally stepped out of the throng of engineers, holding Patricia's hand. She was using a tissue to dab at her eyes.

He held his hand out. "General, or should I say, 'Mr. Reynolds?'"

Lance smiled at him, and used his left hand to reach over and grab Kevin's. Winking at him, Lance didn't release Patricia's hand so he could shake.

Kevin nodded his approval and smiled at them.

"Kevin, you've been with me long enough, call me whatever the hell you want."

Patricia let go of Lance's hand and stepped forward to receive a hug from Kevin, "Good to see you again." Patricia stepped back and grabbed Lance's hand again.

Lance looked Kevin up and down. "Keeping trim I see."

"Trying my best."

"I need you here, if you're willing." That was Lance, ever the straightforward type with him. Kevin had always appreciated it.

"I can be, if all of this," he waved a finger in a circle, "isn't just a money grab."

Lance's face went from fun to frowning in a quick second. "Kevin…"

Kevin was quick to put up his hands. "Sorry, General. But I needed to know how much you might have changed and you've answered my question." He looked over at Patricia. "What with you finally getting a clue about some things."

Lance grumped, "Had a little help with the clue. But I get your point."

Patricia added, "A clue that was connected to a two by four."

Kevin's face scrunched up. "That bad?"

Lance looked a little embarrassed. "Yes, pretty much."

Patricia came to Lance's aid. "In his defense, it wasn't a long time from two by four to being a gentleman."

Lance looked over at his fiancé. "Lady, I can't risk you on the market! Someone without my hard head would recognize your worth and I'd lose my chance. Hell no." He reached around her shoulders and pulled her in tighter. She rested her head on his chest. He looked back over at Kevin. "I'll bring you in as soon as you're out of the service. I don't want a conflict of interest on your conscience."

Kevin put his hand out. "We out to save something big, General?"

Lance smiled and shook his hand. "Think bigger than big, Kevin." With that, he winked at Kevin and he and Patricia walked towards the operations area.

Kevin let his hand drop to his side. Lance had never been much of a kidder, why would he say he should think bigger?

Then, Lance yelled back to him as they went through a door, "You're not thinking big enough, Kevin!" Kevin caught Lance's wink before he disappeared.

———

Turkey

Michael had moved on once he had taken out the vampires that controlled the Nosferatu. He continued his search and found the PKK contingent. Capturing the leader, he killed the rest.

He found the equipment that they had been using to block the communication signals. He 'turned it off' by picking up the hundred pounds of equipment and casually flinging it off the cliff to land three hundred feet below, shattering it into pieces that would probably be unearthed centuries in the future.

Bethany Anne translocated the three snipers down from their nest. Lucas and Scottie's faces were awed when they went from cliff face to ground. She had given Chris a little blood to help his brain heal. She asked Stephen why he hadn't done so. He explained that he hadn't been aware of the wound.

She confirmed for him that he was safe giving blood for just about any wound, it was the amount that was a concern.

The pods had been back earlier for the wounded Chris, Chet, Ecaterina and finally Paul's body. Nathan went with Ecaterina. Bobcat had accompanied Chris back.

Bobcat had spent a few minutes with the wreckage that

had been Shelly, gathering a few mementos that he found in the burned out shell.

Bethany Anne went over to talk with him for a minute, to let him know what would be happening in the near future. He nodded his head in acknowledgement and a few minutes later had been back in the camp.

Soon, the rest of the Guardians had left along with Scottie, Art, and Lucas. Leaving Bethany Anne, her Guard, Ashur and the vampires.

Bethany Anne was looking over the town, grey in the early morning light. She was reflecting on all of the death and despair that had been wreaked upon it by David, in his quest for power and control. Michael came up to stand beside her.

Michael spoke quietly, "It is this which I looked upon, time after time, sometimes created by humans, sometimes Wechselbalg, sometimes Vampires that caused me to create the Strictures."

Bethany Anne looked at the bleakness. "I understand."

Michael nodded. "I think that you do."

They stood there, silent for a few minutes. Taking in everything as the light grew brighter, colors coming back into the valley, shining a ray of truth upon the scene. A truth that had left the corpses of untold hundreds. Innocent people who had been used in David's effort to create the perfect trap.

Bethany Anne said in a small voice, "He has to die, Michael."

Michael answered, "That was foretold already, Bethany Anne. That isn't something I thought we would be discussing."

"No, not really discussing it. More like saying it so that I hear it. I will focus all of our efforts towards finding him. He can't be allowed the time to build another trap like this again."

Michael looked over and down at the woman beside him. "And what about those that helped them?"

"Hmmm?" She looked up to Michael, "Who?"

"The mole on the American Pack Council and those who wish to push their own agenda."

Bethany Anne pursed her lips, and considered what her teams needed to do. They had the beginnings now, the very beginnings to enable the push into space. There was so much more to accomplish. They could not afford to be constantly fighting subversive guerilla actions around the world while they were focused on saving it at the same time.

"Well, it doesn't make me happy, but I only have one answer for that."

Michael waited, he had learned patience.

She exhaled. "They will either kneel, or they will die."

She took one more look at the valley, and turned towards the waiting pods.

TOM, do you have the extra pod ready?

Yes, I moved it into a low earth orbit earlier.

Take us out of here, please.

The rest of the teams boarded the remaining pods, Michael needing to be shown how the doors worked. Ashur jumped into Bethany Anne's pod and growled when Michael acted like he was going to come too close. She smiled at Michael and closed the door.

Frankly, Bethany Anne wanted a little time to herself, even if it was only the ten minutes it took to get back to the ships.

No one was able to get any cell phone video of the pods. But there were some people who swore that they had seen little black helicopters screaming overhead, just a few feet above the treetops.

UNDER MY HEEL

Five minutes after they had left the valley, a 'meteorite' came flashing through the sky. It impacted dead center in the middle of that valley, destroying everything.

CHAPTER TWENTY-FIVE

The Queen Bitch's Ship Ad Aeternitatem

It was a somber crew that paid their dues to their fallen comrade, Paul Stevens, out at sea. They had played taps and gently laid him to rest in one of the pods before consigning it to the deep.

Bethany Anne had watched Paul's coffin, the first of many to come, slip beneath the waves. It was the first death for one of her team, it was just one of a long list of grievances that she had against the Forsaken. And against the Kurtherians, who had brought their war to her world.

They would get a chance to meet her soon enough, she thought. She would make sure that Paul Stevens' sacrifice was honored.

She stayed around for a while on the yacht, before she and Ashur took Michael back to Argentina. She surprised him by giving him a hug and a quiet 'thank you' before reaching down to grab Ashur, and they were gone.

Michael stared at the place that the two had occupied just moments before. His soft, "Your welcome," floated through the room.

He changed into myst, sweeping through the house and out into the night. He needed to find out what his uppity technician had gotten into while he was gone.

Stephen had held a meeting on each ship, with the crews. He wanted to make sure that everyone had a chance to review the operation. They discussed what had happened, what went well, and what could be changed.

All of the children, Art, the two ladies and the minister had their memories tampered with, to keep the details of what had actually occurred fuzzy. Michael had worked on Art for a while, to make sure everything he planted was correct. Michael had plenty of experience with military brass that kept poking when they couldn't get answers they liked.

The Polarus cruised west to arrive at Antalya before ferrying the rescued people over to a pier, using a boat from the Ad Aeternitatem.

Bethany Anne gifted the minister who had been chaperoning the children with a sizable anonymous donation. One that easily paid for anything that the ministry would need to do for the children for the next five years.

The two women received first class tickets and another two weeks paid in Antalya at one of the ritziest hotels. It was waiting for them three weeks later, after they had finished helping to get the children settled back into their homes.

Nathan had sent an email to Bethany Anne. It had a link that showed both Diane and Dorene in a photograph. The caption was about how both women had almost been arrested for pinching a man's butt as he passed by. They had sworn, the article said, to be good girls for the rest of their trip.

Art had arrived at a NATO military base riding on a bus. He could never explain how he had gotten back. It had taken him several hours to prove he was the person he claimed to be.

Both Scottie and Lucas had asked for reassignment to Todd's group.

Dan approved both reassignments.

Bobcat, William and Chris gathered together in the shop on the Ad Aeternitatem and raised a toast to Shelly.

Bobcat looked over at the original pod that William had built as he drank his beer. William and Chris followed his gaze.

William asked, "What's on your mind?"

"I think we have a new designation, guys."

"Oh?" William was confused. "For what?"

Bobcat pointed with the beer in his hand. "Not IZTAs... These will now be designated 'SHLYs.'"

Chris asked, "What does that stand for?"

Bobcat shrugged. "Beats the fuck out of me. But it sure as hell will be easier to dream up something that doesn't have a 'Z' in it." The guys' laughter met Marcus as he walked into the room.

As always, William had stuck with soft drinks and, unlike Chris and Marcus, didn't have a headache in the morning.

———

Key Biscayne, FL USA

Bethany Anne walked upstairs, drinking a glass of milk. John had arrived and called up to her ten minutes before. She was surprised when she went downstairs to find that John left a cake box with a note attached. She put the box on the table and pulled off the note.

It was from Mary, who was visiting her new home.

Mary noted that she didn't have much to say at the moment, but she would 'come visit' soon. She hoped Bethany Anne loved lemon cake, but it looked so good Mary had eaten a piece first 'just to make sure.'

Bethany Anne smiled while opening the box and found Mary was right on both accounts. The cake was missing a piece, and it was delicious.

Bethany Anne walked into her suite, setting down her milk to pick up her tablet computer when a headache hit her hard, again. She sat down on the couch and rubbed at her temple.

TOM, can't you do something about this fucking headache? God, it's killing me.

I'm sorry, Bethany Anne, but I'm not doing anything right now. As far as I can tell, the problem is an issue with the matrix computer in your brain.

Fuck! Shit almighty. If we can't figure out how to stop this... wait ... wait, it's gone. Thank God! What did you do?

Bethany Anne, I keep telling you, I'm not doing anything to cause it, or anything to stop it.

Both of them were shocked when a third voice entered their conversation.

>> I apologize. I was testing the capabilities of this computer I am housed within. I will not do so again without first consulting the power source I have inadvertently harmed. <<

Bethany Anne sat shocked, her whole body going numb as she considered the ramifications of what she thought she just heard.

TOM, tell me you're pulling my leg?

She was really, really hoping that TOM thought up a great April Fool's joke. Even if it would be months early.

Bethany Anne, I'm not in any position to pull anything. That wasn't me.

Bethany Anne put her head between her knees.

Oh, fuck my life.

MICHAEL'S NOTES

Under My Heel - The Kurtherian Gambit 06:
Written February 2, 2016

Thank you, I cannot express my appreciation enough that not only did you pick up the sixth book, but you read it all the way to the end and NOW, you're reading this as well. Since this book is part of a series, I am presuming you have blessed me by reading them all and what a fantastic feeling that is for any author!

Can you believe I'm writing another one of these in just twenty-two days from the last one? If you believe some on the author boards, this is heresy. If you believe some of the fans, they are wondering what the H#LL is taking me so long?

:-) <FANS WIN>

This book that you have just completed (Right? Because if you didn't and I throw a spoiler (*Lance proposed to Patricia*) then SHAME ON YOU!)

Mwuhahahaha… That will teach you not to jump to the end first.

My plan is a book about every 30 days. Not that I've accomplished that goal yet, they are always earlier than 30 days, but that is my goal. I do expect it to take over 30 days between book 7 (the next book) and the following Book 8. Why? Because I have to (gasp) add a bunch of front matter to 'catch up' those who haven't been reading the series (off with their little pinkies for that).

We Will Build - Book 8 is what I understand to be called an 'entry point' for a reader. A book that allows readers to get into the story without missing too much. If you would like to know the titles for the next few books, check out the very, very end of book 5. I did that whole 'Marvel ending' where I added stuff past the credits and the reviews.

The tales of a newbie author - part six. (Or, what has Michael been up to lately?)

I've worked with some editing help and beta readers for Under My Heel that has been pretty freaking cool, I have to admit. I have written chapters for this book and then at a stopping point, dropped that info to my helping editor who tries his dead level best to clean up my writing. I move his comments back into the main file and then drop a file to the Beta reading group who reviews and finds the huge amount of mistakes I STILL didn't catch.

While the beta readers are reviewing, I'm busy writing more story. Beta catches are integrated into the file and I drop the new chapters back out to the helping editor and the virtuous cycle begins again.

This means that when I was 'words complete' (a totally made up phrase by yours truly), the beta team had already completed 11 chapters of review and had the first 20 chapters under review the very next day. They are getting the full manuscript with a first pass completed tonight (48 hours after I completed the story).

That is FREAKING FAST. I swear, it seems like I completed this story a week ago, not 48 hours ago.

I explain all of this to let you know that we are all working on an amazing system to turn these books around with a couple of legitimate review passes to catch mistakes in … <author adds the sums, carries the four… gets a calculator… looks at the calendar…> off the top of my head? About twenty-four days.

Purchased vs. Kindle Unlimited update. As we go into book six, the Kindle Unlimited side is ahead in gross sales vs.

The Kindle purchased group. Income is still 55% Unlimited vs. 45% purchased (after Amazon's cut). I'm still considering going wide when I hit the 6 month mark with Death Becomes Her. By that time (Early April) I should have the first in the NEXT Arc going which I will have in Kindle Unlimited for three months minimum.

Then again, Kindle Unlimited has been very good to me. Besides book sales, there have been over a million pages read of the five books so far. My feeling is that at some point, I will have hit all of the KU readers with the first ARC I'm likely to easily attain. Then the KU pages read will go down to where I *need* to go wide and get the books in front of the people who don't read Kindle books (I know, you're asking, "Who doesn't read on Kindle?") It's mainly Apple iBooks right now. Plus, there are a bunch of non-United States English readers who use their phones as a reading device... Apple reaches these readers very well I'm led to believe.

Plus, Kobo in other countries.

But WAIT, Mike, how will I go about getting my Bethany Anne fix if not on KU? All new stories WILL be on KU for 3 months, minimum. One thing I have to consider, is that if I choose to continue 'All In' with Amazon I need to believe that the 800 lb Gorilla is looking out for the tiny mid-list author like yours truly. Right now, they keep dropping the amount they pay for the pages read in KU. I was not involved when it was 'amazing' at 0.0058. I came on board at 0.0048 per page (a little under 1/2 a cent). Last month, it went down to 0.0046. I'm ok with this, but if the future is a constant drive to lower and lower amounts, I need to stick a leg out and test the waters at some point elsewhere. Better with the first Arc than the latest Arc, I would think.

Speaking of surprises in this book (I did, look WAY above at Lance and Patricia getting hitched.) Anyway, I had NO idea that was happening. I hadn't planned it, I hadn't considered it in this book. There Lance was, telling the engineering group about building up the base and when he introduces Patricia I was thinking, 'You B@astard! You're going to propose right in the middle of my scene!'

I might have teared up while writing. I also might have had to go and find a proper proposal speech online. One of those statements is absolutely true.

I'm not admitting anything.

I love the Tabitha addition to Michael's team. Her comment "*Well, slap a bitch and make her howl,*" just cracked me up. I'm worried I might have multiple personalities (no one has ever told me this) because I don't personally think like this.

No, truly. You can stop laughing, I'm not joking here.

The stuff that flies off the keyboard comes from somewhere… deep and mysterious in my unfathomable mind. <— < *Author is HOWLING in laughter at that comment. His wife as well if / when she reads this.*>

At the very end of this book I have cut and pasted reviews from book 1 (to date) - I respond and I'm f'ing fun! Still reaching for a minimum of 50 reviews for the books, ESPECIALLY book 1. When we reach 50 on book 1, I won't be placing review comments in the back of the book. If you would like to forever be captured in (e)print, *don't* hesitate to put up your review today! (I'm shilling like a villain <smile>).

Every single review is a badge of honor I own proudly and thank you from the bottom of my heart for writing them. Occasionally, you drop a note to let me know you put a review on ALL of the books, thank you for that as well.

I've mentioned before, my writing is more escapist. I love a good action story, but more than that I want to engage with the characters. I want to feel what they are going through if possible. I want situations that make me get excited, worried, laugh and say 'take that, sucka!' out loud. The challenges faced by the protagonists don't have to be life threatening, it could be a challenge to ask that special someone out for a date that keeps the story flowing. I'm not really into books that keep you constantly afraid for the characters. If I care about a character, I'll turn the page, and buy the next book, just to see them reach a personal milestone that is challenging to that character. However, having said that, all of that action is what drives the story forward.

Please, if you enjoyed this book give it a good rating on Amazon? Your kind words and encouragement help any author. I will continue to the next story whether you provide an OUTSTANDING review or not. But it might get done a wee bit faster with the encouragement (wink).

** Note: If you would like the $0.99 pre-official-full-price-release message, please sign up on the email list - I'm going to keep doing this for each new release moving forward, so when released early, the price is $0.99 for a minimum of 24 hours **

If you want to help make the books better and receive an advanced copy, please consider the Advance Team project please catch me on Facebook and let me know your interested.

You can find book links on my Amazon Author Page here: http://www.amazon.com/Michael-Anderle/e/B017J2WANQ/

Want to comment on the best (scene, comment, event, shoes or gun for Bethany Anne, weapon Nathan would prefer... you name it) join me on Facebook: https://www.facebook.com/TheKurtherianGambitBooks/

Want to know when the next book or major update is ready? Join the email list, get that $0.99 24 hour bonus knowledge in time to SCORE.
http://kurtherianbooks.com/email-list/

Software used to write this book is Scrivener (Windows and Mac):
https://www.literatureandlatte.com/scrivener.php

Book Cover Images purchased at PhotoDune.net: http://photodune.net & http://www.dreamstime.com
(Sometimes better selection on www.dreamstime.com - TKG05)

Image software to make the cover (Mac): http://www.pixelmator.com/mac/ (1.6 ratio @ 300dpi)

Image software to make the 3d book Covers: http://www.Adobe.com/photoshop

3d Template Script: http://www.psdcovers.com

Thank you,

Michael Anderle, Feb 2016

*All credit for me having ANY shoe knowledge goes to my wife, who still works to provide me with even a finger's amount of fashion sense. Why she asks me to comment on her outfits in the morning still confuses me to this day.

P.S. ** Rough Translation for Giannini when she spots Tabitha w/her laptop on her car hood: "How rude! Do you Americans always act in this way in your own country? Simply placing equipment wherever it suits you?"

REVIEW REMARKS

I'm a REBEL, Not listening to 'The Man' when I do this… Because I can… Because I can…

Review Comments

This is my 'Middle Finger Salute' to **being told to not** say 'thank you' to reviewers on reviews. Even if your review isn't… nice (sniff, sniff).

But then, if you have made it to book SIX and are reading this far, I doubt that you wrote a one or two star review (back on Death Becomes Her) and continued reading… So I guess this will be for Reviews with three stars and above. If you did put a 1 or 2 star review and are reading the end of this book, what the h#ll?

Ok, sorry, I just thought that was funny. Let me know on Facebook and I'll included your review and republish w/ the next version.

Michael Anderle

———

Wow, blending some of my favorite genres and a great way with great pacing, characters and fast release schedule!

By Amazon Customer on January 13, 2016
Format: Kindle Edition

I have just finished book 5 (via Kindle Unlimited). This

series is great! I have read hundreds of kindle books both purchased and thru unlimited and this is one of the best. By best I don't mean the most meaningful or deep but certainly the most fun in quite a while. These books have cost me a lot of sleep and productivity at work and I love it. I can't put them down! Thank you so much for this series and the great pace of releasing books. Reminds me of P.S. Power at how fast he sends out content!

Just so people know for their own buying decision. I love 'world building' fiction, urban fantasy, and science fiction. This series blends all three in a very interesting and engaging way. Sometimes you have put up with a slow pace in world building books to account for the tech development and character power advancement but you get that here with great action and cheer to yourself moments. I really love the series so far and can't wait for the next installment! Going to start over and read again from the beginning and hope it holds me over until the next book.

Thanks again! You are awesome

(btw, there are some editing issues but to me they are minor and I can read thru them easily. I am pretty impervious to those in good, fast, inexpensive books) I would much rather he spend time on speed and content than get too bogged down in editing. Perfect is the enemy of good!

Michael - Thank you Amazon Customer ;-) - I have to give a bit of Kudos to P.S. Power myself. It was during his Alternate Places (Mr. Hartley) series that I really 'felt' that if I enjoyed a book such as this one, with mistakes etc. etc., that I could probably write a series others might enjoy as well. At least, it gave me the permission to try, which was super important.

Anytime I'm told (reviews, email, Facebook) that someone has gone back through and read the series again? Priceless! It means I've created characters which mean something to you. So, a person or team I would want to be around, is the same sort that you would like to be around. Thank you!

———

Five Stars

By Dot Little on January 14, 2016
Format: Kindle Edition

A great read from start to finished. Looking forward to more books from this author.

Michael - Thank you Dot! Also, I appreciate your dropping by on Facebook and engaging on the page. It isn't like I stalk or anything (the author is saying no, but his head is nodding yes?) <— *Not* concerning or anything…
I hope to keep you entertained for MANY, MANY more!

———

Loved this book

By collegechick88 on January 16, 2016
Format: Kindle Edition

Loved this book. That being said there is a lot of editing that still needs to be done. Story a solid 4 stars. Lack of editing took away a star. That being said the author does say that he publishes his books without editing them first. He says he does this so that readers who are eagerly awaiting the next book don't have to wait as long. After the new book is out he goes through and edits previous books. So if lack of editing is driving you nuts try again in a couple of months.

Michael - Thank you CollegeChick88! You are absolutely right on the previous editing. I have book #3 coming back today from an edit. The problem (which I didn't understand before) is that my edited books CAN'T seem to get out to those of you who have purchased them before. I've tried everything and I can't figure out how to get an update once I've downloaded a book.

———

Great story

By Kris R England on January 16, 2016
Format: Kindle Edition Verified Purchase

Will definitely read more of this series. Enjoyed the twists and turns in the story line. Like the writing and a tough female lead character.

Michael - Thank you Kris! I'm pretty partial to tough females as well. Not that I have anything against tough males, but they are kind of expected a lot of times. I've met some pretty tough females in my life that I admire. My biggest issues with some female lead characters is all of the 'should I do this, should I do that' questioning. This goes for both male and female leads.

I've never understood those with power and a purpose being indecisive. Maybe if they don't have a purpose, or lack some level of maturity you might vacillate on what to do, but when reading I'm ready for them to do something already!

Bethany Anne 'did' something with Nathan to help out, but she failed to give an update to the leader. So, she made a mistake. She accepted the responsibility and admitted she should have told him and then she moved on. No need to either be a jerk and ignore your mistake or think about your mistake for half a book. At least, that is my opinion.

———

Great Concept

By Kindle Customer on January 16, 2016
Format: Kindle Edition Verified Purchase

New take on vampires and aliens. Great characters and story. Looking forward to the next book to see what new twists the author creates.

Michael - Thank you, Kindle Customer! ;-) New twists… I mentioned earlier about Lance proposing to Patricia, and Stephen back in Queen Bitch being complete surprises when writing them. There are others if I thought about it long enough. This writing is not what I though it would be, exactly.

I figured as the author, I would always be able to direct the story. However, my subconscious (and wife) sometimes have ideas that should be integrated that I hadn't considered. I have also deleted a paragraph or two when I send a character on a path and I realize they wouldn't *DO* that. It does make it easier to write scenes.

For example, when Bethany Anne goes after the Nosferatu in the village and Eric comments, "Here we go again!" - It was super simple to know 'who' would say that. Eric just has the mouth out of the group. Scott is quieter and more introspective, generally. I'm not sure how much of what I know about the characters makes it to the page, but I hope all of the characters eventually get their moments in the spotlight.

———

A good read.

By Elizabeth adams on January 19, 2016
Format: Kindle Edition

Not sure what I expected when I started this series. But was very pleasantly surprised. It takes a different and enjoyable plot twist and make for a fun read.

Michael - Thank you Elizabeth! I am going for a fun read. It's hard sometimes to realize where we are in the story and just how much everything has grown (people, plot, abilities, resources). We have all read over 400,000 words to get where we are.

That's a lot of words. We have two yachts worth hundred's of millions, places in multiple places around the world and I've been TRYING to keep the locations relatively consistent without just sending us everywhere.

We still haven't even made it back to Michael's house… Which I had *planned* on blowing up back in Bite This.

I'm curious about Michael's house in New York. Not sure why that didn't go 'boom', must be some reason.

You will find out when I do!

———

A five star story despite the imperfections

By Big Ben on January 20, 2016
Format: Kindle Edition Verified Purchase

There are a few pages of author's notes at the back of each of the first three books I've read. Therein he repeatedly states that he's writing fun stories, not great literature. Much like Star Wars isn't great cinema, but it is hella fun ... His words, or close enough.

And he is exactly right, both about Lucas' work and his own.

These are superbly fun stories, combining modern paranormal, sci-fi and military action into a cohesive whole that blasts through the imagination like Han and Chewie in the Falcon.

The author never promises technical perfection - states it right up front in each of his books, in fact. But for me, at least, the quality of the storytelling overrides such minor concerns.

Plus, he's cranking them out at a rate of one or more books per month - and while these aren't epic novels, they're each a few hours of very enjoyable reading.

They say that quantity has a quality all it's own. When you can get a healthy dose of both, it's worth five stars.

Michael - Thank you for making my evening when I read this, Big Ben. I had forgotten about writing 'hella fun' in my author notes until you referenced it above in your review. I can't say say much more or I'll feel like I'm tooting my own horn w/ your review!

You do make one point I like, they are *fast* books. By that, I mean that the action is constant and something is happening. Even if the action is the President of the company bringing his two children to work with him. It isn't always about someone shooting someone else, or other 'high' action. But sometimes it is the small stuff, like going to a grave site.

<I had tears during *that* chapter more than once.>

———

Loved it!

By Zeus on January 21, 2016
Format: Kindle Edition Verified Purchase

I'm going to be lazy and cut n paste this review for the first five since they were all great. I found this gem at the back of a rather blah book I recently finished. Sounded interesting so I tried the sample. Hooked me immediately so I purchased this one. Half way through I purchased the next two. Half way through the second I purchased the rest. Less than two days later I finished all five. All I can say is, these books are a lot of fun with great characters and lots of action. Try the sample and if it interests you go for it. They only get better. Make sure you read the authors comments at the end. He is pretty straight forward about the editing etc. which is why I didn't really ping it in my review. Enjoy!

Michael - Thank you, Zeus! You mention here that you finished all five in 2 days. I've had other reviewers talk about reading their set in 36 hours (I imagine it is about the same for you).

Holy crap people, I thought I read fast! That is perseverance at its best. When I get the chance, I have to create something for those who shot-gunned the books when you first found them.

I tried doing a background for computer screens but I don't think it hit the mark. Just wasn't 'special' enough, you know?

I just need some feedback what the fans might want. Kind of like a card for those who 'drink the worlds beers' at a bar when they have tried them all? I can do something digital, and digitally sign them.

———

Wow!

By Mrs.T on January 23, 2016
Format: Kindle Edition

This book put a huge smile on my face as I read it. Sure, there were mistakes such as "there" instead of "they're", as well as dropping a word or two in a couple of sentences. But when you stack editing misses against a great story, great story wins out with me. The story has a nice switch on the vampire world, and Bethany Anne is not only a strong character but is also a likable one. Initially it was kind of confusing having different storylines happening, but they came together nicely and from there the book took off. This was such a fun read that I can't wait to tear into the next book.

Michael - Thank you, Mrs. T! I presume based on your comment above that you read Queen Bitch. I'm curious if you are reading this (and continued to this book?) Reach out and let an Author know! ;-)

Working on the editing, always. I hope the you enjoy the great story and I don't falter, I don't waiver, and I don't let all of you down!

———

Entertaining

By William W. Cotterman on January 23, 2016
Format: Kindle Edition Verified Purchase

Very good with entertaining use of profanity.

Michael - YES! Thank you William. I have SO much fun w/ profanity. There actually isn't much profanity in this book. Just not the same call for it, I guess. Maybe I got it out of my system? Man, I hope not. 8-o
  Yet, the very last sentence is 'Fuck my life'... Ooops ;-)

———

A 411 for interested parties:

By Lisa on January 23, 2016
Format: Kindle Edition

Ok here is a 411: if you are a perfectionist reader stop now, otherwise this an outstanding story. I'm already on book three and I started reading them today. The negatives: sometimes knowing which character is talking; happens a lot in the first book but evens out in the second, still happens but not as much. Sometimes inserts the wrong character name while they are talking or thinking. I do like that this is from an multiple characters point of view, but it can be difficult occasionally to follow because the transition is not always seamless. The grammar is ok but not perfect but did not take away from the story. The PROS: love the story line, love that is a continuation with lots of laughs and action. I'm looking forward to see where the author is going with this. I'm stopping now to read the third book, but because I'm digging this author I wanted to send a shout out!

Michael - Thank you Lisa! I sure hope that books 3,4, & 5 got better on the character names. I realize (as I have gone back through my own writing) how often the character names are messed up during my drafts. Lance and Frank are a particular problem for me. Not sure why. I love that you are 'digging the author' and wanted to send a shout out quickly.

Feel free to do that Every. Single. Time. ;-) (Not really, well - maybe… if you want to…)

———

Awesome

By Amazon Customer on January 24, 2016
Format: Kindle Edition Verified Purchase

Keep it coming

Michael - Thank you, Amazon Customer! (Boy, this 'Amazon Customer' writes a lot of reviews…)

Short, sweet, to the point. I don't suppose you are one of the fan's with the pitchforks and matches? (Grin)

I had one fan get on me about 9 days after the previous release to 'hurry up'. I had to go back to the calendar and ask myself just when I had dropped book #5… I'm thinking, "I'm pretty sure I should be allowed a little break between books."

I was dissuaded from that notion later in the evening

over on the Facebook page.

I have NO idea how someone like Christopher Nuttall or P.S. Power drops so many books. Even using dictation software (Dragon) to start writing some of the story, I don't think I want to can keep my head in the stories that much every day. I enjoy the marketing and other aspects too much.

I just checked, I started actually putting fingers to keyboard for Under My Heel on January 17th (thank you Facebook Page). Finished on January 31st. So, 71k words in 14 days. I didn't write every day (had a BIG project in the middle of all of that). So, call it 5k words a day on average.

———

Great read. Kinda found by accident 4 days ago

By Larry V. on January 24, 2016
Format: Kindle Edition

Great read. Kinda found by accident 4 days ago, tried it for free thru Kindle Unlimited....now I've purchased and read the next 4 in the series and waiting impatiently for #6. As well written as other "name authors" with established series in similar genres. Great characters, awesome story lines, and the world he has created is coherent and flows believably from a single factor (nanocytes that can be programmed to alter operate at the cellular level).

Michael - Thank you Larry! This review brings up an interesting question I've wondered. How many readers start with Kindle Unlimited, but then go and purchase the books?

Personally, I do one or the other. Perhaps, if I was going back to read something and the author had pulled out of

Kindle Select (which is for Kindle Unlimited) so they could sell in other ebook stores I might find and purchase the books. However, if I was reading the series I wouldn't think to purchase the series if I started in Kindle Unlimited.

As a Kindle Unlimited Author - If someone reads the books on KU, then goes and purchases the books for their own library I end up getting paid 2x. For six books in the series, that is both Starbucks and a ... Well, it is Venti Starbucks Vanilla Bean Frappacinno Double-Blended with whipped cream and a cake slice.

Twice. In Las Vegas.

Because, let's face it. The Starbucks in Las Vegas are more expensive than the one in the strip center near the grocery store. I can only imagine the cost of a Starbucks in downtown New York, so maybe only once there.

———

Awesome series! Read them all!

By starlight on January 25, 2016
Format: Kindle Edition

I just finished reading all five of the available books in this series, so I am reviewing them altogether since they are really one story. They are fabulous. Fast-paced, great characters, interesting story. I highly recommend them. The first book starts a little slowly but soon picks up and we are on our way.

Michael - Thank you Starlight! Really, aren't we all just one story? One little slice taken out like a Jackson Pollock painting from a large canvas?

<O.K., true story. In H.S. I had to do a 'Jackson Pollock' style painting on a posterboard. It was incredibly difficult. It wasn't until after H.S. that I found out Pollock would do these MASSIVE paintings, but cut out the pieces he liked. Not that I am bitter about it… still…. decades later… > :-)

Truly tho', thank you Starlight for your review and your comments on the great characters! I've often wondered about readers opinions, if Bethany Anne isn't your favorite character, who is?

I would think either Pete or Stephen would get the nod. Maybe Ashur. Just curious myself.

————

New favorite series!

By Kimmer17 on January 25, 2016
Format: Kindle Edition Verified Purchase

I am writing this review after reading both books 1 & 2. The first book is typically the set up and I wanted to verify the story was as great as book 1 lead me to believe. Yes, I love both the story and the heroine. I am very critical about how the h is portrayed in books, I can't stand TSTL, whinny, immature so called female leads. I want the h to be the h and not window dressing to be rescued. This book has a great storyline and an even better kickass h! I will definitely be buying each new release! Highly recommend!

Michael - Thank you Kimmer17! You wouldn't believe this, but I've been beating my head against the wall every time I read your review and saw 'TSTL'.

I just used this new thing… called the Internet? … To

look it up (I feel so stupid). "Too stupid to live."

Agreed! Can you be called a hero/heroine if you need rescuing all of the time yourself?

In this story, Bethany Anne gets some support, but she didn't 'need' Michael to save her. She was just pissed. More of a 'Oh! You think you have the problem solved? I'll be right back.' then bringing another big gun to the party.

Let's face it, Michael would have been bitching for a while if he hadn't had a chance to kill a few, too. As the author of the books, I didn't want to hear his !#!% in my head all of the time.

But did she 'require' Michael to help? No.

———

Really like the books

By Mike Garrett on January 26, 2016
Format: Kindle Edition

Really like the books, only drawback is the EXTREME language. Think about a book with a lot of swearing, then multiply it by 27. Not that it stopped me from reading the series, obviously. Character reminded me a bit of Chris Gordon and the other Vampire books where the vampire turns into Mist, can't remember the name off the top of my head.

Michael - Thank you Mike! Have you ever had something that would usually offend, but it is SO over the top that it is ludicrous? I hope that is how people enjoy the cussing.

I'm really familiar w/ Chris Gordon, one of my favorite series (I've mentioned elsewhere, at one point John Conroe spoke about how he saw Twilight (or read it?) and decided if that was a vampire book, he could write better!) I just got my kids on The Demon Accords a couple of weeks ago. One read them all, another stopped after book two or three as he felt Gordon was too powerful.

The other (I would guess) is possibly Connie Suttle. I've read a bunch of her stuff, but eventually had to stop because it seemed her heroines were always getting beat up and generally were wet noodles, yet had all of this power? Didn't make sense to me. That and the amount of names - I just couldn't keep track of them all.

Which reminds me, I need to do something about that for my fans as well. :-(

I do try to keep the names unique… Except Tom Billings and TOM. Heck, I don't have a ton of Mikes / Michaels or Jeff's in here. There were two Paul's, but one died in Turkey.

————

Great new Author!

By Amazon Customer on January 27, 2016
Format: Kindle Edition

Fair warning, there are some editing issues with this book and the next 2. At least there was when I read them. The Author is getting them fixed and so you might have a better copy. For me it can be annoying to have these kind of errors, as they can pull you out of the story. But I love the story and characters so much that I was not bothered by it. Other self published books that had these kind of errors would make we stop reading but I did not feel that way with this series.

I also really like that the author does not repeat a lot of descriptions from book to book like most authors are doing these days. It always seems like authors think we just jump right in at book 4 and skip 1-3. I have never known anyone that does that. I personally think it is the mark of a lazy writer that wants to increase their word count. I end up skipping paragraphs or pages when this happens, I did not feel the need to do that with these books. The really amazing part is how fast he is writing these books. He has produced 5 books in less than 3 months. I sure hope he can keep up the pace :) LOL.

Michael - Thank you Amazon Customer! (You get around, I swear). I think maybe your the first review (that I can recall) that mentioned the lack of previous story 'reminders' from book to book. No, wait, there is another - there has to be because otherwise I wouldn't have added 'YOU PRETTY MUCH HAVE TO' otherwise. But, I'm not sure about the lazy writer thought. I read like you do, skipping whole paragraphs and pages, which is why I don't do it in my books.

Not to mention I'm all about the story, not dredging up something you have probably just read, or read within the last 30 days. It is a personal preference based on my reading style. I'm confident that other fans miss the method and appreciate it. As I mentioned in the author notes, I'll be doing that as a BIG chapter one in Book 8 (2 books from this one) so new readers can start when we go L.E.O. If they don't want the story so far.

Episode IV - A New Hope anyone?

I sure hope I can keep up the pace! ;-)

———

Unusual but intriguing

By Lisa M on January 30, 2016
Format: Kindle Edition

I loved his character strong emphasis on the characters. The only thing keeping it from a 5 was the frequent breaks to Change locations, and while I can't figure out how it could have been done better, I did find it jarring. This looks like a series I will enjoy following ... We'll see.

Michael - Thank you Lisa "M"! How in the world did we get two Lisa's in these reviews? I understand your comment on the change locations. I've tried to mitigate that issue; however, I didn't come up with a good solution either.

I do that because I'm kind of older now, and my elastic mind doesn't appreciate filling in the blanks. So, I add it to the beginning when we change major locations to allow me to quickly understand where the action is taking place (as a reader I appreciate it more than it bugs me). I'm open to listening to any suggestions that the fans might have.

An additional issue is that often, these stories are all happening at the same time, so I can't do two weeks of story and then go back and talk about the same two weeks in another plot line. You get issues when the two overlap (like a phone call) and you receive too many hints about what is coming up - or what has happened.

I hope later stories weren't as bad for you.

———

Five Stars

By TAMMIE MCCALLIE on January 31, 2016
Format: Kindle Edition

I just finished the fourth book, and I can't wait for the next installment.

Michael - Thank you, Tammie! I read your review and was thinking 'Great! She has book five already available. I'm one ahead, the stress is off.'
;-)
Especially since I had JUST attained 'words complete' the day of this review for book six. Talk about nice timing on *your* part. That worked out for me amazingly well. I really appreciate every review (even the bad ones), but reviews that ask for books when it is available or will be really, really soon? Priceless!

———

Five Stars

By James Parke on January 31, 2016
Format: Kindle Edition

I like the straight forward approach too everything and I was hanging onto every word.

Michael - James! Your the most recent review I have for book one. Thank you for your review and I love that you are personally enjoying the series to hang onto every word.

Truth be told, I'm a closet introvert and the amount of nice things people have said about the books is slightly overwhelming. I rather changed in my teenage years from when I wanted to be a rock singer (read 'rock god') and found out I can't sing for @#%@#. Not only that, but I got up in front of a choir to make sure I showed everyone how bad I could sing. My desire to make a fool out of myself in front of my peers took a hard turn to 'let's not do that again … ever.'

I say 'closet' because I've had to be out there and in front of people for my company. However, I push through the uncomfortableness to get the job done. I'm sure I can overcome my uncomfortableness when receiving glowing reviews in an effort to support you being comfortable when you write your reviews on Amazon! ;-)

Man, that is SOOO much easier to type than say out loud. <— Still shilling like a villain. <Grin>

———

Thank you for reading these comments. Please know that I appreciate all of my readers who have spent your time with my stories. I hope that I'm capable of keeping the Bethany Anne saga up to your expectations.

Michael Anderle - February 3, 2016

SERIES TITLES INCLUDE:

KURTHERIAN GAMBIT SERIES TITLES INCLUDE:

First Arc

Death Becomes Her (01) - Queen Bitch (02) - Love Lost (03) - Bite This (04)
Never Forsaken (05) - Under My Heel (06) Kneel Or Die (07)

Second Arc

We Will Build (08) - It's Hell To Choose (09) - Release The Dogs of War (10)
Sued For Peace (11) - We Have Contact (12) - My Ride is a Bitch (13)
Don't Cross This Line (14)

Third Arc (Due 2017)

Never Submit (15) - Never Surrender (16) - Forever Defend (17)
Might Makes Right (18) - Ahead Full (19) - Capture Death (20)
Life Goes On (21)

New Series

THE SECOND DARK AGES

The Dark Messiah (01)
(Michael's Return)
12.25.2016

THE BORIS CHRONICLES
* With Paul C. Middleton *

Evacuation
Retaliation
Revelation
Restitution *2017*

RECLAIMING HONOR
* With JUSTIN SLOAN *

Justice Is Calling (01)
Claimed By Honor (02)
Judgement Has Fallen (03) *Feb 2017*

THE ETHERIC ACADEMY
* With TS PAUL *

ALPHA CLASS (01) *Dec 2016*
ALPHA CLASS (02) *Mar 2017*
ALPHA CLASS (03) *May 2017*

TERRY HENRY "TH" WALTON CHRONICLES
* With CRAIG MARTELLE *

Nomad Found (01)
Nomad Redeemed (02)
Nomad Unleashed (03)
Nomad Supreme (04) *Mar 17*

SHORT STORIES

Frank Kurns Stories of the Unknownworld 01 (7.5)
You Don't Mess with John's Cousin

Frank Kurns Stories of the Unknownworld 02 (9.5)
Bitch's Night Out

Frank Kurns Stories of the Unknownworld 02 (13.25)
With Natalie Grey
Bellatrix

AUDIOBOOKS

Available at Audible.com and iTunes

THE KURTHERIAN GAMBIT

Death Becomes Her - *Available Now*
Queen Bitch – *Available Now*
Love Lost – *Coming Soon*

RECLAIMING HONOR SERIES

Justice Is Calling – *Available Now*
Claimed By Honor – *Coming Soon*

TERRY HENRY "TH" WALTON CHRONICLES

Nomad Found - *Coming Soon*

ANTHOLOGIES

Glimpse
Honor in Death
(Michael's First Few Days)

Beyond the Stars: At Galaxy's Edge
Tabitha's Vacation

WANT MORE?

Join the email list here:

http://kurtherianbooks.com/email-list/

Join the Facebook group here:

https://www.facebook.com/TheKurtherianGambitBooks/

The email list will be sporadic with more 'major' updates, the Facebook group will be for updates and the 'behind the curtains' information on writing the next stories. Basically conversing!

Since I can't confirm that something I put up on Facebook will absolutely be updated for you, I need the email list to update all fans for any major release or updates that you might want to read on the website.

I hope you enjoy the book!

Michael Anderle - February 4, 2016.